"I want you," he said

Do you understand what I m

Amelia swallowed. "Yes,

He pulled away, kneeling upright and gripping the edge of the bath. Her first instinct was to pull him back to her. But with each breath, the fog around her mind cleared.

"I need you to want this," he said.

Did she want this? She'd enjoyed it, every second. But it was all so much. So fast. She took another deep, clearing breath.

Benedict didn't make her say *no*. Her hesitation had been enough. Instead he stepped out of the bath and offered her his hand.

She wrapped the robe tight, keenly aware that it clung to her every curve. He handed her a towel.

"I'm going for a walk," he said.

"Now? It's freezing out there."

He smiled. "That's kind of the point."

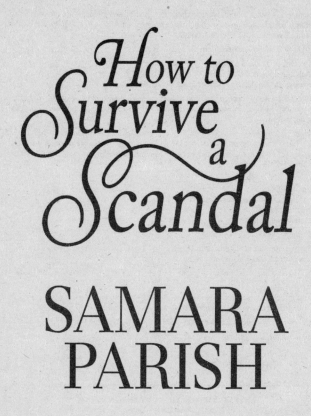

How to Survive a Scandal

SAMARA PARISH

FOREVER

NEW YORK BOSTON

Cover design by Daniela Medina
Cover photography and illustration by Sophia Sidoti
Cover copyright © 2021 by Hachette Book Group, Inc.

Forever
Hachette Book Group
1290 Avenue of the Americas, New York, NY 10104
read-forever.com
twitter.com/readforeverpub

First Edition: May 2021

Forever is an imprint of Grand Central Publishing. The Forever name and logo are trademarks of Hachette Book Group, Inc.

The publisher is not responsible for websites (or their content) that are not owned by the publisher.

The Hachette Speakers Bureau provides a wide range of authors for speaking events. To find out more, go to www.hachettespeakersbureau.com or call (866) 376-6591.

ISBN: 978-1-5387-0448-6 (mass market), 978-1-5387-0446-2 (ebook)

Printed in the United States of America

CW

10 9 8 7 6 5 4 3 2 1

ATTENTION CORPORATIONS AND ORGANIZATIONS:
Most Hachette Book Group books are available at quantity discounts with bulk purchase for educational, business, or sales promotional use. For information, please call or write:
Special Markets Department, Hachette Book Group
1290 Avenue of the Americas, New York, NY 10104
Telephone: 1-800-222-6747 Fax: 1-800-477-5925

For my love, the rock on which I could build a lighthouse. For my mother, who always believed I could.

Acknowledgments

This book has been a long time coming. I want to thank my husband, Elliott, for his constant, unwavering support, and for all the gentle nudging (yes, love, I should be writing). My deepest appreciation also to my mother, who helped me in so many ways I can't name them. Also to Jo, Stu, and Dad for your heartfelt encouragement.

A massive shout-out to my Romance Roomies: Miranda Morgan, Lauren Harbor, and Michelle Somers, without whom this would not be written. They are my brainstorming buddies, critique partners, and conference roommates, and I'm so lucky to have them. Thanks also to the Melbourne Romance Writers Guild—there is not a better writing group in the country. I have learned so much from you wonderful ladies.

I want to acknowledge the incredible RWAustralia community, including the competition judges who took the time to help me learn my craft, thank you. Especially all those dreaded *third* judges, whose feedback served me better than any score could.

Thank you to my agent, Kari Erickson, for deciding that Amelia was a heroine she was willing to fight for, Madeleine Colavita for taking a chance on this story, and Alex Logan for helping to shape it into something I'm so, so proud of.

And thank you to my readers, for picking up this book by an unknown author and giving it a shot. I'm so very happy to meet you. I hope this is the beginning of a long friendship.

How to
Survive
a
Scandal

Chapter 1 ——————

Benedict Asterly kicked in the door to the Longmans' empty farmhouse. Despite the crash of splintered wood, the chit slung over his shoulder was as silent as a sack of last season's grain.

Lady Amelia Bloody Crofton. Half dead, soon to be all dead if he couldn't warm her up.

He lowered her onto the cold, uneven stone floor before the fireplace.

Damnation. There was no fog of breath, no flicker of pulse, no sign of life at all.

He'd almost ridden past the snow-covered carriage in his effort to get out of the storm. He'd been an idiot for traveling in this kind of weather but apparently not the only idiot on the road.

Why the devil was an earl's daughter alone in a carriage all the way out here?

He pressed two fingers against her neck. Nothing. He pressed harder.

Th-thump...th-thump. It was faint. It was slow and erratic. But it was there.

Thank God.

He sagged with relief. The ropes around his chest, that had drawn tight the moment he'd seen her pale and unconscious, loosened.

He turned to the hearth and struck flint into the brush with shaking fingers. The scrape, scrape, scrape of steel on stone faint against the howl of the wind.

It caught, and he began the methodical task of building a fire. With each carefully placed stack, his racing heartbeat slowed. Thank God, Aldrich had restocked the wood supply before taking his children to visit their grandparents. Benedict had no desire to reenter the tempest.

Behind him, Lady Amelia muttered.

"I'm here. I'm with you." He turned back to the woman who'd previously declined to acknowledge his existence. After all, a man like him was beneath her notice.

He tossed aside the coarse traveling coat he'd thrown over her and removed her gloves and pelisse, struggling with the weight of her ragdoll body.

Bloody hell she was cold.

How long had she been trapped in that broken-down carriage? At least she'd had the good sense not to leave it.

He took her soft hands in his calloused ones, bringing them to his lips, but his breath did little to warm them.

Unbuttoning the cuffs of her sleeves and rolling the fabric up her arms, he exposed as much of her bare skin to the seeping warmth as he could. Her skin was more than pale. It had a blue pallor that caused his heart to skitter.

"Just stay with me. Please."

In a cupboard by the bed, he found some blankets. He pulled a knife from his boot to cut a piece and wrap the ends of her sodden blond hair. The rest he tucked behind her head and shoulders.

He untied the laces on her ankle boots and pulled the boots off, pausing at the sight of her stockings.

They were cold and damp. They needed to come off too. But a footman's son had no place touching a lady. And this particular lady? The ice princess would skewer him with the poker if she knew what he was contemplating.

He turned his head aside, giving her all the modesty he could as he reached his hands under her skirts, fumbling with the ribbon of her garter.

"I'm sorry." She couldn't hear him, but just saying the words made him feel less of a cad.

He tugged the dark wool off her toes. The skin was red and like wax to touch—but it was only frostnip, not yet frostbite.

"You mustn't... giant calling." Her words were so slurred he struggled to understand them.

"I'll bear that in mind, princess."

Of all the idiotic things he had done, tonight's escapade was the worst. The carriage had barely made it to the posting house. Instead of thanking God for the solid roof and warm fire, Benedict had left the carriage and its driver to go the last mile home on horseback.

He'd promised his sister he'd be home tonight, after a month away. Instead, he was stuck.

Feeling was slowly returning to his body, if not warmth. He covered Lady Amelia in his coat and then staggered to the bench that ran along the edge of the room. There was a kettle filled with water, sloshy and semi-frozen.

He dumped a small amount of tea inside, grabbed two mugs with his other hand and staggered back to the fire.

The intensifying flame was the best damn thing he'd ever seen.

He hung the kettle from an iron hook and turned back to his biggest problem.

She couldn't stay on the floor.

There was a large, worn armchair in the corner. He moved it in front of the hearth, as close as he dared. What she needed was heat—and fast—but the fire hadn't taken a chink out of the bitter shroud of the room.

There was one thing he could do, but damn she was going to flay him alive when she woke. He took off his jacket, pulled his shirt over his head, and picked her up off the floor.

He settled into the armchair, holding her against his naked chest, his bare arms resting along the length of hers. His body heat had to work.

The cold air was whiplike against his skin, and goose bumps covered his arms.

Think warm thoughts. A steam engine furnace. A hot bath. A warm brick under his bedsheets. A warm woman under his bedsheets...

He looked down at the chit on his lap. Lady Amelia Crofton. Diamond of the *ton*. Leader of the fashionable set. Cold as the ice shards on the window. And Wildeforde's bloody fiancée. Damn, this was a mess.

He exhaled hard, trying to steady his shivering through slow, even breaths.

"That's not what I asked for." Lady Amelia's eyes flickered but failed to open. "I said blue."

His laugh was shaky. "Well, tonight's not what I asked for either. And I'm partial to grey."

Her eyes fluttered open. The deep jade green caught the light of the fire.

"Put it under the horse."

He snorted. Even half-dead, she was giving orders. But he would take them, if it meant she would live. Her eyes closed again, the long dark lashes resting against pale skin.

"You're welcome, by the way."

Her grunt was accompanied by a soft sigh—as innocent as a babe. If you were fool enough to believe it.

"Why the devil were you traveling alone?" The snow had been so deep around the broken-down carriage that only a glint of metal from the wheel had given any hint that someone might be in trouble.

There was no response, just a twitch of her nose.

After a long few minutes, warmth finally traveled up his legs. It was a superficial heat, not the bone-deep warmth that came from a hard day's work, but hopefully it was enough to warm her.

"Lemonade."

She put a hand on his thigh and pushed herself up, faltering on her weak legs toward the fire.

His heart leapt to his throat as he lurched up and grabbed her dress, jerking her backward before she could fall into the flames. A dozen buttons popped free and scattered across the floor.

"You will be the bloody death of me." He maneuvered her back to the chair, slumping her over it, her limbs sprawled like a green boy's after his first trip to the pub. Not taking any more chances, he dragged the chair farther from the flames.

"I'll get you your damn lemonade," he muttered, turning back to the boiling kettle. Using the tongs by the fire, he poured tea into the two mugs.

She was every bit as high-horsed as he remembered. Although at least she'd deigned to speak to him—an improvement upon their last encounter.

The first few gulps burned a satisfying trail down to his belly. It was the best thing he'd ever tasted.

"I have your lemonade, princess."

He turned and nearly dropped the mugs.

The bodice of Amelia's dress had pooled at her waist, leaving her in nothing but stays and a chemise so fine it was nearly translucent. His mouth turned to coal dust.

"I'm hot, too hot." She yanked at the neckline of her chemise.

Bloody hell. He picked up the coat he'd tossed on the floor and tried to wrap it around her shoulders as she struggled to escape.

"It's for your own good." Of course, she would refuse help. It didn't come on a gilded plate.

He wrapped one arm around her, pinning her to him. With the other, he stuffed the coat between them and tucked it beneath her armpits.

The fewer layers between her and the heat the better, but she was going to strip his hide with her barbed tongue as it was. Heaven help him if she woke half-naked.

Her struggling subsided, and he managed to lower the two of them back onto the chair. Her ribs expanded and contracted against his chest with increasing force, and the vein on the side of her throat thrummed with more regularity in rhythm.

She was getting stronger. Color was creeping into her skin. Her cheeks began to flush, and her lips slowly changed from blue to white, to a light pink.

No longer looking like she'd been pulled dead from the Thames, she was every bit as beautiful as he remembered.

Confident that she was going to pull through, he closed his eyes.

The door crashed open.

"I'll have your rutting neck, you rutting bastard."

Chapter 2 ————————————————

Amelia woke with a ringing in her ears—a head-throbbing sound like a cymbal wielded by a mad chambermaid. There was distant yelling and a thudding crash accompanied by the rapid, uneven chatter of her own teeth. Last week's Appleby debutante recital, which she'd foolishly attended, had been unrivaled wretchedness. Until tonight. Whatever this was, it was worse than six tone-deaf society hopefuls.

She sucked in a breath, pulling her knees closer to her chest. So. Cold.

The yelling continued. Maybe Lord Chester had finally been caught with Lord Macklebury's wife? Maybe the simmering tension between Miss Hamilton and Miss Clarke had finally boiled over.

She would investigate. The second she could open her eyes.

Crockery smashed. "I will kill you, you rutting bastard."

That was her father…Someone must have been serving the good brandy. Or any brandy, really.

She dragged her eyes open, struggling to focus. *What in heaven's name?*

She'd never been in a room like this. It was large-ish, roughly the size of a small ballroom, but it seemed to be a bedroom, drawing room, and kitchen in one. The walls were unadorned and tinged black with soot, the floor frightfully uneven. The overturned chair beside her was heavily worn.

But the tableau of characters in front of her? That was the most bewildering of all.

Her father was straddling a half-naked man with a broken table leg, raised and ready to strike. And Edward—

Why was he in town?

He should have come to call.

You'd think he'd be a better fiancé by now. Her stomach rumbled. *Roast pheasant would be so nice…*

"Settle down, man," Edward said in his duke-ish tone. He had one hand clenched around her father's wrist, preventing him from murder, the other arm wrapped around her father's chest.

The flames from the fire beside her created shifting patterns of light on the stone. Why was she lying on the floor?

It was time for answers. "Enff." The word was thick, and her tongue wouldn't make the shapes it needed. "Eee nwaaaf." She ran her tongue around her mouth trying to remind it of what it was supposed to do. "Eee. Nuff." Only one word, yet so much effort.

All three men stopped to stare at her.

Clumsily, she pushed herself into a seated position, the pins and needles in her arms making it barely possible. As she sat, a coarse blanket fell to her lap. She reached down, her fingers fumbling with the fabric. For the life of her, she couldn't grasp it. Couldn't even feel it. She looked down.

Her chest was bare but for her loosened stays and thin

chemise. Her lungs tightened as though her lady's maid was pulling at her laces in a fury.

What in heavens?

Panic got her fingers working. She clutched the wool and yanked it to her chin.

"W-w-what is h-happening?"

Her father's face turned purple. Spittle burst from his mouth like little pellets. He shoved himself off the undressed stranger and bore down on her.

"You..." He jabbed his finger inches from her face. "You little whore."

She flinched and looked around. Every movement felt sullen and slow, at complete odds with her heart, which beat overtime as if trying to spur the rest of her to flee. She tried to sift through her memories, but as soon as her brain grasped an image, it let it go.

"Step back from her." It was a quiet warning that promised unpleasant consequences from anyone foolish enough to ignore it. And it didn't come from Edward. The semi-naked man had made it to his feet and now, sensibly, was putting the rough-hewn table between him and everyone else.

He had her father pinned with a glare hard enough to cause actual damage. Hard enough to force the esteemed Earl of Crofton to take a few steps back from her.

She slowly exhaled.

The stranger leaned against the shack walls, and a blond lock of hair fell over his forehead. Deep blue eyes, the color of a twilight sky, stared into hers. He was not the sort of man she was acquainted with. He wasn't pretty or refined; he was granite and rock. He looked rough—south side of Cheap Street kind of rough—an image intensified by his bloodied nose and sheer hulking size.

His chest, all brawn and sinew, bunched beneath his

crossed arms, and her eyes dropped to the interlocking muscles at his waist, the dusting trail of hair that reached down past the waistband of his breeches.

So *that* was what men looked like beneath their finery.

Despite the cold, a red heat seared across her. She tore her gaze away from his naked torso and found him staring at her, his eyebrows raised as if he knew very well where her attention had been.

Her face grew hot with embarrassment.

"W-well?" she asked, trying to brazen it out. She'd sound more impressive if her words weren't slurred. "Who are you?"

He gave a deep, weary, frustrated sigh. "Benedict Asterly."

"And why am I here, like..." she gestured to the blanket covering her.

"You were in a coach, freezing to death." His voice was flat and unsympathetic.

Yes. It had been cold. The hot bricks at her feet had cooled, and the cold outside had seeped in. Despite piling on every layer she could, she'd been freezing, and it had become harder and harder to stay awake.

"And I'm undressed because...?"

"That's a darn good question." Edward's bearing mirrored the stranger's—grim, autocratic, guarded.

The stranger—Benedict—sighed, raking his hands through his hair. The muscles of his chest stretched as he did so. "You disrobed yourself."

"I did not!" The nerve of him. "It takes my maid half an hour to get me into this dress."

Her father rounded on her again. "And took him half a second to get you out of it." She was well acquainted with his temper, but never had he been so furious that he'd lost his composure in public.

The stranger pushed himself from the wall. His was a different species of anger. Where her father exploded like fuel-fed fire, the stranger was controlled, lethal.

Every inch of her was startlingly aware of him, of his immense size and the surprising fluidity of his movement.

"I said, step back." He placed himself firmly between her and her father. "Rather than yelling at a girl, why don't you tell me which of you idiots left her in a carriage alone?"

"She was supposed to be in London, minding her own bloody business," her father said.

The shouting began again, all three men obstinate and determined to talk down the others. The noise was too much.

For heaven's sake, stop beating your chests and pour me a hot bath.

She ignored the lot of them and wrapped her arms around her knees, focused on taming her shivers. Taking deep, measured breaths, she closed her eyes and let their words roll over her. Nine. Eight. Seven. She shuffled closer to the fire behind her. Six. Five. Four.

The frigid floor disappeared from under her as the stranger swooped her into his arms as if she weighed little more than a wisp of lace.

"You're too close to the flames, princess. Wilde, drag that chair over here."

Did he really just call Edward, Duke of Wildeforde, Wilde?

A muscle ticked along Edward's jaw, but he did as the stranger asked.

"This argument is ridiculous," the stranger—*Oh, what was his name?*—said, lowering her to the chair. "I've not compromised her, and you damn well know it."

The words hit like a heavy reticule swung by a careless debutante. She sat back. *Compromised?*

Edward fixed the stranger with a frustrated stare. "Of course you didn't. But you have made a mess of things."

"*I've* made a mess of things? Why the devil was a lady traveling alone? Where was her chaperone? Where was her coachman? Where were the people who were supposed to be looking after her?"

Edward stared at her. Her father stared at her. The stranger stared at her. Heavens, she was tired.

"That's not of any consequence." The voice came from a dark corner of the room. It was loud and low-pitched and seemed to settle on the room like a copper snuffer extinguishing flame. An old man in an overly ornate, embroidered and fur-covered coat, clearly from the previous century, stepped into the light. She hadn't noticed him earlier and was glad for it.

His lips were twisted into a sneer. "The chit has debased herself. The only question now is what's to be done about it?"

A chill prickled across her neck. That didn't bode well. Best to cut that line of conversation short. "I hardly see that anything needs to be done about it," she said. "Whatever it might look like, we all know—"

"It looks like you are alone in a house, unchaperoned, with him half-naked and you...disheveled."

The prickles spread as a shiver that had nothing to do with the cold coursed through her.

"Now wait just one minute. Perhaps we should give them a minute to explain." Finally, her father had caught up to the potential ramifications of this ludicrous situation.

"What we've witnessed is explanation enough. We left the comfort of Lord Wildeforde's library to rescue an innocent girl in peril. What we found was a harlot engaged in a wanton act of lust." The man turned to Edward, who was rubbing the spot between his eyes. He rarely did that. Only when his mother was particularly trying. Or when Amelia was trying to lock him in to a wedding date.

The man continued. "You have responsibilities to the family name, to your title, and they include choosing a duchess who hasn't tupped half the county."

Her chest tightened, and she scrambled to catch the threads that were unraveling around her. "You wretched cur." She turned to Edward. "How can you let him say these things? You know they're untrue. I was unconscious, for goodness' sake."

He rubbed a hand over his eyes. "I know that." He sighed, as lost for words as she'd ever seen him. "This is all a confounded mess that looks a sight worse than the truth. But Lord Karstark is right. There's my family's reputation to consider."

"Lord Karstark is a jackass." He could not do this to her, dash it. After all these years. "We have been engaged since I was *five*."

"Amelia."

And there it was, the tone he used whenever he thought she was being irrational.

"Amelia, you need a Season before we wed. Be reasonable."

"Amelia, we can't possibly marry in the same year as the Duke of Rushford. Be reasonable."

"Amelia, we can't possibly wed at all because your carriage got stuck and you almost died. Be reasonable."

"Don't 'Amelia' me. I've been waiting for you for years." She tried to stand, to go and shake some sense into him, but her legs crumpled.

He examined the pressed cuff of his coat, running a thumb over the embroidered edge. "You've always known the conditions. No scandals. It is in the contract we all signed." His voice carried a tinge of disbelief, like he couldn't quite believe what he was saying.

She squeezed her fingers into tight fists. Her nails dug into her palms. "There isn't a bloody scandal if everyone in this room keeps their mouth shut."

Edward's eyes widened in shock, but if ever she should be permitted to use profanities, surely this was the time. They were quite surprisingly satisfying. No wonder men used them.

She looked over at the half-naked stranger. He was rubbing his eyes with his thumb and forefinger, strikingly similar to the way Edward did.

"Well?" she demanded.

"By noon, it'll be all over the county." The stranger looked pointedly at the ancient peacocking Lord Karstark, and she felt a sudden, all-consuming urge to rake her fingernails down those powdery, tissue-like wrinkles. Her entire life ruined by a gossipy centenarian.

Edward finally looked at her. "I'm sorry," he said. "I'm so, so sorry." It was the first time she'd ever heard him apologize for anything. His tone was bleak, as though he knew full well the pain he was causing and regretted it.

Bile crawled up her throat, and she fought the urge to retch. She couldn't breathe, and the ringing in her ears grew louder.

"I'll be ruined," she choked out. "Please." Her voice caught. She'd never in her life thought she'd plead for anything, but she'd plead now.

His face twisted. He knew it to be true, yet the truth didn't change his mind. "We'll say you ended it. You threw me over. You got tired of waiting. I spent too much time in parliament and not enough time courting you."

But that's not what they would say. Not when this story got out.

Edward could confront a difficult and contentious parliament without hesitation, but if there was one thing that could bring him to his knees, it was the slightest hint of gossip. And tonight would be more than a hint. He would step away, stay out of the scandal, and she would have to defend herself.

She searched his countenance for something to give her hope, but there was nothing. "Are you actually doing this?"

"I'm sorry," he whispered, and he turned away, pulling his hands through his hair as he left.

And with his exit, a fissure appeared. She was Lady Amelia Crofton, daughter of an earl, diamond of the *ton*, third cousin to the King, and the future Duchess of Wildeforde. Or at least she had been.

Lord Karstark smirked and turned to her father. "If Wildeforde sends one of his men to Canterbury now, you could have a special license before Sunday's Christmas service."

A bubble of horrified laughter caught in her throat. The situation had spiraled from awful to borderline hysterical.

"Excuse me?" The stranger's voice rose five octaves. "Now see here."

"No. Now *you* see here," her father said. "Someone is marrying my daughter, and if it isn't the Duke of Wildeforde, it will be you, damn it. God knows no one else will have her now."

She looked at the stranger—Benedict—waiting for him to say something. Do something. He just stared at the palms of his hands.

Useless men. "Father, I can't marry him...I've never even seen him before tonight." Her eyes pricked with tears.

The stranger rolled his eyes with a look of unadulterated scorn, which she was wholly unused to having sent in her direction. "We've been introduced, Lady Amelia."

Had they? She searched his face, the unfashionably tanned skin, the harsh stubble on his jaw, the strong, broad nose with an unseemly bend where he'd clearly come out worst in a tavern brawl. Nothing about him was familiar. "We have?" Surely she'd remember a man of his lumbering size.

He shook his head, clearly disgusted.

Her father nodded. "We can do it after the Christmas service."

By the time Amelia woke, the orange glow of the coals was battling with descending dark. By the time she was dressed, the day had fled.

The maid she'd been assigned by Edward's housekeeper arrived with a tray. The toast was burnt, the eggs were cold, and the mushrooms she'd asked for were nonexistent.

"I realize I'm asking for breakfast during the early evening, but I was hoping for something that wasn't actually cooked at breakfast time."

The past twenty-four hours had been beyond humiliating. Never in her life had she felt less in control of a situation. And the cold, congealed mess before her was her mood manifested.

"Yes, ma'am," the maid muttered.

Amelia raised her chin, thankful for her extra height. "My name is *Lady* Amelia Crofton."

The only response was a clenched jaw.

"The correct term is *my lady*."

"Yes, m'lady." The words came through gritted teeth. The

milksop chit scuttled out. No doubt the gossip below stairs was out of control.

As she choked down the rubbery eggs and tepid tea, Amelia assessed what was left of the hours ahead of her. Damage control was needed. It would take a nauseating amount of flattery, but there was no reason the situation couldn't be rectified. It's not like she was *actually* compromised, just apparently compromised.

With any luck, her father had fixed the disaster while she slept. That had been the point of his visit to Abingdale in the first place—to convince Edward to set a date. Every conversation they'd had over the past fifteen years had somehow referenced her approaching marriage to Edward.

> *"Don't wear yellow. The Duchess of Wildeforde is not cheerful."*
> *"Don't skimp on the sugar. The Duchess of Wildeforde is not a pauper."*
> *"Don't laugh. The Duchess of Wildeforde is not a barmaid."*

Her father was as invested in this marriage as she was. The whole situation was most likely solved already.

She knew the way to the study. She'd been here briefly just after her first Season. And her third. She waved off a footman's reluctant offer to guide her and strode down the stairs and through the hall to where Edward generally conducted business. Taking a short, determined breath, she pushed open the door.

Edward's study was much like the man himself—grand, richly appointed, and meticulously presented. The curtains fell in even lines. The journal on his mahogany desk was perfectly parallel to the edges.

Except her father, slouched in the leather wingback chair by the window, deep into his cups. She could smell the brandy from here. The other chair was empty; Edward was absent.

"Well, here she is." Her father tipped his near-dry glass in her direction. "The lady of the hour. The key to our family's salvation and the whore that threw it in the ashes."

"I see you found the liquor cabinet. Again."

He stared at her, eyes glassy. "You had one job."

And here it was, the lecture she'd listened to more times than she'd care to count.

"Marry the Duke of Wildeforde. Become the perfect duchess. Bring..."

She rolled her eyes. "...honor and prestige to the House of Crofton. Yes. I know. I'm working on it."

He let out a long, gaseous burp. "This never would have happened if you were male."

It was truly unfair that her greatest failing in life was something she had no control over. "If I were male, I could have taken one of the horses and saved myself."

His eyes narrowed. He hated it when she spoke back to him. "You're a selfish creature, just like your mother. All I asked for was a son."

"And all she delivered was a daughter. We've had this conversation." Over and over and over. Every time he got deep in his cups.

"All I asked of you was to marry well. Now look at the shit we're in."

"I take it you haven't managed to rectify the situation."

He snorted. "Oh, it's rectified. You'll be married in the morning, after the Christmas service."

She pressed a palm to her chest, noticing the weight she'd been under only as it lifted. "Well, that's a relief. Truly, if all it took to speed things up was the threat of scandal, I would've half-frozen myself years ago. The way Edward has dragged his feet is intolerable."

Her father laughed, the mean, snide laugh he made coming home half-drunk from wherever he'd been gambling—if he'd won. The hairs at the nape of her neck rose.

"You seem to be misapprehending the situation. You'll be married. To Mr. Benedict Asterly of the...Abingdale Asterlys? Do half-breeds come from anywhere?"

She grabbed at the back of the chair as her knees buckled. "You are joking."

"No."

Straightening, she clenched her hands into tight, fury-filled fists. "This is absurd. I can't believe Edward would do this to me."

"You were found in the arms of another man, with your dress..." He waved his hand at her bosom. "What's so difficult to believe?"

"For a start, he'd have to find himself a new bride. That's an awful lot of effort for him."

He certainly hadn't put any effort into their engagement. In fifteen years, she'd received one letter, and that was to ask the name of a composer she'd mentioned his mother might like.

"Well, he did. Rejected you as if you were a fish gone bad at the markets." Her father poured himself another drink.

"Oh, don't be ridiculous. You've never stepped foot in a market."

She walked to the window and back. And again. Her father was useless. It was up to her to set things back on course.

In the background, the ranting continued. "I told you. Be the perfect duchess. Say the right things, do the right things—"

She swatted his words away.

Lady Wildeforde was in residence. Could she convince Edward's mother to stand beside her? She'd always been supportive—if somewhat acidic—in the past, and had been instrumental in establishing Amelia as the younger set's preeminent figure.

"—had to keep yourself out of scandal, and you would be—" Her father wiped his mouth with his sleeve.

"I can't see why there needs to be a scandal," she snapped. Could he not see that she was trying to focus? "It was just you, Edward, me, and... what was his name?"

"Mister Benedict Asterly."

She shuddered. *Mister.* Ugh. "Right. Well, surely you can pay him off. Marrying an earl's daughter might seem attractive, but he's a country lummox. Give him a thousand pounds and assure him that I'm more trouble than he expects." Because she would be. That was certain.

"You're forgetting Lord Karstark."

Hell. The blasted lord with his vile sneer. "For goodness' sake, give generously to whatever cause will put the funds into his pocket, promise my firstborn child to the relative of his choice, and send him on his way. Really, must I do everything?"

Her father held the snifter up to the light and gave it a nonchalant swirl, studying the brandy as it clung to the sides of the glass. "Karstark. Brother-in-law to Lady Merwick."

Her heart gave way like slippers on ice.

"Cousin to the Duke of Oxley," he rattled off, "and rich as Croesus. The only things he values are power and gossip, and you just gave him both."

Dash it.

He sniggered. "Face reality, Amelia. Abingdale is your new home. I don't believe your future husband owns a London residence."

This couldn't be. It wouldn't be. Amelia spun on her heel. If Edward wasn't in his office, where would he be?

Maids fled as they saw her approach. She didn't stomp—a duchess's footsteps are never heard—but her clenched fists and brisk pace ensured no one got in her way. Edward could be made to see reason.

He entered the foyer just as she did. Judging by his heavy coat and Wellington boots, she'd caught him just as he was escaping. He stopped, tapping his hand against his thigh. He was uneasy. Good.

She rushed to him and buried her face in the soft linen of his cravat.

Hesitantly, he stroked her hair. This was the most intimacy they'd shared throughout their entire courtship. Typically, it was a stiff embrace. The few times she'd pressed him for a kiss, it had been a perfunctory peck on the cheek.

"Edward." She sobbed. "What is happening? I don't understand." She took in rapid, shallow breaths that made her chest press against his. "I don't know what"—gasp—"to do. Please tell me it isn't true."

Looking up at him, she allowed one tear to roll down her cheek.

"I just can't," he said, his voice catching.

"But we can weather the gossip. You are the Duke of Wildeforde, and I am Lady Amelia Crofton. There won't be a scandal if we forbid it, not one they'll remember. You aren't your father."

Edward stiffened before he pried her hands from his lapel and stepped back.

"I can't take that risk. It's not just me I need to think about. I have my sister's future to think of. My brother's. God, my mother—"

"Ugh, your mother. Your mother will be sour and spiteful

regardless. She might as well have something to be sour over."

He shook his head, although whether it was at her comments or at the thought of the current duchess, she couldn't tell.

"Why did you do it?" he asked, as though the fight was lost, and he was trying to work out where it all went wrong. "Why leave London?"

Every muscle tensed. Yes, she'd departed London in a madcap state—so hot with fury she hadn't noticed the cold. But she was not responsible for this situation. How dare he insinuate that she was.

"Why, Amelia?"

"Miss Josephine Merkle announced her engagement. To Lord Cossington. I thought you would want to know," she bit off.

His brows knitted as though she'd spouted off some complex riddle. "Why would I want to know?"

And there was the crux of their problem. He couldn't see anything beyond his dry, demanding duty. Beyond managing his estates and serving in the House of Lords.

"For goodness' sake, Edward. I was annoyed. And embarrassed. Even Moany Merkle is getting married before me, and she only came out this year. I'm sick of waiting. I've been waiting for you my whole life. Just do it. Keep your word. Marry me." She beat his chest with those last two words. He let her.

"I'm sorry." He refused to meet her gaze, fixating on the painting on the wall behind her. "I must think of my family. When you're a duke, society holds you to a whole different level of standards."

She inhaled deeply, counting backward until she was sure a snarl wouldn't erupt with the exhale.

"Standards? I am the daughter of the Earl of Crofton. Our lineage goes back to the Normans. I can name every peer in Debrett's as well as their conversation preferences. Ladies *beg* me to attend their balls. I'm not the most fashionable young lady. I *am* fashion. The Incomparable. The diamond. And *you* worry about standards?"

Edward at least had the good sense to look ashamed. "I know Asterly. We haven't been close lately, but he'll do the honorable thing."

She struck at him, a soft *thwap* sounding as her hand connected with the padding of his waistcoat. "I'm more interested in you doing the honorable thing, you wretched cur."

Blood drained from Edward's face, but he continued. "He's a good man—a better one than me in many ways. And he'll treat you well."

"He's a country simpleton with the manners of a goat and the breeding of a donkey. You'd have me stuck out here in some godforsaken backwater, married to a mere mister and eating what, potatoes and blood pudding? Do commoners even drink tea?"

There was a cough from the doorway. Edward's face flushed red, and she knew immediately who was behind her.

For heaven's sake. A brief wave of mortification assailed her.

"We commoners drink tea. Courtesy of the West Indies."

Chapter 3 ————————————

Benedict's cheeks burned as he strode into Wilde's study, the sharp-tongued harpy at his heels. The esteemed Duke of Wildeforde had escaped out the front door.

Benedict had spent the day hammering steel sheets—a departure from his usual work with a sketchpad designing his steam engines. But he'd needed the *thunk, thunk, thunk* of a hammer. Needed to sap the fight from him until he had the exhausted acceptance of a man ready to meet his maker.

A country simpleton with the manners of a goat and the breeding of a mule.

The words blazed across his skin, a stinging reminder of decades-old insults. They could have been taken straight from his mother's diary. Well, to hell with them both.

The aristocracy could hang itself. He didn't care a whit for its good opinions. To think he'd walked in with an intention to marry the ice princess. Now he was just here for the entertainment.

Her father didn't bother to stand as they entered. There

was one chair opposite him, and Benedict took it, crossing his legs lazily. He plastered an apathetic smile on his face—a "go to hell" smile he'd not used since he was a bull-headed youth.

Lady Amelia's nostrils flared, but it was the only hint of anger she showed.

Last night, she'd been pale, drab, disheveled. But this evening, awake and furious, she was striking.

It wasn't just her beauty that was arresting. No, it was the crisp intelligence in her emerald eyes that had him transfixed. Pinned down. It was the set of her jaw, delicate but determined. The straight back and squared shoulders that weren't quite disguised by her soft, ladylike lines. That was why she was a force to be reckoned with. Why her reputation preceded her. She was too bullheaded to have it any other way.

"Amelia, you don't need to be here." Her father dismissed her with an unsteady wave of his hand.

"Because you've done such an excellent job in my absence?" She stood, arms akimbo, like a veritable Amazon.

Her father's hand tightened around the glass he was holding, the only sign he'd heard her. He fixed his gaze—as best a drunken man could—on Benedict. "Wildeforde has arranged for the special license. The wedding can proceed as planned on Sunday."

Benedict slouched farther down into the chair, trying to look detached and uninterested. "I'm unconvinced a wedding's necessary."

The words were directed to Lord Crofton, but it was Lady Amelia's response he was watching for.

He wasn't expecting the warm smile or satisfied nod she gave. "Mr. Asterly, on this we are agreed. Thank you for your time."

With that thorough dismissal, she turned to her father, her voice switching from friendly to cast-iron hard. "Now can we be done with this business and focus on bringing Edward around?"

Benedict laughed. He couldn't help it. She couldn't honestly think she still had a chance with Wildeforde in the face of such a scandal? They'd been engaged for over a decade, and she still didn't understand her fiancé's fears. "He *won't* marry you." He reached over to the small table between them and poured himself a drink. Now that he'd decided he wasn't going to marry her highness, the situation was almost enjoyable.

"Pardon?" Her smile was no longer warm. How many men had shrunk under the force of her cool look? Too many if that had become her expectation.

He sat up straighter. "He wouldn't risk a scandal in order to marry the woman he actually loved. There's no chance he'll risk it out of some obligation to you. His family's happiness means too much to him."

Lord Crofton lurched to his feet, stumbling. He bore down on Benedict with a fist raised. "Listen here, you mongrel. You are—"

Benedict stood, and the older man stopped. He had nearly a foot on Crofton and no cause to be reasonable. "*I* am no longer half dead with cold. Nor am I inclined to put up with threats from a man so brandy-soaked he struggles to stand."

Lord Crofton's eyes narrowed. Benedict could see him debate the pros and cons of throwing a punch and hoped the pros would win. Smashing something would feel gratifying.

Lady Amelia stepped between them, placing her palm firmly against Benedict's chest.

It was unexpected. Few men would put themselves in his path when he was angry. This willowy chit had a set of bollocks of her own. Even through the fabric of his waist-coat he could feel her hand—surprisingly hot for someone cold-blooded.

She looked up at him, meeting his eyes, and for the first time, he saw a crack in that ruthless exterior. A hint of uncertainty. A trace of vulnerability.

"Edward won't marry me?" Her voice, quiet and direct, formed a winch around his heart and pulled.

Perhaps she wasn't so frigid and dispassionate. Perhaps it was a mask to hide her fragility. He'd been there. He understood.

He shook his head. "I know him, better than most, and he would never have hurt you on purpose. But what he went through when his father died? That left a wound that won't ever heal. He won't put his family through that same anguish."

She took a deep breath, nodded, and walked across to the window. Good. He hated to see any woman cry.

"Then you will have to," her father said.

It was arrogant and presumptuous and everything that was wrong with the aristocracy. To be dictated to—as if Benedict's life was not his own, as if he had no agency—lit within him a dangerous furnace. "I don't *have* to do anything. I am not your employee. I am not your subordinate. I do not answer to you."

Lord Crofton waved a hand, as though brushing off an insect or some other low-level irritant. "An honorable man would live up to his responsibilities."

Benedict could barely keep the rage from his voice. "I fail to see how I benefit from this arrangement."

Lady Amelia whirled to face him. If she'd been crying, there was no sign of it. Her green eyes flashed sharp and spiteful.

Oh, there's nothing fragile about you at all…

She looked at him as if he were a chimney sweep asking to dance with a queen. "I am the daughter of the Earl of Crofton. You are a…man in a patched coat."

He crossed his arms, brushing the patches at each elbow with his rough, working man's hands.

"Marriage to me raises your standing to something almost acceptable in polite company," she continued. Her words were the punishing thump of a blacksmith's hammer.

"Polite company? Out here in some godforsaken backwater?" he lashed out.

She swallowed at her own words thrown back at her.

"There isn't much 'polite' company out here, princess. Other than Wildeforde, and somehow, I don't see how marrying his fiancée is going to raise my standing with him. You have no use to me as a wife."

She brushed a nonexistent loose hair from her brow. "I can run a household of fifty servants. I can host the perfect tea party."

"Can you make tea?"

She sputtered.

"Can you light a furnace? Boil water? Cook a meal, mend a tear, clean a hearth?"

She flinched at each word.

"Do you have any skills at all?"

"I am an excellent watercolorist," she said through gritted teeth.

"Well, I'm sure that will come in handy."

He didn't need a wife. And if he were forced into marriage, he wanted one who could help raise his sister to be a kind and useful woman, who wasn't afraid to pitch in and get filthy next to everyone else on his estate.

"You've made your bloody point." Lord Crofton had

collapsed back into the chair and was pouring yet another drink. "Ten thousand pounds if you marry her tomorrow."

Benedict's throat constricted as if a noose were slowly drawing tight. If he married her, he was facing a lifetime of his father's loneliness. If he didn't marry her, she'd be ruined. He shouldn't give a damn, but he did.

"I want the same terms as Wildeforde."

"What?" his soon-to-be fiancée shrieked.

Her father spat out the brandy in his mouth. "You grasping—"

Benedict interrupted him. "He wouldn't have accepted a penny less than thirty thousand. Your signature on paper will do."

Crofton swore and stumbled across the room to Wildeforde's desk, where he pulled out paper from a drawer and began to scribble.

Amelia stared at her father, incredulous. "What, no bonus if I successfully breed within a year? No extra compensation if my children are male? What if I run five furlongs in under a minute?" She turned to Benedict. "Would you like to see my teeth?"

He sighed. Devil help him if he were making the wrong choice. "He made the same negotiations with Wildeforde. Would you be complaining if I were a duke?"

"I would if he didn't think to negotiate an allowance or have any money put aside for my own use in case you lose my dowry at the local fair bobbing for apples."

He bit the inside of his cheek to hold back a retort.

Her father looked up at her. "Really, Amelia. Out here, what could you possibly do with an allowance?"

She pressed her lips together. Then she turned away to stare out the window once again. Had those been tears in her eyes? Or an illusion?

Her father thrust a scrawled note in front of him. He read it over slowly, folded it, and slid it into his jacket pocket.

"Crofton, Lady Amelia. I will see you Sunday morning."

⌒

Snow was falling lightly outside, yet Amelia was ready to suffocate from the heat. The small church with its rough wooden pews was densely crowded, and the smell of unwashed bodies made her nauseous.

It took every ounce of self-control she had not to pull at the fur collar of her coat or strip her hands of the white silk gloves.

In front of her, Edward and his mother sat alone on the first pew—precisely where she and her father should be sitting. From the throbbing vein in her father's neck, it was clear the snub was getting his temper up.

She took a deep breath and turned her attention back to the pasty, bulbous man in front of her.

It was a traditional Christmas sermon. The local clergyman talked on and on in a tone of voice that scraped like chalk on board.

She ground her teeth.

Looking dead ahead of her, she examined the back of Edward's head. As she'd lain in bed the night before, she'd convinced herself that Edward was going to change his mind. They'd been engaged for more than a decade, since she was just a child; surely that counted for more than some fear of a little gossip.

Those hopes faded when she'd entered the church. He hadn't looked over when she'd entered. Hadn't chastised his mother when she refused to stand and let Amelia and her father join them. Hadn't even flinched when Amelia had slid into the seat behind him. The muscles in his neck and shoulders were stiff and hadn't moved since the service started.

He was not about to rescue her. So what was she supposed to do now?

She snuck a look at her intended. He sat stony-faced across the aisle. Next to him sat a child—a girl of perhaps ten years? Twelve? She couldn't tell. She'd never interacted with children, not even when she was one.

They were clearly related. Short of the broken nose and despite the long blond braid, the child was the spitting image of him. Tanned and freckled, she had her blue eyes trained on Amelia, brow furrowed.

Amelia stared back.

The girl cocked her head, her lips pursed.

Amelia cocked an eyebrow. The girl was bold. Most debutantes wouldn't dream of staring at Amelia so brazenly.

The stare-off continued until, seemingly satisfied, the girl gave a quick nod of her head and turned to Benedict, whispering in his ear. His eyebrows rose, and he turned to look at Amelia in surprise.

She quickly turned her attention back to her lap, her hands twisting in the grey fur muffler that contrasted with the pale pink of her pelisse. It was pretty, but hardly the pearl-encrusted creation she'd planned to wear on her wedding day. No, that dress was at home in a trunk, along with the rest of her trousseau she'd been building over the years—every piece carefully embroidered "Lady Wildeforde."

As the sermon ended, people stirred in their seats, waiting for the priest to step down so they could leave. It took everything she had not to be the one leading the retreat. She pressed the soles of her trembling feet hard into the floor.

The clergyman paused for a long painful moment before clearing his throat.

"Before we depart, let us stand together for the union of Lady Amelia Elizabeth Crofton and Benedict Asterly."

There was a collective gasp among the parishioners. A furious muttering almost drowned out her thumping pulse. Almost.

She looked across at Benedict. He stood and then bent down to whisper something in the young girl's ear. The girl patted *his* hand—as if *his* life were being demolished—and stood to allow Benedict to make his way to the altar alone.

How had she gotten into this?

She should move. She should stand. But her body flat-out refused to comply—until her father elbowed her in the side. Hard.

She stood and moved into the aisle. She would not give the congregation further gossip. She walked toward the altar, head high, her light steps at odds with the heaviness of her insides.

Taking her place, she was once again reminded of Benedict's hulking size. She was hardly a petite woman, yet she was barely as tall as his chin. He was a bear of a man, quite unlike the gentlemen she was used to.

She cast a last glance at Edward. His eyes were averted.
Coward.

The eyes of the rest of the congregation were fixated on her. It was a sea of suspicion and contempt. To hell with them. Whatever their objections, they couldn't possibly be stronger than hers.

The priest's rasping voice cut through the chaos of her thoughts. Good grief, it had started.

"…is not by any to be enterprised, nor taken in hand unadvisedly, lightly, or wantonly…"

To Amelia, this marriage was highly unadvisable, but her thoughts didn't signify, apparently. She bit the inside of her lip, considering what little information she'd gleaned of her husband in the past twenty-four hours.

Benedict was a landowner.

"...It was ordained for a remedy against sin..."

He was on familiar terms with the Duke of Wildeforde.

"Both in prosperity and adversity..."

He had enough money to warrant a man of business in London.

"...if any man can show any just cause why they may not lawfully be joined together, let him now speak, or else hereafter forever hold his peace..."

Tears pricked her eyes, but that was where they stopped. Weakness was for lesser women, and she would not cry.

She was not without wealth. She had jewels. It would break her heart to sell them, but she could rent a small house in London or escape to the continent until the gossip died down.

She closed her eyes, pressing her lips together. Her nails bit into the silk of her gloves.

Large hands covered hers, warm even through two layers of fabric. They teased at her fingers, loosening her death grip, unlacing them until she no longer held tightly to herself but to him. She looked up. His expression was unexpectedly kind.

"I take thee, Lady Amelia Elizabeth Crofton, to be my wedded wife, to have and to hold..."

Goodness, were they up to this part already?

Her heart began to pound. The ringing in her ears reached a crescendo.

Benedict looked at her intently.

Was it her turn? What was she supposed to say?

The priest repeated himself.

She took a deep breath. "I take thee, Benedict Asterly, to be my wedded husband. To love, cherish, and to obey..."

A handful of words only—choked out. And inside, beyond the walls that kept her safe, something shattered.

Chapter 4 ———————————

At the pub on your wedding night? Your choices have been interesting lately." Edwina slid another pitcher of ale toward Benedict with more force than usual. The drink sloshed over the lip, adding to the sticky layer on top of the chipped and marred wood.

The barmaid's words had the same edge all his conversations tonight rested on. Even the men he worked with were stiff, their playful teasing forced.

"Their blood is blue for a reason, Ben. They're ice cold," one said.

His foreman, Oliver, dug an elbow into Benedict's side. "From what I heard, there was nothing cold about the way they were found. On dis-hab-ill, as the French say."

The men around him laughed, the sound lost in the general din of men talking. It seemed his marriage was the most amusing thing to happen in Abingdale for years, but he couldn't find anything funny in their teasing.

"You didn't lose anything that night, did you? And that's

why you're here instead of there, you know—" The blacksmith made an explicit gesture with his fingers.

"Ben took Wildeforde's fiancée; maybe the duke took something in return?"

The mention of Wildeforde made Benedict's blood boil even more than the mention of his damned wife. The whole damned debacle was his fault.

Benedict pushed back from the bar. "Excuse me if I choose to enjoy my own company tonight, boys."

He walked away from the group, but not before one last, loaded comment reached him. "That's what you get for marrying out of your class."

The blow hit so hard he almost stumbled. He'd known marrying her highness was going to lay waste to his life at home, but he'd been naïvely hoping the problem would remain confined to his property and not follow him here.

He zigzagged his way around patrons in the packed bar. It was busier than usual, but there was still a corner booth available at the back of the room.

Everyone was packed tight, closer to the stage to see tonight's invited speaker, a short, muscular man whose political fervor made him seem six feet tall. Charles Tucker hadn't spoken to the men of Abingdale before, but his reputation preceded him. He was an agitator for change, and tonight he would find a receptive audience.

Benedict had been looking forward to hearing the man talk, but tonight he was too distracted.

Not a wisp of emotion had shown on his wife's face during the ceremony. She'd been like a perfect porcelain doll, beautiful but cold and lifeless. Standing next to her, he'd been awfully aware of the contrast they presented. Her, delicate and gently bred. Him, with his common lineage writ clear across his oxlike frame.

The carriage ride home had been long and tense, filled with Cassandra's earnest attempts to engage with her new sister-in-law and Lady Amelia's terse replies. He hadn't said two words to her. And after showing Amelia to her room, he'd made a poor attempt at comforting his sister before escaping to the firm—Asterly, Barnesworth & Co.—hoping to lose himself in his work.

Then he'd come to the tavern to lose himself in drink. "Keep them coming," he said to Edwina, who'd arrived with another ale.

If he was being honest, it wasn't anger that had pushed him out of the house—it was terror. History seemed hell-bent on repeating, and he could almost hear the devil cackling away. Benedict took another long gulp and tried to swallow down the nausea that always appeared when his thoughts turned to his mother, a woman who'd been born into the aristocracy but had left it when she'd foolishly fallen in love with a footman.

A woman who had regretted her decision so deeply that she'd chosen to abandon her own child to try and establish herself among the *haute ton* in France. Dying alone in Paris had been preferable to living a life in Abingdale with him.

And now he was set to live his failures all over again.

An upswell of applause grabbed his attention. The men were standing. Jeremy, the apprentice engine stoker at the firm, climbed onto a table and shouted. "Down with the bloody toffs. The land is ours! *Vive la France.*"

The comment was met with a clamor of pints against wood, and the young man beamed. Benedict would need to talk to him. He didn't necessarily disagree with the senti-ment, although he'd like to avoid the need for a guillotine, but there were dangers in expressing them so openly.

Alastair McTavish slid into the booth opposite him. His

grey hair was pulled back into a rough queue, and there was a ring of dirt and sweat along the old man's hairline.

"Ye nae standing. Did ye nae appreciate Tucker's fine words?" the grizzled man said in his thick Scottish brogue.

"I was distracted."

"Perhaps now ye've got yerself a fancy wife, the plight of the working man no longer interests you."

Benedict tightened his grip around the glass. Of all nights, tonight was not the night to press him. "The plight of my men will always interest me, McTavish."

The grooves in Alastair's face deepened. A decade ago, the man's frown could make Benedict stand up straighter, square his shoulders, brush the dirt from his breeches. It didn't have the same effect it once did.

"You should nae have done it. There was nae gun at yer head."

It was the same statement he'd thrown at himself over and over in the past eight hours.

"I had no choice. What do you think happens to ladies who are ruined? Should I have that on my conscience?"

Not that his conscience was clear either way. If the past was any indication of the future, he'd condemned her to a life of misery. Riding out a wave of gossip might have been the better choice for her. She might still have found happiness with a man closer to her station.

"Ye've fucked yerself, ye ken that? Ye've gone from a respected independent businessman, the top o' the rung, to a desperate hanger-on that will never be accepted. Not unless ye annul the marriage and get this farce over with."

A hot shame crept up Benedict's neck. His mind had traveled to that same thought every time his insides twisted in a desperate urge to escape. "Annulment is not an option. I may not be a lord, but I am a gentleman. And my catastrophes are not your business, so I suggest you leave."

The older man's face, normally soft and paunchy with the slight yellowed tinge of a man who's known too much drink, reddened. He slammed the mug he was holding on the table. "Nae. Ye're a damn fool. But s'pose blood always tells. P'haps ye're more like yer ma than ye let known."

Each word was more fuel in the furnace that had been burning for days. As the heat and fury and pressure had built, there had been no easy release. Now the room around them dropped away, and all Benedict could see was the sneer of a man who could've—should've—been a bit more damned understanding.

It was the work of a moment to drag the Scotsman out of the booth and thump him—days of frustration finally finding relief. With one hand, he lifted the man back to his feet, ready to deliver a further blow before his foreman captured him in a viselike grip. Few men matched Benedict's size. Oliver dwarfed him.

"Easy now, boss," Oliver said.

Alastair slumped back against the booth, a scarred hand to one eye, a look of pure contempt from the other. "You'll regret this."

Benedict looked around. The whole pub had gone silent, everyone staring at them. Charles Tucker, watching from across the room with his arm lazily across Jeremy's shoulders, had a gleam of speculation in his eye.

"Go home, McTavish," Benedict said, though as his blood settled, guilt crept in. McTavish wasn't the problem, and the man he'd once looked up to had just borne the brunt of Benedict's true anger.

"I'll take him," one of the boys from the firm said, taking the older man by the arm. "Not to worry, boss."

The hum and bustle of the inn began again, and Oliver shoved Benedict roughly into the booth.

"Cool down, lad. The world's not coming to an end. Things are not as bad as you think."

"How can it not be that bad? She's the daughter of a bloody earl."

Oliver shook his head. "Despite what we heard tonight, they're not all the devil."

Benedict went to interject but Oliver stopped him with a hand. "I'm not saying there aren't some right bastards among them, just as there is in any group of people. And you've more reason to hate them than most, I know. But look at our Johnny-boy. His blood's as blue as any of them."

"John doesn't count."

"And Wildeforde. I know the two of you have had your differences lately, but you can't deny that he looks after his people."

"Wildeforde's the ass that got me into this mess."

"That he did. He has his flaws. I'm just suggesting you take a moment. Give your lady a chance before you decide to write her off."

Benedict grunted. He could give his wife a chance, but he wasn't expecting anything to come from it. Her type were what they were.

"Have another drink, lad." The foreman passed him a pint. "There are things that need celebrating."

"Like what?"

"Like the fact that you all but secured the contract we needed. The locomotive you designed is going into production. *Asterly, Barnesworth & Co.* is growing. It's an achievement. One worth honoring if you refuse to celebrate your wedding." He clicked his glass on Benedict's.

Oliver was right. He should be rejoicing in his success.

They'd worked for two years to develop a new and better-performing steam locomotive, and the Americans were ready to sign a deal for three of them.

But the knowledge didn't spark any sense of joy. Not when it was overshadowed by the disaster of his marriage.

~

Amelia twisted, arms bent behind her back as she tried to undo even one of the buttons trapping her in her gown. It was no use. Ringing for help was pointless. The rope had fallen into her hands as soon as she'd yanked it. Apparently, her options were to venture downstairs or sleep in her gown.

A thud sounded on the door that separated her from her husband, and she straightened. Her heart skittered and pranced beneath her too-tight stays as she held her breath. With a lump in her throat, she trained her eyes on the brass doorknob, but it didn't move.

Thank goodness. Her breath escaped with a loud *whoosh*.

She looked around the room again. She'd attended enough house parties to become accustomed to sleeping in strange beds, but she was the daughter of the Earl of Crofton, and she was always given the best room—not one with a lumpy mattress, creaking floorboards, and a threadbare rug.

She pressed her lips together, catching them between her teeth as she realized this probably *was* the best room.

It was plain, outdated, and practically *frugal*. Other than the bed, there was just a chair covered in last century's fabric and a dresser that she supposed must double as a writing desk given it had both a cloudy mirror and a dusty writing set.

The only comfort that she could take was that her things would be arriving soon and then she could leave.

There was a knock at the door. One tap, an awkward

pause, and then two more. Her pulse throbbed in her ears until she smothered it with a deep breath.

She was Lady Amelia Crofton. She could do this.

She stood and smoothed her dress as best she could given the wrinkles worn into it from the day. "Come in."

The heavy wooden door opened, and Mr. Asterly—Benedict—entered. He had to duck his head to avoid hitting the frame. But as he straightened, his size once again overwhelmed her. She knew he was tall; she'd stood opposite him at the altar, but here in her bedchamber the man was a behemoth.

He clasped his hands behind his back. Despite his feet planted firmly on the floor, she got the impression that he would prefer to be anywhere else. "I thought to inquire as to whether you had what you needed," he said.

What she needed. To reverse time. To wake up. For someone to tell her it had been an elaborate prank. "A hot bath wouldn't go astray." She stared pointedly at his damp curls.

He flushed, his copper cheeks taking on a reddish glow. "Of course, I should have thought. Forgive me. I'll see to it." He turned and turned back again, lips pursed.

"The bath is...uh...it's in there." He pointed to the door that separated their bedrooms. "I can go downstairs."

As much as she wanted to soak herself in hot, rose-scented water, entering her husband's bedroom, being surrounding by his things, was more than she was willing to bear at the moment.

"Never mind. It can wait until morning."

"Well then, good night." He half bowed, an uncomfortable jerking movement, like he wasn't entirely sure how to interact with her. Which was fair enough. She had no idea what to do with him either.

"Good night," she said. "Except..."

He raised an eyebrow, waiting for her to stumble out the rest of the sentence.

"I can't get out of my dress."

He blinked. "You can't get out of your dress."

"My lady's maid is in London."

"Your lady's maid is in London."

Good God, had she married a halfwit? Was she destined to a life with a man no better than a parrot? "Do all your conversations consist of so much repetition?"

He ran a hand through his blond locks. "I'm struggling to understand what Lady Amelia Crofton is doing in Abingdale without a maid."

She held her head high but couldn't stop her fingers from rubbing against the textured lace of her long sleeves. "Reid had a family emergency. She was to follow in a few days with my things."

"Why didn't you hire a companion?"

Because I tore out of London in the middle of the night...

She lifted her chin. "A companion was unnecessary. I can take care of myself."

He snorted, crossing his own arms; they were like solid logs. "Because that worked out so well."

His sarcasm rekindled the frustration that had been ever-present since that night. "I had a coachman."

"Who left you alone on the side of the road to freeze to death."

"Who left to get help. My goodness." She clasped her hands primly in front of her in an effort to smother any outward sign of emotion.

His throat bobbed as though swallowing a retort. He was trying to be civil. She could be civil.

"I can't see how it signifies now anyway," she said. "That's yesterday's bread, so to speak."

They tumbled into awkward silence. What in heaven's name was she supposed to say to a husband she didn't know? On her wedding night?

His face softened a fraction. Not into a smile, nothing that welcoming. Just as if he were made of soft soapstone rather than granite.

"Come stand by the light." He gestured toward the dresser. "I'll get you out of your dress."

Her cheeks warmed—never had she been spoken to so intimately—yet they were married now, and she had no desire to sleep in her gown.

She stood in front of the dresser, her back to him as he reached for the top button.

The touch of his fingers against the nape of her neck ignited shivers that travelled the length of her spine and set goose bumps running across her skin. He was so close, his very presence sucked the air from her lungs. One button came free, and then another, the coolness of the night air across her neck a stark contrast to the heat from within.

She looked at his reflection in the dusty mirror. His brow was furrowed in concentration as he worked on one fabric-covered button after another. The candle threw a wash of golden light over one side of his face, throwing the other into shadow. The line of his jaw was harsh, the skin roughened by short stubble a shade darker than his hair and slightly reddish. His complexion, already tanned, took on a fiery glow. In this light, his eyes looked midnight blue. Everything about him was rough, nothing like the soft, elegant men of London.

"How many blasted buttons are there?" His voice, low and gruff, reverberated through her. He caught her eye in the mirror. "How attached to this dress are you? I could just…" He made a wrenching motion with his hands.

She gasped, her heart yammering wildly at the thought of

his tearing the dress from her body. "One ruined dress is quite enough for the week, don't you think?" she managed.

"Of course, my lady." He gave a small smile, and a dimple formed in the granite plane of his cheek. At least *he* found it amusing.

He managed another button. "How did you get into this thing without a maid?"

"The duchess loaned me hers for the day, which was kind of her, under the circumstances."

The look on his face suggested he thought otherwise. "Kindness from Lady Wildeforde? It *was* a special day."

She swallowed hard. "Thank you. I can take it from here." She turned toward him, her hands tucked tightly under her armpits to keep the dress from falling.

He didn't move, and she found herself standing far too close to him. His collar was open at the neck, and wiry strands of hair curled below the deep v that formed at the base of his throat, drawing her eyes farther down. She forced herself to look into his eyes. His heated gaze ignited a shivering that began at the deepest part of her and rippled outward.

"Is there anything else?" he asked.

The words were barely a whisper, but they buffeted through her.

He dragged a thumb lightly across her brow, shifting a stray hair. His touch was nothing like she'd experienced. No gloves, just the heady friction of long, warm, calloused fingertips.

No man had ever stood so close—not even Edward. His lips were only inches from hers, as if waiting on her permission to close the gap. Half of her wanted to lean into the kiss. The other half wanted to shrink back.

He seemed to sense it, pulling away, taking in a deep ragged breath as he did so.

"If that's all, I'll leave you."

She inhaled, an earthy scent of spice and grass setting off something she didn't want to acknowledge. She was exhausted and lost and wasn't quite ready to be alone. "You said we'd met before?"

He stiffened, the warmth in the room slipping away.

"Twice, actually, the first time you visited the Wildeforde estate. But it's no surprise a lady like you wouldn't remember a man like me."

Chapter 5 ———————————

The sitting room was a jumble of mismatched furniture. Books were scattered in small piles. The table had parchment and an abacus, and an empty teacup balanced precariously on the edge. The settee wasn't even facing the center of the room. Instead, it had been dragged in front of the window facing the outside. Stockinged legs hung over the back of it.

Amelia coughed quietly. There was a soft *thunk* of something hitting the floor, and the legs slithered out of sight. A quick second later, the sister—Cassandra—appeared from behind the couch, coming to stand in front of Amelia, book in hand.

She dipped into a shallow, wobbly curtsey. "Good morning, Lady Amelia. Did you sleep well?"

Tall and lanky with a smattering of freckles across her slightly tanned face, she wore a dress two inches too short in a simple fabric. Unlike her brother, Cassandra looked at her with the open admiration of a new debutante.

"I slept very well, thank you." She had slept terribly in fact—something she wanted to put down to a sagging mattress but in truth was more about the memory of Benedict's breath, hot on her neck. The thought of his hand tracing a line across her brow.

No. She had not slept well at all.

"I put the flowers on your breakfast tray. I thought they might cheer you up."

"That was very kind of you. They were very pretty." It had been touching, actually. They were hardly the hothouse flowers Edward sent each week—at least his secretary sent each week—but the gesture was sweet.

Goodness. Sweet. When was the last time she'd met anyone like that? London and sweetness were not common bedfellows. But then, she wasn't in London anymore. No. She was in Abingdale, and her best way forward was to gain as much insight into her situation as possible. And Cassandra was her first step.

"I thought perhaps you and I could have tea. Get to know each other." Amelia reached for the bell rope to summon one of the maids.

"That doesn't work," Cassandra said, scooting around Amelia and ducking her head into the hall.

"Daisy, can we please have some tea?" she yelled. She turned back to Amelia. "It shouldn't take long. Mrs. Greenhill leaves a kettle on the stove all day in winter." Cassandra cleared off the center table, stacking the papers in a pile on the floor. She dragged two seats to face each other.

Amelia took her place neatly on the edge of the seat, her hands folded into her lap. Cassandra did the same, studying Amelia's hands and mimicking their placement.

There was a long silence before Lady Amelia gestured

toward the book in Cassandra's hands. "What are you reading?"

"The final Princess Lionberry novel. Have you read them?"

"I can't say that I have."

Cassandra blossomed into animation, her expression brightening, her hands gesturing wildly. "They're splendiferous. Princess Lionberry lives in an enormous castle, but it's bewitched and things are alive that shouldn't be and are causing all sorts of problems."

"Oh my. How...troublesome."

"You don't need to worry. Nothing's alive in this house that shouldn't be." She patted Amelia's hand in a surprisingly comforting gesture.

"What a relief."

"What are you reading?" Cassandra asked.

"I don't read."

Cassandra's jaw dropped open. "You can't *read*?"

"Of course I *can* read. I've read Debrett's cover to cover a dozen times. I *don't* read."

"Why not?" The girl's face was one of horrified curiosity.

"Novels are frivolous. And men don't like bluestockings. There's nothing appealing about a woman who might be more intelligent than he is."

Cassandra pursed her lips, her face the epitome of confusion. "But Fiona says that girls are as smart as boys and should learn all the same things they do."

"And is this Fiona married?"

"Well...no."

"I rest my case. If you want to be a success on the marriage mart, you need to avoid books like they're wealthy young men with trade backgrounds. Tempting but entirely unsuitable."

Cassandra's eyes filled with tears, and she began to twist the fabric of her skirts.

Darn it. Even Amelia balked at making children cry. "I'm sure it's perfectly fine to read books at your age. I won't tell."

Cassandra looked at her hopefully. "Did you read books as a child?"

"Of course. I read *Lady Quinn's Guide to a Perfect Household*, *Social Graces* by Miss Megan Dunley, *The Language of Flowers* by Charlotte de la Tour."

Her governess had given her a new book to read and memorize each fortnight. She'd hated every page of them. It was only now that she saw the benefit of such strict tutelage.

"But they're instruction books." Cassandra wrinkled her nose.

"And very good ones. You can borrow my copies when they arrive." Regardless of one's station, there was no excuse for not managing a strict and effective household. Amelia wouldn't be here for long, but she would do what she could to teach the girl in the meantime.

A thin gawky maid who couldn't be more than fifteen stopped in the doorway, looking ready to collapse under the size of the unpolished tray she carried. Her eyes darted between Amelia and Cassandra. Hesitantly, she entered and put the tray on the table between them.

Amelia looked at the tray and then looked at the maid. "I'm sorry. We asked for the tea service."

Confused, the girl looked from the tray to Amelia and back again. "Yes, m'lady. And I've brought it."

"You've brought a teapot and some cups. Where's the coffeepot?"

"P . . . Pardon, m'lady. I thought you wanted tea."

Amelia sighed. The staff were clearly going to require a lot of work. "It's fine. Please bring it now."

Her housemaid bobbed a quick curtsey and picked up the tea tray.

"What are you doing?" Amelia asked.

The maid froze. "Taking back the tea to get you coffee, m'lady."

Amelia rolled her eyes. If the girl couldn't get tea right, how on Earth were they supposed to handle a larger party?

"Leave the tea. Bring the coffeepot."

The girl nodded and scurried out of the room.

"I don't drink coffee," Cassandra said.

"Neither do I." Amelia poured tea into the two cups. "Deplorable stuff. Goodness knows why anyone drinks it."

She had a second cousin that drank coffee, but he also held on to last century's obsession with wigs, so he could hardly be considered a barometer of taste.

"Then why did you ask for coffee if you don't want to drink it?" Cassandra stirred sugar into her tea with youthful vigor. Amelia delicately dipped her spoon once, twice into the brew.

"Because when you serve tea, you also serve coffee for those who prefer the latter." She sipped. Divine. If she closed her eyes, she could almost imagine she was in London and the past few days were just a bad dream.

Cassandra slurped at her drink, sending shudders down Amelia's spine. "That seems dreadfully wasteful. Ben would never approve."

"It's the aristocracy, my dear. If we insist on watching our pennies, we might as well be middle class."

The housemaid came in with a coffeepot on a tray, face falling when she saw both of the girls drinking tea.

Amelia acknowledged the housemaid with a slight nod. "Thank you—?"

The girl turned a deeper shade of crimson. "It's Daisy, m'lady. We met yesterday."

"Of course. Thank you, Daisy."

The maid left, and Amelia turned to her new sister-in-law. What she needed was information. Then she could form a plan.

"I thought when the weather cleared, we could go on a tour. You could show me Abingdale."

Cassandra nodded. "I'll take you to Mrs. Duggan's bakery. She makes delicious apple tarts."

Amelia counted backward from five. Were all children this frustrating? "I was more thinking the estates *around* Abingdale. A tour of the grand houses nearby."

"Eh." Cassandra shrugged, suddenly less interested. "There's Wildeforde House, I suppose. But I heard Mrs. Greenhill say you have already visited there."

Amelia swallowed. "Any houses *other* than Lord Wildeforde's?"

The girl tapped her finger against her cheek as she thought. "Lady Karstark has a big house, but she's in the next county."

Amelia's thoughts immediately shifted to the decrepit Lord Karstark who'd condemned her to this life. His was not an acquaintance that she particularly wanted to pursue. But she was also a pragmatist and could recognize that there weren't many other options.

"I made Ben promise to take me to see their library one day. He says it's heaps bigger than our study, with thousands of books. It's dusty, though."

"Does he visit often?" Perhaps his relationship with them was not as frosty as it had seemed at first. Maybe he could introduce her to Lady Karstark, and Amelia wouldn't be as alone out here as she first thought.

"No. He only went once—with his mama when he was my age."

His mother. That explained the age gap between brother and sister. "You both look so similar I wouldn't have guessed you had different mothers."

Cassandra flushed red. "His mother was very pretty. There's a painting of her in the attic," she whispered.

"How exciting. You'll have to take me up there." Not that she was remotely interested in rummaging through a dusty attic. She *was* interested in learning more about the increasingly intriguing background of her husband, though.

"And was Benedict's mother close to Lady Karstark?"

Cassandra shook her head. "I don't know. I think so. He doesn't like to talk about her."

"Lady Karstark?"

"His mama. He rants about the Karstarks all the time. He thinks Lord Karstark's the devil."

It was a sentiment Amelia shared. Although she rather thought the devil had the better end of the comparison. But surely there was more to it. "Why does he think that?"

"I'm not sure."

Cassandra was proving a frustratingly poor source of valuable information. "Does your brother have any fancy visitors?"

"Not really."

"Does he go visiting?"

"Why are you asking all these questions?"

Amelia scoffed. "Don't be silly. This is just conversation."

Cassandra looked at her suspiciously. "If it were a conversation, wouldn't I get to ask questions?"

"Very well, what would you like to know?"

"Do you love my brother?"

Amelia choked on her tea. "I barely know your brother."

Cassandra frowned.

"But I'm sure he's a lovely person."

"Then why did you marry him?"

Because she was an idiot, Edward was a coward, and Karstark was a jackass. "I believe it's my turn to ask a question." And since the child was asking the tough questions so would she. "What happened to your parents?"

Cassandra dropped her gaze and began to fiddle with the handle on her cup. "They died. There was a carriage accident two years ago."

Two years was fresh. It had taken Amelia at least that long to be able to speak about her mother with anyone. "I lost my mother when I was about your age. It's not easy. I'm sorry."

And she was. It was a hard thing as a girl to grow up without a female hand to guide you. A governess could only do so much.

"Ben takes good care of me."

"I don't doubt. You're very lucky." Amelia hadn't had that fortune. Her father had made it clear within days of her mother's death that she was a nuisance, and other than giving her strict instructions on the appropriate ways to behave, he'd paid very little attention to her.

"What happened to Benedict's mother?"

Cassandra shook her head. "He doesn't like to talk about that."

Getting information out of a child was like getting a decent rendition of Serenade Number 13 out of a country orchestra. "Come now. That's hardly fair. I thought we had an agreement."

"Ben really doesn't—" She stopped and looked up at the

sound of the drawing room door swinging open; her face was that of a child caught sneaking an extra sweet.

Dash it. Just when it was getting interesting.

Amelia turned to face her husband. Everything about him was iron and stone, from the expression on his face to the muscles exposed by his rolled-up shirtsleeves and open collar. She was not fooled by his casual lean against the doorframe. Every inch of him was tense.

"Good day," she said. There. That was perfectly polite. This man might bring out the absolute worst in her, but she would make the effort. Last night, he had been rather gentlemanly for a commoner. Perhaps they could make it through the next few days without drawing blood.

"An inquisition before lunch, Lady Amelia?" There was nothing gentle about his tone. Whatever truce they'd come to last night was clearly over.

From her seated position, she was forced to look up at him, an abdication of power she wasn't happy to bestow. She'd lost enough this week. She didn't want to lose the upper hand as well.

"Hardly. There's not a chain or stale bread in sight."

"Yet an interrogation nonetheless."

She rolled her eyes. Her husband was proving to be quite dramatic. "I wasn't aware interrogations involved tea and lemon cake—the fuss about those prison hulks is clearly overstated."

Benedict's eyes bulged, and she felt some small satisfaction. She shouldn't goad him. She knew she shouldn't, but she'd tossed and turned half the night. The memory of his breath against her lips as he'd almost kissed her made her skin tingle, and every movement against the thin cotton sheet had been a reminder that prodded her awake.

And a lack of sleep did nothing to improve her mood.

Clearly trying to put on a good front for his sister, he moved out of the doorway and took the seat next to Cassandra. He looked ridiculous relaxing back against the delicate floral chair, which looked ready to collapse beneath him.

"I hope you're enjoying your first day in your new home, my lady."

"It might have started with a tour of the house, don't you think?"

If he wanted to exchange sarcasms, she was more than ready. She was stuck, sleep-deprived in a strange house, in the middle of nowhere, married against her will, and with no more than a handful of dresses to her name. And he had the gall to be offended at the direction of her conversation?

His patience clearly splintered. "I would have offered, but you didn't come down to join us at breakfast," he said, his voice laden with false courtesy.

"I didn't know the way." She took a long sip of tea. He could be as sore-toothed as he liked. She'd withstood worse.

He smiled. "Ah, of course. My apologies. So we can expect you tomorrow then? We breakfast at seven."

Seven? Not a chance. She placed her teacup back on the table between them and leaned forward. "Married women breakfast in bed." And not at seven in the morning. Good grief.

"Of course." Two words, but he used them as an obnoxious victory flag she wanted to smother him in.

"For goodness' sakes, I've been looking forward to breakfast in bed since I was twelve. Must you take this from me too?"

"I'm twelve!"

Both of them turned toward Cassandra, who was giving Amelia a tentative smile.

Amelia swallowed the frustration, reining in the volume

of her voice. The last thing she needed was to alienate the only ally she had in this house. "Twelve is a perfectly lovely age. I advise you to remain there for as long as possible."

"We can take you for a tour now, if you like," Cassandra said.

"That would be lovely," Amelia replied, standing.

"Yes. Let's." Benedict also stood and offered Amelia his arm.

She didn't want to take it. Maybe she was balking at the inherent power imbalance in him taking the lead, maybe it was because she wasn't sure she wouldn't burst into tears.

"Are we going?" Cassandra asked, taking Amelia's other hand in hers, completely oblivious to the standoff.

Releasing a frustrated sigh, Benedict swept his arm wide. "This is the sitting room."

"I had gathered," she replied as dryly as she could muster. Cassandra giggled. He gave the two of them and their shared camaraderie a suspicious glare.

Out in the foyer, he indicated the room next to it. "That's the dining room. Should you care to join us this evening. Through it is the kitchen." He turned to indicate the rooms at the back. "This back room is the library."

Then, as if rudeness didn't come easily to him, he added, "You're welcome to any of the books in it, obviously."

And even though she was perfectly capable of delivering a cut direct, she inclined her head. "Thank you."

"Amelia won't need the library," Cassandra said. "Did you know ladies don't read?"

He blinked. Twice. Bewildered.

"I read," she ground out, in case he thought her unedu-cated. "I don't read novels. It's not the done thing."

"How...utterly unsurprising."

Amelia had the sense that she'd just failed some sort

of test, and it rankled. She was not used to failing at anything, let alone failing to meet a set of social standards. She *set* the standards. Who did he think he was? Before she could respond, he'd dismissed the conversation and moved on.

"Upstairs on the left is your bedroom, my bedroom, the nursery and the playroom. Welcome to The Cottage."

Amelia indicated the doors on the right side of the hall they were standing in. "And the east and west wings of the house?"

Cassandra shook her head. "There are no wings."

"Please." She crossed her arms. "I may have been half asleep when I arrived yesterday and more than a little wishful, but even I can't have hallucinated two thirds of a building."

"The wings are closed." He stood with his feet set wide as though he could block her from seeing what was plain in front of her face. Three tall wooden doors that were certainly not decorative—nothing in the house was—so were presumably functional. Which meant they very much led somewhere.

Amelia skirted around him and pushed on one of the brass handles. It didn't budge. "I'd like to take a look," she said, turning to face him.

"It is closed."

She huffed. *Ludicrous.* "Unless you bricked up each doorway, closed can become open. Goodness, Mr. Asterly, one would almost think you're hiding a hoard of dead bodies. Or are they live ones? All your previous wives locked away forever?"

"You're being ridiculous."

"Ridiculous is living in ten rooms instead of fifty." She turned to Benedict's sister. "Cassandra?"

The girl shrugged. "I've never been in there. Father used

to say that big houses were lonely houses, and we should move to a real cottage."

In Amelia's experience, all houses were lonely ones when you took away the guests and the orchestra. Better a lonely and well-appointed one. "Then why didn't you move?"

"Mama liked the gardens."

There was no deep grief in the words, but nevertheless Benedict put a protective arm around his sister. "That's enough. I'm sorry the house doesn't meet your elevated expectations, Lady Amelia. But you're just going to have to live with it."

Chapter 6

Maybe she's not coming down for dinner." Cassandra fiddled with her water glass. "You weren't very nice to her today."

Benedict grunted. He hadn't been very nice to his wife today. He'd come in with every intention of making her comfortable, building on their moment together the night before, and instead he had walked in on her discussing his mother and snapped.

For the umpteenth time, he sighed. It was only natural she'd want to know about his family. Hell, it was probably a good sign that she was interested enough to inquire.

But he'd been on edge all day, ever since that blasted almost-kiss, and it had taken just the thought of his mother to push him over.

His mother, the woman he'd never been able to please, trapped in a life she didn't want. His wife, in the very same position.

"Maybe she doesn't know dinner is ready. Maybe she thought it was earlier. We are eating really late tonight."

"It's seven. People in town eat at seven. She knows dinner's ready." He was a damned fool for changing their dinnertime to begin with. Amelia was a country woman now and would need to get used to country hours. "She didn't come down for breakfast; my guess is she's not coming down for dinner."

Damn. He was going to have to apologize. That much was clear. The only thing worse than marriage to a woman who didn't love you was marriage to a woman who detested you.

"If she doesn't want to join us, then it's your fault for yelling at her." As Cassandra threw the accusation out there, her voice wobbled. It had been easy for him to spend the afternoon wallowing in self-pity. He had to remember that his sister's life had been upended just as much. And she didn't have the thick skin needed not to take this disaster personally.

The thread of regret that had sat with him all afternoon twisted some more. "I'm sorry, poppet. I'll be nicer tomorrow. I promise." He'd spent the afternoon finding the heaviest things in the firm and moving them in an effort to distract himself from thoughts that plagued him every time he stood still.

The slow reveal of her skin as he'd undone each button.

The flare of heat as she'd turned, so close he could feel her breath.

The ache of desire as he'd leaned in to kiss her.

He rubbed the space between his eyebrows, but the thoughts could not be pushed from his mind. "We'll wait another few minutes."

"But you just said she's not—" Cassandra broke off as Amelia appeared in the doorway.

His chest tightened at the sight of her. The evening gown she wore was creased but hugged tight across her breasts. The dress hid her figure, but he'd already seen the gentle tapering of her waist, the silhouette of her body beneath her shift. Somehow knowing what was unseen beneath the fabric was just as arousing.

He stood as she entered, Cassandra following suit.

"I'm not interrupting, am I?" Her voice was tart, her demeanor cool and aloof. It made a mockery of his attraction to her, and only the look of hope and welcome on his sister's face stopped him from responding acerbically in kind.

"Not at all," he managed.

Amelia stayed in the doorway as if she hadn't quite decided to join them yet. "I didn't hear the dinner gong," she said.

Cassandra cocked her head. "What's a dinner gong?"

Amelia paused, and the briefest flicker of confusion showed on her face. "It lets people know when it's time to dress for dinner."

"Why were you undressed?"

"In London, people put on nicer clothes for dinner," Benedict interrupted, attempting to cut the conversation short. Amelia could think what she liked about him, but it would devastate Cassandra if Amelia thought her uneducated.

"Huh. Is that why you changed, Ben?" Cassandra asked. "I thought you'd burnt another hole in your shirt."

Devil save him from troublesome sisters.

He had changed. He'd gone through practically every shirt in his closet, ninety percent of which were discarded immediately, before he'd found something somewhat suitable.

"Nice" clothing was a waste of money when they'd likely be covered in soot within minutes of entering the firm. Not that he cared.

He walked the length of the table and pulled Amelia's chair back. As she sat, he got a whiff of the same jasmine perfume she'd been wearing the night before, the scent causing an unwelcome stirring in his groin.

"Thank you," she murmured, completely unaware of the maddening effect she had on him. "I take it Greenhill is not waiting on us tonight."

"We generally serve ourselves."

She made a noise in her throat, somewhere between a cough and a gurgle. But her face remained impassive as she reached for the spoons and served herself.

"Did you enjoy your afternoon?" he asked as he piled his own plate.

"Yes, thank you. I was writing letters." She took a delicate forkful of meat and gravy. "Oh my." She pressed fingers against her lips, and her eyes scanned the room.

Blast. He hadn't thought to warn her off the sauce. Would the elegant Lady Amelia dare spit out her food? Or would she soldier through?

She fixed him with a glare and chewed once, twice, and swallowed hard before giving him another polite smile and reaching for her wine glass.

"Is this a joke?" she asked after a long swallow.

"It's best not to try the sauces," Cassandra said.

Hesitantly, Amelia ate a small forkful of the potato. "Well, on the bright side, not tasting like anything is a step up from tasting like that." She wrinkled her nose at the sauce. "Your cook is away, I take it."

"Daisy Greenhill is our cook. Mrs. Greenhill struggles with her eyesight these days."

"Daisy is your cook and your housemaid? Perhaps she got her jars mixed up. Silver polish in the salt tin."

"She's gotten much better," Cassandra said. "Only one side of the toast gets burnt now."

"And have you considered replacing dear Daisy?"

In the one sentence, she demonstrated everything he hated about her kind. "I'm afraid people aren't as disposable in our world as they are in yours."

Amelia rolled her eyes. "I'm not saying chop off her head, but expecting one to do the job she's paid for is hardly unreasonable."

He stabbed his fork into the beef. "Daisy is an excellent housemaid."

"The dust under my bedroom rug say otherwise." It may have been said under her breath, but there was no doubt he was meant to hear it.

Benedict ground his teeth. Yes, Daisy struggled in the kitchen, and her attention to detail was not the best. But she was a sweet girl, and her grandparents had been working here since his mother and father had married.

In truth, he had been thinking about hiring a cook. Though he wouldn't do it now and give her the satisfaction.

"Is there anything on this plate that's safe to eat?"

"You're exaggerating," he bit out. He'd come in to dinner this evening fully prepared to raise the white flag if it meant restoring some peace and comfort to the house. But damn his wife was aggravating.

She folded her napkin and placed it on the table beside her. "Mr. Asterly, there were plenty of things I thought I was going to miss, living out here in the middle of nowhere. I didn't think eating was one of them."

Enough is enough. "Well, you'll be pleased to know you needn't suffer Daisy's cooking tomorrow."

"Well, that's a relief."

Cassandra looked at him, confused, but he ignored it. "Tomorrow is your turn to cook."

Amelia's tight smile went slack. "Pardon?"

"We take turns in this house to do the primary chores. Cooking, shopping, cleaning of the common areas. Your personal rooms are your responsibility, of course."

"You are joking." His wife looked as aghast now as she had when their marriage was first proposed.

"I'm not." Benedict was glad that Amelia had her horrified stare focused on him because his sister's face was just as shocked. "I'll have Daisy bring you the new roster in the morning."

"If you think I'm going to scurry about in the dust, you are a bedlamite."

He watched to make sure her hand didn't twitch toward the dinner knife. Instead they were clasped together in front of her so tightly her knuckles had whitened. *Good.* "You were fool enough to travel alone and, in the process, upturned my life as well as yours. You've married into this world, my lady. The sooner you accept it, and everything that comes with it, the better."

"This...I..." Her mouth opened and closed like a trout gasping for air.

It didn't bring the satisfaction he was expecting, to see her speechless. So he toned it down. Slightly. "There are worse things than a life in the country."

"Hmph. I daresay it's an improvement on city slums or"— she shuddered—"Australia."

Brilliant. Now she was comparing his house to a colony of thieves and murderers. He'd been a fool to soften. It made it easier for her to find a place to pierce.

She pushed back from her chair. "Cassandra, it has been

lovely…eating…with you. I look forward to seeing you tomorrow. Good night, Mr. Asterly."

With a swish of her skirts she stormed from the room. Cassandra slowly shook her head.

"It's for her own good," he said gruffly. "I trust you'll keep this secret."

"This is not going to end well."

Chapter 7 ——————

To gird one's loins. According to one of Benedict's tutors, it was a term that came from Africa. Tribesmen would wrap the fabric skirts they wore up tight around their groins before battle to keep them from tripping as they ran.

Right now, Benedict needed to do more than wrap his balls in fabric. He needed steel armor around them.

Taking a deep breath, he opened the door between their rooms. She didn't stir. He was transfixed for a moment as he took in the sight of her sleeping. Blond hair was loose over the pillows, scrunched in rough, uneven waves. She had one pillow hugged close to her body. In sleep, she looked small and innocent. It almost made him regret what he was about to do. But it was for the best. He'd already watched his mother waste away in this bedroom, dreaming of a better life. He'd be damned if he let his wife suffer the same fate.

Which brought him back to his current task. She would engage with her new life until it was no longer new. She would be an active participant in this family until she no longer wanted to leave it. And she would start today.

He coughed.

Nothing.

He banged the door into the wall.

Nothing.

Bloody hell. The woman could sleep through a dozen steam trumpets. He dumped the bundle of clothes he was holding on her dresser and strode to the curtains. "Rise and shine, Mrs. Asterly."

He yanked the curtains open. The sun was just starting to rise, a wash of yellow through the pine trees and over the snow, creating ribbons of light and long purple shadows. It was his favorite time of day. Perhaps, in time, it would be an opinion they shared.

"Mmmhpmph." Amelia turned over to face the wall, bringing the pillow over her head.

"It's eight o'clock," he said in his most annoying, sing-song voice.

"Then why are you awake?"

Awake? He'd been up for three hours, despite a night spent tossing and turning. "You're in the country now, Mrs. Asterly. Time to get used to country hours."

She burrowed so far under the covers that he could barely hear her response. "You have until the count of three to exit this room."

He laughed, leaning against the wall, trying to paint a picture of nonchalance, despite the unreasonable anxiety that bubbled away. "You'd be a little more terrifying if I hadn't seen the trail of saliva on your pillow."

Emerging from her cocoon, she glared at him. "You are no gentleman."

The smile he gave her was intentionally goading. He

preferred her spitting mad; it made him feel less of a cad for doing what he planned to. "I think we've established my lack of breeding well enough. You have a busy day. Time to get up."

She flung herself back down and pulled the blankets over her head.

This is for her own good. With three quick strides, he reached the foot of her bed, grabbed a fistful of downy quilt in each hand and pulled.

Her nightdress might have covered her to the chin, but it had ridden up over her knees and left her long, lithe calves exposed.

Distracted, he didn't see the pillow she flung at him until it hit him square in the face.

"You boor."

He deserved that, but he was pushing ahead regardless. "I'm not going until you're up and dressed, so you might as well get on with it." He grabbed the clothes from the dresser. "These are for you," he said, tossing them to her.

She shook them out and held them up with a sour look. "And what are these?"

"I assume you don't want to be working in your dresses. You only have three."

She clasped her hands in her lap and leaned forward, fixing him with the type of look adults generally used on the very young or the very crazy. "I don't work," she said in a matter-of-fact tone.

"You do today. Here's the roster."

"Roster?"

"Duty roster for the week. What each of us is responsible for." He thrust the timetable he'd been working on all morning at her. With a scowl, she took it.

"Wash the laundry, polish the banisters, buy groceries,

cook dinner. You forget, Mr. Asterly, that I've been in this house for two days now, and I can tell you, that banister has not been polished in recent memory. Don't try to tell me that this roster of yours is common practice."

Damn. He scrambled for an excuse. "You don't feel that polished banisters are appropriate for a household led by a woman of your station?"

She climbed out of bed, pulling on an old robe of his that Mrs. Greenhill must have dug out from somewhere. The sight of her in his clothes did uncomfortable things to him.

She turned her pert little nose up, arms akimbo. "Of course they are. It would be an embarrassment to receive guests in that foyer."

He gave her a wolfish smile. "Well, with an extra person added to the schedule, we can meet your lofty expectations."

Benedict had more experience with steam and pressure than most people, and if Amelia were an engine, she'd be ready to explode. "What do we hire a maid *and* a housekeeper for, if not to polish the banister?"

He shrugged. "Mrs. Greenhill doesn't clean. She's too old."

"She's too old to *clean*?"

"Indeed. She is almost sixty." It was an effort to keep a straight face. Her outraged expression was the first moment of joy he'd had since that blasted night he'd found her. Petty, perhaps, but Lady Amelia managed to bring out the worst in him.

"This is ridiculous. I am a married lady in charge of a household. I delegate. I do not *do*. That's what the lady of the house is for."

At some point in the early hours of the morning while he'd been lying in bed thinking about her, he'd anticipated her response.

He took a step closer to her. "A married lady of the house does a whole host of other things." He grazed her arm with the back of his hand, flinching as desire coursed through him. His cock throbbed as she shivered—a confounding sign that whatever this damnable feeling was, he wasn't alone in it. He barely managed to perform his next line. "If you want to fill a traditional role, just give me the word. Otherwise, the roster is here."

It was a bluff—but she didn't know that. Her eyes widened in outrage. At him? Or how she felt? He let go of her, and she immediately stepped back.

"You are a cur."

He winked, hopefully convincingly, and retrieved the package he'd left on her desk, handing it to her. "I found this book in the library." That was a complete fabrication. He'd gone into town first thing to purchase a copy of Mrs. Baker's *Cookery and Cleaning Guide for the Modern Household.* "Enjoy your day being useful, my lady."

As he turned and walked toward the door that separated their bedrooms, the book sailed past his ear, crashing into the wall.

⌒

"Would you like help?" Cassandra sat on the edge of the long bench that ran through the middle of the kitchen, swinging her legs and holding out a stain-covered cap.

Amelia shook her head. The ill-fitting, coarsely spun work dress Benedict had given her was bad enough; she wouldn't stuff her curls into a filthy headpiece.

"I don't need help, thank you very much." Benedict had accused her of being useless, and goodness, it made her blood boil. "*Good-for-nothing. Pointless. Of no worth other than the marriage I arranged.*" Her father had thrown those insults at her time and time again. To have them echoed here, of all places, was intolerable.

So she would show him. She would prove him wrong. She would make the best blasted pie he had ever tasted, and he would realize that Lady Amelia Crofton—now Asterly— was the furthest thing from useless.

She stared at the pots hanging from the wall and wondered exactly what was meant by "medium to large."

"Have you ever cooked a pie before?" Cassandra asked.

"No, but there are instructions. I can follow instructions."

"It's called a recipe."

"I can follow a recipe." With two hands, she lifted the cast-iron pot off its hook. The crash was loud as it fell to the benchtop. The darned thing was heavier than it looked.

She hefted it onto the stove top. *Now what?*

"You'll need to add more wood to the stove," Cassandra said.

Right. If it wasn't bad enough that she had no idea what she was doing, there was a witness to her incompetence. Not that a lack of cooking skills was frowned on in her circles. But if she could avoid looking like a fool, she tended to take that option.

"Of course. I'm just checking to make sure the pot fits first." The instructions didn't include how to add wood to a stove. She surveyed the room, hands on her hips.

Cassandra sighed, jumped off the table, and grabbed several logs from the metal box against the wall. Opening the stove door, she tossed them inside. The flames under the stove grew. She turned to Amelia. "Didn't you ever make jam when you were my age?"

"No."

"Cookies?"

"No."

"Scrambled eggs?"

Amelia sighed. "I can't say that I've ever been in a kitchen before today."

Cassandra hopped back onto the bench. "What did you do when you were young?"

"I did the same things that I do now—wrote letters, played piano, embroidered." There was no food in the kitchen, just pots and pans, knives and towels.

Where in heavens was the food kept if not in the kitchen?

"What are you looking for?"

Amelia handed her the instructions.

"Larders," Cassandra said, pointing to two doors at the end of the room. "I'll take the dry larder. You take the wet." Together they collected all the ingredients needed to make the meal, piling them on the center bench. Amelia picked up the butter.

The instructions called for a quarter pound of butter. How was she supposed to measure a quarter pound? She shrugged and tossed the entire slab into the saucepan on the stove.

Cassandra continued to pepper her with questions.

"Did you climb trees?"

"Certainly not."

"Go fishing?"

Amelia turned to the slab of meat in front of her, the smell making her queasy. "Cassandra, I'm a lady. Ladies don't climb trees or fish." Or cook, really.

"But you weren't always a lady. You must have been a child at some point."

"Stop your questions and tell me what to do next."

Her childhood did not bear thinking about. She had been in

duchess training from the moment she could walk and talk. She'd never much minded the childhood she'd missed out on because the reward was worth it—but now she'd had neither a childhood nor a title, and that was a bitter, bitter pill.

"Use this knife," Cassandra said, handing a long blade to her.

Amelia held the large kitchen knife awkwardly in both hands and tried to saw through the lamb, but the meat kept moving. Resigning herself, she held the meat still with her left hand, almost dry retching at the cold, sticky texture.

She held up her fingers and shuddered. He would pay for this.

Enjoy being useful.

The nerve. Well, he had a surprise coming. She would make this dratted pie, clean the dratted banisters, do the laundry, and when her things arrived, she would sell some of her jewelry and disappear. It would be a shame to lose any piece from her collection, but it was better than being forced to do manual labor.

She noticed the smell of acrid smoke just as Cassandra gasped and jumped down from the bench toward the stovetop. The butter in the pan caught fire a second later.

Amelia grabbed Cassandra and shoved her away from the flames. The black smoke coming off the pan stung her eyes. Luckily, the fire was small and confined to the pot.

"I am going to kill your brother," Amelia said through gritted teeth as she grabbed the kettle of water.

"Don't!"

But it was too late. Amelia turned around at the shriek, but she'd already tipped the kettle. There was a roar as the fire ballooned and droplets of flame shot away from the pan.

The pain in her shoulder was extraordinary as fire scorched her dress. A lock of hair that hung loose caught alight.

Without thinking, Amelia grabbed at the small lick of flame by her head, unprepared for the searing agony of her hand.

"Aaaahhhh!"

It was unlike anything she'd felt before. She couldn't breathe properly. The burn was excruciating—loud and large and overwhelming. It stretched across her entire palm and three fingers, quickly blistering.

A small whimper escaped her. Why? Why did everything have to go wrong? Was it not enough that she was stuck out here in some godforsaken backwater? Was this torture truly necessary?

She blew on the burn, trying to soothe it, but the stream of air only intensified the pain. "I...Uh..." Her thoughts refused to come together, overpowered by the sheer fierceness of the burn.

"Come here." Cassandra grabbed her by the other wrist and towed her toward the scullery, where she dunked Amelia's hand in a bucket of cold water. "Let it sit in there until the water warms up. I'll go fetch another bucket."

The twelve-year-old grabbed an empty bucket that sat by the scullery door and rushed outside.

The sudden emptiness of the room, the unfamiliar setting, the impact of the day and the days before that defeated her. Tears became huge wracking sobs. She struggled for breath.

She was lost. She was without purpose.

Her entire life she'd had one job, knowing her only value was in the power and influence she would marry into, and she'd failed.

At what point Cassandra came back in, she didn't know. The first she was aware of it, the child was rubbing giant, gentle circles between her shoulder blades.

"It will be all right," Cassandra said. "We can go into town and buy a pie from the bakery."

"I…I just didn't want him to be *right*. I didn't want to be *useless*." She tried to wipe away the tears, mortified that she'd been caught in such a state. A duchess presents a calm presence at all times.

"We don't have to tell him. I don't tell him stuff all the time."

Amelia looked at the girl in front of her. Cassandra's face was sympathetic and kind and welcoming. Amelia couldn't remember the last time someone had looked at her with such openness.

"It will be all right," Cassandra repeated.

Amelia nodded. She looked for a handkerchief to wipe away her tears and the snot that was running out of her nose, but there was none in sight.

"Just use your apron. No one will know."

Amelia laughed. Just a little bit. And wiped the corner across her face. If she was going to make a fool of herself in front of anyone in this household, she was glad it was this Asterly sibling.

Then the door to the scullery opened, and the one person she really did not want to see stood in the doorway.

"What the hell is going on?"

Chapter 8 ————————————————

The place was chaos.

Benedict had walked into an empty kitchen on fire. The stove was alight, there was a leg of lamb on the floor, and a smoldering rag had scorched the bench. The room smelled of burnt oil and something more acrid. He grabbed a lid and put it over the pan, smothering the flames. He grabbed a cutting board and tossed it onto the still-smoking rag.

Then he'd gone in search of the girls, his heart racing.

What he'd found stopped him dead.

Tears had left sooty tracks down Amelia's face. A chunk of her hair was missing, the ends fried. Her hand sat in a bucket of water in the sink.

His stomach churned at the sight. "What happened?" he asked, crossing the room in four strides and taking her wrist in his hand.

An angry red mark marred her otherwise perfect skin.

"There was an accident." How his wife managed to sound so composed, so in control, when everything about her appeared so tumultuous, he didn't know. But her voice was steady, imperious, and determined.

But it hadn't been an accident. Not really.

He'd known she had no idea what to do in a kitchen when he'd given her the bloody schedule. He'd wanted a disaster—for her to fail completely. He just hadn't expected she'd get hurt doing it.

He should have known better. "I'm so sorry."

"*You're* sorry? I didn't realize that you owned my actions as well as my person, Mr. Asterly. Pray, do let me know when I have some sort of autonomy, even if it is just over my mistakes."

He let go of her hand and stepped back. "I apologize."

She arched an eyebrow. If he hadn't seen the tear tracks, if his sister hadn't been shaking her head in warning in the background, he might not have realized that the woman in front of him was, in fact, presenting an exceptional façade.

One that he would let her keep, since he'd managed to take everything else from her.

"Cassandra, go ask Daisy for a salve," he said. "I'll cook tonight."

⟍

Standing at the sideboard, Benedict layered a thick spread of jam over his burnt toast, followed by an equally thick layer of marmalade.

An enjoyable breakfast had become a science since Mrs. Greenhill had become too blind to cook. Enough jam to mask the taste of burnt bread. Enough bitter marmalade to mask all the sugar in jam.

He stuffed a piece in his mouth before he'd even turned away. It was best eaten quickly and without thinking.

Turning back to the center of the room, the sight of Lady Amelia in the doorway set him coughing. She had never come down for breakfast before. And he'd never seen that dress with its slimmer fit skimming over her curves. An absurd number of trunks had arrived the day before. At the time, all he'd thought of was the incredible waste of one person owning so many things. Now he wondered how many of those things were going to set his heart racing.

"Good morning, Mr. Asterly. Have we moved away from using a table? Shall I have it turned into firewood so we can eat like cavemen on the floor?"

Ah, his wife. Never short of an opinion.

"Lady Amelia. You are aware that it is seven a.m.? Are you unwell?" He took his seat at the head of the table, where the tea and chocolate were laid out. There was a small, dark stain marring the white linen. Damn her for highlighting every fault just by being in the room.

"I'm perfectly well, thank you," she said, crossing the room to the sideboard. She wrinkled her nose at the options in front of her and, after exaggerated consideration, put an orange on her plate. "Clearly I'm stuck here in Abingdale so I might as well get on with life."

"Really?" He couldn't mask his surprise. Despite his throwing open her curtains each morning, she'd stubbornly remained in her room until past ten every day. The mornings had become a battle of wills as she flat-out refused to do whatever was on her list, and he refused to let her off chore-free. Yesterday, they'd compromised. She had chosen mending over beating the carpets. Today he'd gone into his dressing room to discover the rips in his shirts had been patched with elaborately embroidered flowers.

"I have much to do today, according to your absurd list. If

I'm to wash all the bedding, dust the cobwebs, and polish the silver, I'm going to need an early start." She took a seat to his left, neatened the place settings, unfolded her napkin, and set his pulse off-kilter. Time had not diminished the physical impact she had on him—if anything it had intensified.

He shifted in his seat. "And you're actually going to do all those things?" he asked, trying to focus on the conversation.

She looked at him in a you-must-be-kidding manner. "Of course not. I'm going to visit the tenants."

"All two of them?"

"Precisely." She picked up the knife and looked at her orange, perturbed as though she had no idea what to do next. For a woman who made condescension an art form, she lacked a significant number of basic life skills.

"Pass it here." He cut into the fruit and began to peel. "What brought about this sudden urge to visit the tenants?"

"Isn't that what we, the country gentry, do? Visit those less fortunate than ourselves?" Her words had a dark bitterness to them.

"And the great Lady Amelia wants to sit in a one-room farmhouse with five children climbing the walls, making chitchat with a woman who's never set foot in London, let alone strolled down Bond Street?"

He pushed too hard on the last bit of peel, and the blade caught his thumb, nicking the skin just enough for the citrus juice to set it afire.

She took the orange from him. "I may have lived my entire life in London, but as Duchess of Wildeforde, it would have been my responsibility to call on Edward's many, many tenants, and although you and I have but two, visiting them is still my duty."

She sliced the orange in half with ferocity. "Regardless of

what you think of those of my station, the vast majority of us take our responsibilities very seriously."

"You do?" In his experience, those of her ilk were more interested in their clubs and brandy and cards than caring for the people that relied on them. That he was forced to help rethatch roofs and fix fences on properties that weren't his was example enough.

"I do. The higher your station, the more people rely on you. You need to provide stability, shelter, income—justice more often than not. It's a heavy burden, something I would have excelled at."

"You *would* have excelled at. So something you've never practiced?"

Her lips tightened. "As I said, I spent most of my time in London."

"And your father?"

There was an almost imperceptible tightening of her hand on the knife. "He had estate managers who worked hard in his absence."

"How certain are you of that?"

She shot him a furious stare. Benedict was tempted to push the matter, but they both knew her father was a bastard, and debating the point was not going to make life any easier.

"And what will you take with you when you call? Has Daisy prepared a basket of foods?"

"And inflict this cooking on others?" She speared an orange segment with her fork. "I plan to visit the village first. From memory, the bakery there is remarkable. They can make up some baskets of food that are actually edible."

"Excellent idea." He paused. "And for the record, they will appreciate your visit. Thank you for thinking of this." He smiled at her and was absurdly pleased to receive a smile in return. Could they be forming a truce? "I didn't see your lady's maid amongst the many trunks yesterday. I take it her mother is still unwell."

Amelia's face twisted for the briefest of seconds before settling into a neutral expression, but her tone was clipped as she replied. "Her mother is perfectly recovered. However, Reid won't be joining me. Apparently, she is now overqualified for the position given my sudden change in circumstances."

Oof. That insult was bound to sting. "I am sorry."

"It's nothing."

It didn't seem like nothing, but she clearly did not want to speak of it. So he turned to the day-old newspaper at his elbow. His fingers smudged the ink as he picked up the pages. At the rustle, Amelia looked up, then looked back to her orange, and then back to the pages.

"Would you like to read it?" he asked.

She grinned. "Just the society pages when you're finished with them."

"Oh, I'm finished with them now. They aren't part of my morning reading."

As he passed the pages, his knuckles brushed her fingertips. That unsettling spark he felt whenever she got too close surged through his body. He shifted in his seat, his breeches suddenly uncomfortable.

It was damnably inconvenient, this attraction he felt for his wife. Any other woman he'd ply with pretty words, a few gifts, and then sate the attraction until it was spent and they could part ways amicably.

How laughable that the one woman he should be able to exercise his lust with was the one woman he didn't dare try it with. He was bound to be rejected, and then life together would be even more uncomfortable.

He tried to focus on the words in front of him but found

himself glancing over the edge of the pages at her. Her hair was in a neat bun at the nape of her neck. Short tendrils curled at her ears. She had a look of eager anticipation on her face as she flipped open the gossip section.

He forced himself to look away and to the words in front of him.

Damnation.

There it was. His marriage had finally hit the newspapers. It was a short article in the business section speculating on the future growth prospects of the firm now that Benedict had married into the upper echelons of society. Had the Asterly, Barnesworth & Co. cofounder changed direction? Would his new connections make the firm first pick for lucrative contracts?

Hell.

If their marriage had made the business pages, it would have made the society pages. He looked up in time to see the blood drain from his wife's face.

"Amelia."

Her hand wobbled. Tea sloshed over the side of the cup, and she put it down with a discernible rattle.

"What does it say?" He could only imagine. He reached across for the pages, but she shifted away from him.

There was no visible indication of the content of the article with the exception of a slight raising of the eyebrows and a barely perceptible cock of the head. She might be reading about the weather as easily as reading about a herd of goats in dresses.

But he knew the jig was up. Lady Amelia Crofton may have found him beneath her notice, but enough of London knew his background that she was sure to find out his connections now.

She finished reading and wordlessly folded the pages

and handed them to him. "Well, that was informative." She poured another cup of tea and sipped it.

He opened the pages. *Fuck.*

SOCIAL CLIMBING REACHES NEW HEIGHTS.
WAS AN EARL'S DAUGHTER KIDNAPPED?
COMPROMISED? FORCED TO MARRY?

Beneath the headline was a sketch, him the size of a giant with Lady Amelia slung over his shoulder.

Blood pounded in his ears. His body shook, and the newspaper crumpled in his hand.

Kidnapping? Forced marriage? He'd been trapped into an unwanted marriage by an earl's daughter who hied off into the country on her own, by a duke who refused to do the right thing by his fiancée, and an earl who spread gossip maliciously, and somehow *he* was the villain?

He slammed the paper to the table.

"Damn." He shouldn't swear in front of a lady, but "Goddamn!"

He pushed back from the table, running his hands through his hair. What was he going to do? He stood and paced the length of the dining room in long, fast strides, spinning on his heel each time he reached a wall. This could jeopardize everything. There would be so many ramifications. He would need to get ahead of them.

Amelia stared at him over the rim of her teacup, not an ounce of emotion showing.

"Does anything ever crack that façade?" he asked.

She raised an eyebrow. "I'm English. We're not disposed to such extravagant displays of feeling."

"*I'm* English."

"Well, there's definitely French blood in there some-where." She returned to staring at the orange segments on her plate as if nothing had occurred that was worth interrupting her meal for. Infuriating woman.

"This is unfair. All I did was save your bloody life."

She stabbed at the orange with her fork. "Of course it's unfair. Life usually is. Now should we discuss this, or shall I leave you to your tantrum? I'd remove the china, but I can't help but think your smashing it against the wall may just improve it."

He ignored that last jibe to turn his attention to the real catastrophe.

Everyone read the society pages—well, every woman—but the husbands would once they heard the rumor from their wives. Not that he gave a rich royal damn about the lords of London, but he had a reputation to protect. Not the ridiculous conceited reputation of the aristocracy, but of an honest, upright, fair-dealing businessman. Rumors of kidnapping could tear that to shreds.

He needed to go into damage control. Now.

He looked over at Amelia, who was now sitting primly in her seat, sipping on tea and watching him pace.

He was loath to admit it, but any rescue from the scenario was going to involve her help.

He took the seat directly opposite her, his arms resting against the white linen, his face as controlled as he could manage.

"What are you thinking?" he asked.

"What am *I* thinking? I'm wondering when you were planning to tell me that I had not, in fact, married a factory worker." Her tone was pleasant, but the look in her eyes told him to reinforce the lock on the door between their bedrooms.

She continued, picking up steam. "I was also wondering why we are living in a musty, rundown half of a house with shabby furniture, no garden, and next to no servants."

And there it was. The crux of her problem, and further proof that she was the most self-centered woman in England.

"That's what has upset you? There are not enough people here to wait on you? You're inconvenienced by the need to brush your own hair and make your own bed?"

She gripped the edge of the table hard, as though her fingers were pressed around his neck. "You are the grandson of the Marquess of Harrington! And wealthier than half of London. And we live like this!" She waved her hand in front of his burnt toast and her fruit. "It is unconscionable."

"Unconscionable? Like false allegations of kidnapping? Like destroying a man's reputation in order to entertain a gaggle of useless, elitist aristocrats?"

"What reputation? You work! Apparently when you don't need to. Some ridiculous gossip that will pass in a week can hardly lower your reputation any further."

He swore. He swore with every measure of frustration in him. He swore to every incarnation of the devil he could think of. He swore in order to shock the look of blasted superiority off her beautiful face.

There was an entire village of people counting on him to deliver a contract for the construction of new steam locomotives. A contract that might fall through because of this gossip. But apparently that paled in comparison to his wife's desire to be waited on hand and foot.

If ever he'd needed confirmation that he was right in not letting his sister grow up with money, this was it.

Amelia smoothed her skirts. "I must say, I'm surprised Lord Harrington hasn't reached out. He usually has such impeccable manners."

Blood pounded in his head at the sound of his grandfather's name.

"This family has nothing to do with that man. And that's nonnegotiable. I forbid you to engage with him."

She smirked. "You clearly don't know me if you think forbidding anything is going to work."

"I mean it. That man is the lowest form of life there is. He's a cruel, heartless bastard, and nothing about him is welcome in this house. Not his presence, not his money, not his name."

"You are a fool. You claim to be a businessman, yet you turn your back on the advantages and connections that your family background offers. Don't you know that more deals are made in cardrooms at balls than in musty old offices?"

"This is not up for debate." He stormed out of the room, needing to put as much distance between him and his wife as possible. She was everything about the aristocracy that he hated. And marrying her was destroying everything.

Amelia waited until Benedict had left before retrieving the crumpled newspaper from the floor.

She was livid. He had been treating her like a fool from the very first moment. He'd been laughing at her the entire time. To think she'd spent yesterday afternoon in tears because her jewelry had not been sent with the rest of her things when she was married to a man who could purchase her entire jewelry collection ten times over.

To think that she'd lain in bed last night resigning herself to life as low-income landed gentry.

But no matter. At least now she had a clear path. She might not have jewels to fund an escape or a lady's maid to help her, but she was no longer a drab Cinderella scrubbing floors. She would be her own fairy godmother. It was time to turn the marriage—and her husband—into what she'd always expected. Something worthy of Lady Amelia and the grandson of a marquess.

"Daisy! Cassandra! We're going into town."

Chapter 9 —————————

It had been a bloody awful day, so it was only fitting that the snow had turned to icy rain by the time Benedict left the firm to go home for the night. The hood of his cloak kept it out of his face, but even through the sheepskin lining, he could feel the cold. Dark patches stained the leather where water had splashed.

He was going home to a steaming bath and a fortifying meal, and then he was going to sit her down and explain, as nicely as possible, why living a simple life was the best choice for his family.

They had enough privilege—a roof over their head, food on the table, people that loved each other—and they didn't need the fawning and the excess and the waste of the upper class. She just needed to give it some time, and she would see. She could be happy without that opulence too.

He stamped his feet on the mat at the front door, trying to shake off the mud. As he did so, the door opened. Tom Greenhill stood at attention, everything stiff from his posture to his shirt front, which looked to have been starched and ironed.

"Tom, is everything well?"

"Good evening, Mr. Asterly." He bent at the waist. Shockingly, no creaking sound accompanied it.

"What the devil is wrong with you?" Benedict asked as he stepped inside. In thirty years, Tom had never addressed him as Mr. Asterly. Tom stood behind him, reached over to grab the lapels of his cloak, and tried to pull it off him.

Benedict stepped away. "Good God, man. What are you doing?"

"Taking your cloak, sir." The man's face was as uncomfortable as his movements.

"Sir?"

This was his wife's fault. What numskull idea had gotten into her head while he was gone?

"I can hang up my own damn cloak." Hell, the frail, white-haired man would probably sink under the weight of it.

"Of course, sir."

As he hung the cloak in the cupboard by the door, he saw the local lad who delivered the newspaper each morning walk through the foyer, executing an odd bow without breaking stride.

What the devil? He followed the lad through the dining room and into the kitchens. Chaos. Unbelievable chaos.

Half the damn village was in the room wiping pots, cutting food, or sweeping the floor. At the head of it all, using a wooden spoon as a directing stick, was Mrs. Duggan from the bakery, barking orders as if she were a military general.

She hustled over when she saw him, swatting her younger daughter out of the way as she did. "You shouldn't be in here, Mr. Asterly. It's not your place, and you'll just get in the way."

She'd been calling him Benny since he was in knee breeches, and he didn't appreciate her newfound formality. "Mrs. Duggan, what are you doing in my kitchen?"

"It's my kitchen now. Off with you." She hesitated. "Respectfully, sir."

He slammed the kitchen door shut as he left. "Amelia!" he bellowed. "Amelia!"

He was about to take the stairs when he noticed the door to the east wing was open for the first time since his mother had left. Two children sat on the floor in her old sitting room, polishing candlesticks. They looked at him with wide eyes.

"Have you seen Lady Amelia?"

The children shook their heads. "Not this way, m'lord," one answered.

"I'm not a lord." And he sure as hell wasn't going to become one to satisfy the whims of his wife.

He took the stairs two at a time. "Amelia!"

This was insanity. What right did she have to bring people into his home? He didn't bother knocking. He just marched straight into her room.

Three heads swiveled in his direction as he entered. Two wide-eyed with alarm, the third with that damnable cold smile.

"Cassandra. Daisy," he said. Of course Amelia had surrounded herself with a human bloody shield.

Daisy paused, her hands wrapped in Amelia's hair, pins between her teeth. She bobbed. "Mwah Ward."

"I am *not* a lord."

"Daisy is going to start doing my hair," Cassandra said, smiling.

"You wear your hair in braids. How hard is that to do?"

His sister flinched, and he cursed his wife for putting him in such a mood.

"Amelia thinks it's time I start wearing my hair up," she said hesitantly. "Like a young lady. And she says we're to go shopping as soon as the weather turns. I'm old enough to wear more delicate fabrics."

This. This was exactly what he'd spent Cassandra's lifetime trying to avoid. He had good bloody reasons for raising his sister like he had, and no upper crust chit was going to change that.

He took a deep breath. "She says that, does she? Lady Amelia seems to have a great many ideas at the moment."

Amelia sat silent through the exchange—more than happy to have his sister wade into musket fire for her.

"She found you these fashion plates." Cassandra stood and collected a handful of periodicals from Amelia's dresser. Several pages had been marked with ribbon. Cassandra smiled up at him. "I like this one the most."

It was hideous. Blue breeches, purple shirt, green waistcoat. The paisley cravat was tied up in such an intricate knot that no man would have full range of motion in his neck.

He wanted to toss the plates into the fire, but his sister was looking at him with such joy. He was going to wring Amelia's neck for getting Cassandra's hopes up. "Thank you both for your consideration, but I'm happy with my wardrobe as it is. Amelia, a word?"

She sighed and shooed Daisy away from her curls. "Spoilsport."

"Daisy, take Cassandra downstairs to play." There was a tightness to his voice that his housemaid clearly recognized because she grabbed his sister and left the room at remarkable speed.

"For someone who's not a lord, you certainly are acting like one." Amelia's dry sarcasm hit right under his skin, crawling up his neck, causing his teeth to clench.

"Why is my house full of people?"

"*Our* house is full of staff hired to restore it and run it in a manner fit for its occupants."

He ground his teeth. "It has been fit for its occupants for the past three decades."

"Truly?" How she was able to load one word, two syllables, with scorn, derision, disbelief, and challenge, he was unsure.

She continued. "It's fit for the grandson of a marquess and the daughter of an earl? Please don't insult my intelligence."

She turned back to the mirror in short dismissal and began to play with the loose strands of her hair.

Her brush-off was not unlike the first time they'd met, when she'd not even acknowledged his presence. Frustration, hurt, anger, and embarrassment all warred for pride of place inside.

"I wouldn't give a damn if you were King George's daughter. You are a useless pain in the ass. And I don't recognize the marquess as family."

That finally elicited an emotion from her. She slammed the ivory brush onto the dresser and spun to face him. "You may not, but what of your sister? For heaven's sake, Benedict, she has the chance to make an excellent match. She's a natural beauty, well-connected if you can look past your own ego to accept it, and with your wealth and my guidance, she could be a society diamond."

The picture she was creating was Benedict's worst nightmare.

"How well did being society's diamond work out for you, princess?"

That shot landed. He saw it in the way she pressed her lips together, the way she sat back as if to put as much room between them as possible, the way she looked to the side at the faded curtain and threadbare rug and a barely perceptible shudder passed through her.

How he resented her.

"I will not have my sister joining that cesspool of human vice. And I will not have men whom I've grown up with suddenly fetching my meals and shining my shoes and bowing as if I'm above them because I married a damn aristocrat." He spat the last word out.

"You. Are. A. Hypocrite." She stood, her hands on her hips. "You talk about the importance of bringing security and income to the working class, yet what I offer them is exactly the same thing."

"A life bending to your whims and serving others? I'm sorry if I don't see the appeal of that."

She countered, ticking off points on her fingers. "They'll be paid well; they'll develop skills working in a big house, prestige, and good references; they'll have a career path in front of them. If you can't see the appeal, it's because you're blinded by prejudice."

She accused *him* of prejudice? She, who turned her nose up at anyone with pride enough to work. She, who took a week to remember three people's names.

"You have the money to employ dozens of people," she continued. "It's selfish for you not to. Cruel, even. But by all means, you go out there and tell all those people they no longer have work because you're a stubborn goat."

He ran his hands through his hair. He hated being out-maneuvered. Of course he wasn't about to walk out of that room and fire people.

"This wasn't your decision to make. You should have spoken to me about it first."

"Would you have agreed?"

"Of course not."

She shrugged. "Then speaking to you about it would have served no purpose at all. I'm hardly going to ask permission when I know it won't be granted."

He paced the room. With every lap, it got smaller, the walls looming. "Amelia, you need to fix this."

She gave him a pitiful look. "I just did. You can thank me for it when you've calmed down."

He bristled at the gentleness of her tone—as though the fight was won, and she was consoling the defeated. Because this was a battle he had lost before he even knew it was being waged.

Unable to look at her, he walked out, almost running into a young girl from the village. She jumped. One look at the furious expression on his face and her eyes widened.

And now he'd been turned into a monster terrifying young women.

"Sorry," he said, trying to keep the gruffness from his voice.

"It's all right, m'lord," she said as she curtseyed.

"I'm not a lord."

"Yes, m'lord."

He sighed and walked toward his bedroom door.

"I want to thank you," the girl called from behind him.

He turned. "Thank me?"

"For this opportunity. Me mum's sick and hasn't been able to wash sheets like she used to. She was right thrilled to hear I had a position. And Lady Amelia says it's all right for me to work here and go back to me mum at night. She's kind."

Kind? She was the devil incarnate. Was he the only person who could see that?

"Good night—" Damn, he couldn't recall the girl's name.

"Sarah, m'lord—sir, I mean."

"Good night, Sarah. I hope this job turns out to be everything you expected." He doubted it, though, but there was nothing he could do. His wife had trapped him. Again.

Chapter 10 —————————

If this really is supposed to be your brother, we are going to need a lot more snow." Amelia regarded the giant, half-made snowman in front of her.

"You only need to make the head," Cassandra said, standing in front of an almost-finished snowwoman.

"Exactly." Her bear-sized husband had an equally large ego. The snowman should reflect that.

Cassandra rolled her eyes then trotted off toward the trees to collect more sticks.

Amelia squatted to start packing her ice ball, the bottom of her skirts already sodden. She'd initially taken the role of sculpture supervisor, but it was freezing, the cold was seeping through her boots, and Cassandra seemed intent on creating their entire dysfunctional family out of ice. So after a five-minute lesson on snow-building basics, she'd gone to work on her first-ever snowman in an effort to speed the whole process up.

"Well, this is a sight I didn't expect." Her husband's

low voice sounded from behind her, and she jumped. "Lady Amelia Crofton playing in the snow."

She looked up at him, suspicious. After last night's argument, what mood would he be in? So far, he'd been more tolerant than any man she'd met—with the exception of his idiotic chore roster—but she had pushed it yesterday by hiring staff without his consent. Hopefully, a good night's sleep had helped him see reason.

There was a boyish, sheepish look on his face, and he held his hands out in mock surrender. Perhaps they would actually get through the day without an argument.

His lips were quirked to the side, their softness a stark contrast to the hard planes of his face. The late afternoon stubble on his jawline caught in the setting sun. The long shadows only served to highlight his flint-sharp features. Whatever his faults, her husband was an attractive man.

Brutally attractive.

What would it be like to stop arguing and instead run her hands over him? It was a question that made her toss and turn at night. A question that made it unbearably hot beneath the bed covers. A question that made her eyes travel to the door that separated them more often than she'd like.

Each day of their marriage, these questions intensified. Yet he'd made no move to kiss her. Not since he'd pulled away on their wedding night. Sometimes he tensed and his throat bobbed, and his hands stiffened at his sides and she was *sure* he was about to reach out.

But he didn't. And neither did she. And the awkwardness continued.

And she still didn't know what it would be like…

She flushed, heat creeping up her spine, and she wondered how it was that the snowman to her back wasn't melting.

"We're making snow families," she said, praying that he had no idea of the thoughts running through her head.

He looked at the snowman. "Is that supposed to be me?"

"It will be if you help me lift the head onto it."

He stared at the giant ball in front of him and raised an eyebrow.

She flushed. Perhaps her intentions behind her design were somewhat obvious.

"Dare I ask how you were planning to decorate it?" He lifted the head onto the body.

She pulled out the cravat she'd tucked up the sleeve of her pelisse. "I raided your wardrobe."

"And this was all you took?"

"It was all I liked," she said wryly.

"You wound me." His fist thumped against his chest.

Ignoring his teasing, she faced the snow giant in front of her. Wrapping the cravat around its neck was one thing. The actual tying of a knot was another. Despite being an expert on fashionable knots, she had no idea how to actually create one.

"Here." His breath was warm against her ear as he reached past and took the loose ends. Encircled in his arms, goose bumps prickled over her skin, and it became more and more difficult to breathe. She was aware of him in a way that she'd never been aware of a person before. It was infuriatingly paralyzing.

She tried to focus on what he was doing, but the press of her back against his chest overwhelmed every other sense. He tied a hunting knot with startling speed, but it was a long moment between finishing and dropping his hands. When he did, they rested on her hips.

"There," he said. His voice was as strangled as she felt.

She turned to face him, pivoting within the embrace of his

arms. She didn't step back, though, and from this distance, she could see the bob of his Adam's apple as he swallowed hard. His eyes sparked with the heat she felt.

"You are a man of surprising talents." Hopefully he couldn't discern the effort it took to verbalize a comprehensible sentence.

"I went to Oxford."

"Really? I was unaware." A distant part of her registered this new information as highly agreeable, but the primal present part could only focus on the soft curve of his lips as he spoke.

"It wasn't a good fit. I only stayed a year." He sounded equally distracted, and his eyes didn't leave her mouth.

"Why did you go? It doesn't seem like you."

"I was trying to please my mother." He didn't elaborate but his jaw clenched, and he diverted his gaze.

It was an unexpected sight, this big brawny male so vulnerable. It elicited a tenderness she rarely felt. Impulsively, she raised a hand to his face and stroked her thumb along his cheekbone. "You are stubborn and frustrating, Benedict Asterly, but you're a good man. I'm sure your mother would be proud."

"I don't want to think about her right now." His hands tightened on her hips and set her insides tingling.

"What do you want to think about?"

He didn't answer. And in the heavy silence, every one of her senses heightened. The smoky, earthy scent of him made her dizzy. His breathing filled her ears. Every inch of her was drawn to him.

Kiss me. Kiss me.

He cupped the back of her head in his hands and leaned down, his lips drawing closer.

Kiss me.

She swayed toward him. As his lips touched hers, a shiver coursed from her frozen toes to her snow-flecked hair. They were every bit as soft as they looked. And warm. She leaned into him, surrendering to her body's need to be closer.

He groaned and wrapped an arm around her, his fingers tightening in her hair. Her body responded by drawing tight—her toes curled, her hands crushed his lapels, and her stomach tensed.

It was everything and nothing. A pleasure that made no sense and complete sense. It was a feeling of floating and a grounding earthiness all at once. It was an experience logic could not explain.

Then he ran his tongue past the curve of her lips, teasing at them until they opened. Tentatively, she responded.

This was why women fell. She'd never understood what could make a woman risk her reputation, her future.

But this. Now she understood.

"Ben!" Cassandra yelled. "Are you here to help us?"

Her words were like a bucket of ice water dumped over them. Amelia stepped back swiftly, brushing at her gown and tucking a strand of hair back into place.

Her fingers itched to tug flat the wrinkles she'd created in his coat.

Benedict coughed and turned to face his sister, who was stripping twigs free of leaves as she walked toward them.

"Yes, poppet. I'm here to help." He flashed Amelia a hot and wicked smile.

Goodness. What did that mean?

Her heart raced as her mind sifted through all the possible consequences of the kiss. None of which was territory she'd explored before.

At least Benedict was having as much trouble concentrating as she was. He'd been looking at his sister a full five seconds before he actually saw her. She could tell because surprise flickered over his face, followed quickly by resignation.

Cassandra may have spent the past hour playing outside, but the morning had been spent taking the first steps toward being a young lady. "Your hair looks lovely, Cassandra," Benedict said gruffly in response to the lopsided curls piled high on her head. "Daisy has done an excellent job."

Daisy had done the job that could be expected from a housemaid—an awful one—but Cassandra beamed anyway. "Doesn't it look pretty?" She patted it gently.

She'd been so pleased that she'd insisted they not wear bonnets outside, and the curls had sagged somewhat under the snowflakes that had quickly turned to water.

Amelia watched Benedict breathe deep. It was to his credit that he bit back whatever his actual opinion was. Progress indeed.

"Amelia says we may share a lady's maid until I'm sixteen, and then I'm to have my own. Except for when we're in London. We will be too busy to share one then." Cassandra seemed oblivious to the tension building in her brother's shoulders or the tightening of his mouth.

"London? Have we got plans to go into town now?" He turned to Amelia.

"Not now," she said, hoping their recent kiss would blunt his frustration. "I daresay it would be best to wait until the gossip dies down. But certainly later in the year, once the Season is over, it might be nice. It would be good for Cassandra to start meeting people."

He was near his limits. First the servants, and then Cassandra's hair. Throwing in news of a trip to London in the same forty-eight-hour period was perhaps a bit much.

Benedict took a deep breath. "You may have a lady's

maid, Cassandra. To do your hair and play with dresses. But you're to clean your own room and make your own bed, as always."

Cassandra nodded quickly, as if to agree before he could change his mind. "Absolutely."

"And if you fall behind on your studies, Daisy is not to assist you at all."

Cassandra screwed up her face in a completely unladylike manner. There was so much work to be done with her.

"Why would I fall behind? I love my studies."

The twelve-year-old was a strange creature. Goodness, the extremes Amelia had gone to in order to avoid her studies.

Benedict turned to her, his eyes falling to her lips. "There's no harm in a trip to London, but what we'll do and who we'll see there is a discussion for another time."

"Dare I press my luck and ask if the staff are allowed to stay?"

Benedict rubbed the back of his neck. "There has been an overwhelming amount of support for your decision to employ some of the locals, and while it makes me uncomfortable, I can see its benefits. Besides, breakfast was... appreciated."

Breakfast this morning had been a far cry from the half-burnt toast and sausages of the day before. The sideboard had been covered in hot pastries, glazed ham, buttered croissants, and poached eggs. If anything was going to convince Benedict that hiring some extra help was a good thing, Mrs. Duggan's food would be it.

"I'm glad you enjoyed it. Now I think it's time to head inside for some hot tea." Now that the heat of his kiss was dissipating, she was getting cold.

"Really? I think it's time for something else." Benedict reached down and grabbed a handful of snow, packing it into a ball. "This snowman needs a little more..." He spun and lobbed the snowball at Amelia.

It hit her chest, ice crystals smacking her in the face and finding the sliver of bare skin above her collar. She blinked. "What on earth are you doing?"

"Have you never been in a snow fight, princess?"

"Absolutely not." What kind of barbarians pelted each other with snow?

Benedict and Cassandra exchanged grins, simultaneously kneeled, and gathered up snow.

"Don't you dare." Amelia took a few backward steps.

Their grins just widened.

"Benedict Asterly—"

Cassandra's snowball hit her on the shoulder. It was followed quickly by his. The kiss had been confusing. This was incomprehensible. And apparently not over—the siblings were stockpiling snowballs, so she turned and ran.

Benedict stood between her and the house, so she fled for the trees, but Cassandra intercepted her.

"This is not funny." Amelia stood, arms akimbo, and infused as much authority into her voice as possible.

Cassandra didn't move.

"Miss Asterly," she said calmly, "a lady never—" A snowball hit Amelia in the back of the head, leaving a cold, wet trail down her neck.

To blazes with calm. "That's it." She turned and scooped up her own handful of snow, flinging it at Benedict. It disintegrated in the air in front of her. "Drat." She scooped up another handful, patted it into a solid ball, and threw it.

He didn't flinch as it hit him directly in the chest—simply smiled. A snowball came flying over her shoulder and hit him in the jaw. His smile faded.

Amelia couldn't help herself, she grinned as Cassandra

whooped with joy. As long as it was the two of them against him, this game had some appeal.

She grabbed another handful and formed a ball as Benedict stalked toward them. She ducked out of his reach, skirting behind him, and launched, getting him in the back of the knees.

"Aha! I win," she said as he lost his balance.

He recovered quickly and shook his head before resuming his approach.

Or maybe not…

"Nowhere to run now, princess," he said when he was only a couple of feet away. They faced off, each with a ball in hand.

His face was so full of mock outrage that she laughed. She hadn't had so much fun since…Actually, she'd never had this kind of fun. Fun that wasn't tightly laced and formally packaged.

She let the snowball loose as he closed the gap between them. It splattered over his face, leaving snow caught in his eyelashes and on the stubble of his jaw.

Then he dumped his snowball on the top of her head.

"Oh…Oooh…" The cold was entirely unpleasant. "You are…"

He grinned triumphantly and then grabbed her around the waist, scooping her into his arms.

"Come on, poppet. Time to get our ice princess inside."

Chapter 11 ————————————

His bedroom smelled like jasmine and pear. In the ten days since their marriage, her scent had become annoyingly, arousingly familiar. His cock twitched at the memory of her curves beneath his hands.

Kissing her had been the most terrifying thing he'd done in years. He'd been convinced—right up until she leaned into him—that she'd pull away, chastising him for daring to think a man like him could kiss a woman like her.

And now he was even more terrified. Because their kiss had answered one question and raised a thousand more. Instead of getting her out of his system, it had planted her at the heart of it. He needed more and—frighteningly—he suspected he always would.

A lifetime of kissing her would not be enough to sate the need that consumed him.

The door between their rooms taunted him. It was everything he could do not to walk right through it and sweep her into his arms.

But she was a distraction he didn't need, especially given

the news he'd received while she was bathing, and he was downstairs trying not to think of her bathing.

The Americans were backing out of their agreement with the firm.

Sitting on the edge of the bed, he yanked off his boots and tossed them. Bloody. *Thud*. Hell. *Thud*.

The deal with Grunt and Harcombe had been as good as done. He'd already ordered the additional steel, already hired more men. The entire damn village knew about it. They were expecting big things, expecting production of the new steam locomotives to begin. How the devil was he going to explain that years of work had been undermined by marriage to Lady Amelia Crofton?

He stripped to his smalls. A hot bath would be good. It would clear his mind so he could focus on finding a solution to this disaster.

He just prayed his wife had left him some hot water—or at least had one of their new footmen bring some more water up to boil.

He pushed open the door to his dressing room and went stock still. The sight of his wife, naked in the bath, cemented his feet to the floor. The only part of him that could move was his jaw, which dropped open.

"Get out!" Her typically measured tones became a shriek. A bar of soap sailed past his head. She sank neck-deep below the waterline, one arm crossed over her breasts, another reaching to cover her sex.

But enough of her naked body showed through the water that he was captivated.

"Benedict, out."

The imperiousness in her tone brought him back to his senses. And as usual, pricked enough that he needed to prick back.

"You are *still* bathing?" He crossed his arms. Perhaps it would fool her into thinking he had the upper hand.

Her eyes widened, fixated on his biceps. His skin heated under the weight of her gaze.

"I like long baths," she said, distracted.

"Your long bath is up, princess. It's my turn." He tried to keep his eyes on hers, not letting them drift down toward her body.

"Then leave so I can get out."

Benedict couldn't leave any more than he could dance a cotillion. Some primal part of him wanted, needed, her here, naked in his den. He took a towel from the chair and tossed it at her. Instinct made her grab for it, and in doing so, she inadvertently gave him a quick glimpse at her breasts, full and luscious.

"Cover yourself if you must," he said, walking to the basin where he kept his shaving accessories. He could see her in the mirror's reflection, but from the way she relaxed, blowing a strand of hair from her face, she clearly didn't realize.

He studied her in every entrancing detail, waiting to see what she'd do.

She draped the towel across the bath. Damnation. He should have had smaller ones made for her, ones that didn't cover every inch.

She was studying him too. He saw her eyes travel from his calves and thighs fully covered by his thin smalls, over his arse to his naked back. Thank the devil his back was toward her—his cock throbbed as though her roaming gaze drew across his skin like fingernails.

He looked down at the utensils in front of him to avoid meeting her eyes in the mirror. Cowardice, really. He was afraid she'd run. Afraid she'd look at him in disgust at his size, at the body shaped by long hours of manual labor.

Afraid that she *wouldn't* look at him in disgust, because then he'd have no bearings at all.

"You're half naked." There was a hitch to her voice.

He picked up the soap, vigorously rubbing it between his hands, trying to burn through the energy that had seized him the moment he'd walked in the room. "I'm your husband. You were bound to see me this way at some point."

He hadn't pushed her. Restraint had been the hardest damned thing he'd done when every fiber of his body burned for her. But she wasn't some woman to enjoy for one night. They had a lifetime ahead of them, and while they might never love one another, he was hoping for some form of like in his marriage bed.

She didn't answer, which in itself was an encouragement. It wasn't a "stay" but it wasn't a "go" either.

"I promise not to remove any more clothing."

"Fine." She turned the taps, and more steaming water poured into the bath. He was grateful for the hot water system his engineering partner had designed. No footmen could possibly have kept up with Amelia's desire for bathing.

Benedict couldn't tell if the red creeping up her neck was due to him or the steam that dampened the curls by her face, plastering them to her temples.

"You were upset when you walked in," she said.

"You noticed?" He spread the lather of shaving soap over his cheeks and jaw.

"I am well acquainted with the stronger sex's ever-so-fragile moods. They match their fragile egos."

"A damning assessment." He flipped open the razor and dipped it into the basin of water.

"Why were you angry? Other than missing your turn in the tub?"

The firm and his current troubles were not a subject he

wanted to discuss. Particularly not with the cause of said troubles. "Business. Nothing more."

She sat up straighter, her shoulders squared in the confidence he was used to. The movement caused the crest of her bosoms to sit above the waterline. He swallowed. Hard.

"I can talk business," she said. "I'm not feather-brained."

"I'm sure you can. There's just nothing to talk about."

It was a lie, and he could tell she knew it. Her lips pursed, and she cocked her head, no doubt deciding whether or not to call him on it. Keen to divert the conversation away, he interrupted. "Explain to me how you've never had a snow fight before."

"I've never had someone to snow fight with." It was simply said, with a nonchalant shrug of the shoulders, yet it was the nonchalance that rocked him.

"You never played with other children?" He couldn't imagine a childhood so lonely. He'd spent most of his days running amok with Wilde.

Clearly assuming that his turned back gave her privacy she didn't have, she picked up the soap from the table beside the bath and rubbed it over her arm.

" 'The future Duchess of Wildeforde does not "play." ' " She mimicked what he assumed was her father's voice.

"You're joking." His hand froze halfway to his chin.

"Nor does she wear bright colors or"—she fake-gasped—"read novels."

"It's a good thing you're no longer the future Duchess of Wildeforde." He wanted to take the words back as soon as he said them, but instead of the expected cutting retort, she smiled to herself.

"Princess Lionberry and the dancing teacups are infinitely better than embroidery and almost worth the title. Don't tell Edward."

She looked up at the mirror, and he didn't avert his gaze quickly enough. He was prepared for her to screech and chastise him for his boldness. Instead she held his stare, and he was compelled to ask, "Did you love Wildeforde?"

He dreaded the answer. But he had to know. Today, for the first time since their wedding, he'd had an inkling that their marriage might not be the disaster he thought. Today he saw playful outrage and cheeky determination. Instead of her perfect porcelain mask, there had been creases at the corners of her eyes, dimples in her cheeks.

If one afternoon of his normal life could compromise her façade, what would be the effect if he really tried to woo her into his life?

But that was a dangerous thought. If his childhood had proved anything, it was that a woman of her ilk would never be satisfied with this life, nor with him.

And if she loved her ex-betrothed? Well, he wasn't sure how he'd manage to live with that.

She snorted. "I liked him well enough, I suppose. He was respectful—he didn't drink or gamble or flirt with other women." She screwed up her nose. "He turned out to be a bit of a coward, though."

Relief washed through him. He carried on shaving with more confidence. "So you didn't love him?"

She gave him an odd look. "Marriage isn't about love, though, is it?"

There was no good reason for his heart to sink at those words, but it did. "What's it about, if not love?"

She ran a finger along the edge of the bath, making patterns from the water droplets. "Security. Position. Power. Only fools marry for love—to their detriment." Her throat tightened at those last words, and she wiped her hand across her doodles. It wasn't a throwaway comment. She truly believed what she was saying.

He turned toward her, leaning back against the sink. "I thought all young girls wanted love."

She gave a wistful smile. "The last time I thought I was in love, it was with a footman. I was eight years old. My nanny found a love note I'd written hidden beneath my pillow and gave it to my father."

"I can't imagine he was too pleased."

"He took me down to the rookery at St Giles."

Benedict swore. "That's no place for a young girl." St Giles was a seedy part of London where young bucks would pay a thruppence to tup a whore against the side of a building. It wasn't discreet; rather it was an open cesspool.

She cleared her throat. "Yes, well, my father made it very clear what happened to girls who married for love. Watching them sell themselves on the street to pay for food, I vowed that would never be me. For a woman, the only security from that life is money and position."

Benedict swallowed and turned back to the sink, wiping away any traces of shaving soap. Her words had painted an image in his head. Not of the cheap streets of London but of a cheap room in Paris. Of his mother swathed in wisps of fabric, her face pale as snow, her eyes red. She may have had a roof over her head while she sold her body, but she too had married for love and then spent the latter years of her life prostituting herself to the aristocracy. He had barely made it to her bedside before the syphilis claimed her.

He hadn't noticed the time that had gone by until he felt Amelia's hand covered his. She'd surrendered the bath and wrapped herself in his robe.

"Where did you go?" she asked.

"Nowhere good."

"If the newspapers are correct, neither of us need worry about ending up in St Giles. You have money and I have position—and I'm quite adept at leveraging both."

Her words dragged his focus back from his memories of France to the here and now. To his dressing room. To the woman in front of him. "I feel like 'quite adept' doesn't pay deference to your real abilities to manipulate a situation."

She smiled. "Why, that's the nicest thing you've said to me."

"That you consider it a compliment is, frankly, terrifying."

She laughed, an unconscious belly laugh that gripped his stomach and squeezed. It was the same feeling he'd had watching her build her structurally unsound snowman.

She took a seat on the bench by the bathtub, leaving enough space that he could fit beside her. Likely as close to an invitation as he was going to get.

"Tell me more about your business."

His business. The one balancing on a precipice due to their unfortunate marriage. The one that might fail and take down his whole damn village. The one he definitely did not want to talk about.

But she was his wife, and she had a right to know more about him.

"You'd stoop so low as to discuss work?"

She gave him a wry smile. "The more I know, the more I can plan my next trip to Bond Street."

He snorted, but underneath her flippancy, there was genuine interest. "I make steam engines, for rail." He waited for her to recoil or, at best, nod politely.

Instead she leaned in. "For transporting coal? Lord Pallsbury has one of those running from his estate."

"Transporting coal, mail, people even."

That's when she recoiled, almost slipping into the bath in the process. "Transporting people? Isn't that dangerous?"

"It's becoming safer. That's a lot of what we're doing, actually. Creating safer engines. There are too many accidents." Too many working men dying in order to fill the coffers of the aristocracy.

"Do you test them?" There was real concern in her voice.

"Of course we test them."

"You. Do *you* test them? Because I'm not comfortable with that." Her tone became clipped, demanding. It was touching, in an overbearing way.

"Worried about me?" he asked.

She snorted. "Worried about where the money goes if you're blown up. Tell me I won't be dealing with an odious cousin."

"Your concern is noted. You can relax. None of it's entailed. It goes to you and Cassandra. I'd recommend you allow my accountant to help you, but the money will be yours to do with what you like. If it's there."

"If it's there? What do you mean?"

Had she asked the question critically or in a panic that her newfound wealth was at risk, he would have palmed it off. But she was direct. No-nonsense. Businesslike. And he desperately needed someone to vent to.

"There were plans to sell locomotives to an American company. It would have meant considerable growth for the whole village. We invested a lot to make it happen, but I think we're losing the contract."

"Do I dare ask why?"

It took effort to look her in the eyes and answer. "They're unwilling to anger their current British investors by working with the enemy."

"And you're the enemy?"

"I've stolen what was theirs…"

"You've stolen…" She paused as understanding dawned. "Me?" She squared her shoulders, creases forming between her brows. "To begin with, I can't be stolen because I'm a person, not an object. I belong to no one. Don't forget that. Secondly, that's rather spineless of them."

He grunted. "American ties with Britain are only now just reaching a civil enough point for trade to be possible. They won't risk it."

"Then you need to find other partners with a bit more fortitude."

He ran a hand through his hair. "It's not that easy. There are only a handful of companies taking on rail projects of this size. We're not talking pin money."

"Oh, what a surprise." Her sarcasm caused an uncomfortable flashback to the Amelia he'd married.

"Then what do you need to do?" she continued.

"Pardon?"

"You said you're losing the contract, not that you've lost it. What do you need to do to fix this?"

He sighed. This wasn't an easy fix. There was no way of depositing her back on her father's doorstep, scandal-free and once again engaged to Wilde.

"I need to convince them that working with me won't jeopardize all their other ventures."

"Hmm." She nodded and cinched the belt around his dressing gown tighter, as if she were about to march barefoot to the Americans and give them the sharp edge of her tongue. "Well, lucky for you, I am very convincing."

"Pardon?"

"Invite them here. Have them tour your little factory. I'll host a dinner—I've been meaning to call on Lady Karstark as it is—and we'll convince all involved that, not only are you not a villain, but that our marriage is considered an excellent thing."

"The Karstarks aren't well liked in Abingdale."

She reached up and wiped a thumb along his jaw, removing a spot of soap he must have missed.

It was a compulsion of hers, he'd realized. To neaten things. To put things to rights. He shouldn't be surprised that she'd immediately look for solutions to the problem.

"I can't imagine why. Lord Karstark seemed *so* pleasant," she said dryly. "But if the situation is as you say it is, the Karstarks may be the only reason you get your contract, so we and the rest of the village will have to swallow it."

"You're ruthless."

"I'm practical. At the heart of it, an investment is not unlike a marriage. They want to know the money is going to come in and feel secure that the person they're investing with is not going to do something rash and ruin it all."

"And you know this because..."

"Because you'd be surprised how many business deals are conducted at balls and how freely men talk when they see you as a pretty face and nothing more."

"You are definitely more than a pretty face." And it was true. His wife might be the most beautiful woman he'd seen, but she was also one of the strongest, most fearless, and most intelligent women he'd met. And right now, he wanted to do nothing more than sweep her into his arms and make love to her.

He tucked a damp curl behind her ear and cupped her face in his hand.

Her eyes widened, as though the sudden, sensual change of energy in the room had caught her as off-guard as it had caught him.

He leaned forward and place a feather-like kiss on her

lips. And then, with a gentle nudge on her shoulder, he pushed her into the soapy water.

⁓

Amelia sputtered, wiping away hair that was plastered over her eyes as she resurfaced.

"Why you—" She broke off as he climbed into the bathtub with her, kneeling between her thighs. She scrambled up against one end; her heart thumped wildly, as out of control as she was in this situation.

"You've still got your pants on." It was an inane thing to say, made worse for coming out strangled and weak.

His smile was one she hadn't seen before. It promised all sorts of untold things. "Would you like me to take them off?"

"No!" Heat crept up her chest and neck.

He leaned forward, bracing himself on the bath edge on either side of her. His naked arms and chest had been mesmerizing when they were on the other side of the room. Now, encircled by them, they ripped away her ability to breathe.

Up close, there were more curves and valleys to his body than she'd thought a man would possess. Each muscle stretched taut under his weight, and small veins charted journeys across his skin, coaxing her to follow the paths with her fingers.

She drew a ragged breath, but it was as if his nearness changed the air around them. The oxygen she drew in fed tiny sparks that kindled inside her.

"I'm going to kiss you," he said and then paused, waiting for a response.

She nodded dumbly, unable to form words.

It was not like the kiss outside. That had started soft and gentle. No, this was raw and wild. He wrapped one arm around her and pulled her flush against him. His lips crushed against hers, his tongue flicking inside her mouth.

She moaned. Unsure of what to do next but desperate to do something, to have some sort of agency in this, she probed his tongue with hers—tentative, explorative.

His fingers tightened around her waist, and he leaned into her. The hard shaft of his sex pressed against her, and in response, a hot tingle blossomed between her legs.

This was a want she had never experienced, beyond all thought and logic. As if her body knew exactly what to do when her conscious did not, it took over.

She reached one hand up and around his neck while the other explored the muscles along his side. Everywhere her fingers touched, the fine hairs of his body stood on end. It was intoxicating, this effect she had on him.

He broke off their kiss and turned his attention to her jawline, sucking and nibbling, the heat of his breath sending shivers across her.

He let go of her waist, his fingers quickly working beneath the water to untie the belt of his robe. Slowly, gently, he unfolded it and grazed his palm along her ribs. Her chest arched, and the hot tingle between her legs intensified. He moved his hand to her breast, cupping it, kneading it, stoking the fire within at every point.

Her fingers raked down the sides of his body.

"I want you," he said. "I want every inch of you. Do you understand what I mean?"

She swallowed. "Yes," she whispered.

He pulled away, kneeling upright and gripping the edge of the bath. Her first instinct was to pull him back to her. But with each breath, the fog around her mind cleared.

"I need you to want this," he said.

Did she want this? She'd enjoyed it, every second. But it was all so much. So fast. She took another deep, clearing breath.

He didn't make her say *no*. Her hesitation had been enough. Instead he stepped out of the bath and offered her his hand.

She wrapped the robe tight, keenly aware that it clung to her every curve. He handed her a towel.

"I'm going for a walk," he said.

"Now? It's dark and freezing out there."

He smiled. "That's kind of the point. I'll see you at dinner, princess."

He was almost through the door when she found her voice. "Wait," she said.

He hesitated before turning around, and when he did, his expression seemed anxious.

"I...Uh..." She didn't want him to leave thinking she hadn't enjoyed what had just happened or that she hadn't been a very willing participant. She also couldn't bring herself to talk about it. "Thank you. That was quite illuminating."

His face softened in relief. "Let me take you out tomorrow," he said. "I want to share something with you."

Chapter 12 ———————————

Benedict took a deep breath as he dismounted. Bringing Amelia to Asterly, Barnesworth & Co. shouldn't be a terrifying prospect. They would walk in, he'd introduce everyone, do a quick tour, and she could say what she liked about the place and wrinkle her nose in whatever manner she wanted. The firm would survive without her approval.

He took her by the waist and helped her off her horse, the scent of jasmine and pear oddly helping to calm his frayed nerves. He held on a fraction longer than he needed to.

"So this is where you…work." Amelia surveyed the collection of colossal stone buildings in front of them. There was no open expression of distaste; it was more a look of suspicion, maybe a touch of uncertainty.

From inside, his beloved engine let loose a shrill squeal, ear-piercing even through the wall of rock. Amelia covered her ears—her expression of uncertainty devolving into alarm.

"What in heaven's name is that?" she yelled over the noise.

He bent close to her, putting a hand to the small of her back to let her know that he was right behind her. And also because he just liked touching her. "You'll see."

Drawing her hand into the crook of his arm, he pulled her close, taking pleasure in the way she pressed up against him. A streak of protectiveness shot through him.

He paused when they reached the door, allowing her the room to change her mind, to back out if she wanted to.

But damn, he was glad she didn't. He'd never had the occasion to show the firm off to anyone. Cassandra had practically grown up in it, and taking potential investors through was more about business than pride. This was the first time he was emotionally invested in what someone thought about the place he'd spent a lifetime building.

One glance at her face made his stomach flip. Gone was the often-present detached façade she kept in place whenever she was uncomfortable. Instead, she looked around with curiosity as she walked in, her interest roaming from the scaffolding that covered the walls and the roof to the workers grouped around evenly spaced workbenches.

He tried to see it as she might—crowded, busy, definitely filthy. A layer of coal dust coated everything. He'd designed the rooms with large windows for maximum light and ventilation, but dust still hung in the air. Black rivulets ran down his workers' faces where it mixed with sweat. They wore damp cloths over their noses and mouths to prevent breathing in the dust.

"It's...busy."

It became less busy as men noticed them. His comrades, most of whom were bent over workbenches, stood to watch them with an uncertain stare. His attire likely wasn't helping matters. He'd never come to the firm in formal wear. His boots were never this pristine. And only a fool wore a white shirt when working with coal. But today, he'd be a fool. If he was going to take his wife on an outing, he'd do it as properly as he could manage, clothes and all.

"Don't mind us. We'll stay out of your way," he called.

The men turned back to their work, except for Oliver, who shed the thick leather gloves protecting his arms and strode toward them. Amelia shrank backward—most people did when faced with the giant.

"My lady," Oliver said. He grabbed Amelia's hand and pumped it in a forceful handshake.

She tensed, but her smile remained polite.

"This is my foreman, Mr. Johnson." Benedict grabbed Oliver's hand, ostensibly to shake it but really to free Amelia.

She flexed her fingers, checked the white satin of her gloves, and then clasped her hands firmly behind her back. "A pleasure to meet you, Mr. Johnson," she said.

Oliver grinned like a half-drunk idiot. "You're a right pretty one. You've got spun gold hair Rumpelstiltskin would want."

She shot Benedict a questioning look, and he tried to contain his laughter. His foreman was a man's man who told it like it was in plain terms. This flowery speech was unexpected. It was no wonder he was unmarried if this was how he spoke to women.

"You're a veritable poet. What a delight."

His foreman's cheeks turned pink beneath the grime.

"I'm going to introduce her to the team," Benedict said, guiding Amelia away.

He took her around the outskirts of the room, introducing her to the men working at each station and letting them explain their role in the production. Shockingly, she was in her element. It was blatantly apparent why she was such a popular figure of the *ton*. She listened, asked questions, and men relaxed under her apparent interest. She seemed at home, as if this were a ballroom and she was making chitchat with potential acquaintances. If she were uncomfortable, no one would know it.

Eventually, they walked through the giant doors that comprised one side of the building. Outside stood his pride and joy, rocking slightly and shooting steam.

Jeremy was feeding the engine with coal, his hands black from the sooty, sandy material, black streaks across his forehead and cheeks where he'd wiped away sweat.

Benedict had become accustomed to the buffeting force of heat near the engine, but Amelia shrank away, putting her hands up against the hot air.

He bent close to be heard over the roar. "This is Ten Tonne Tessie."

"Tessie? You've named it?"

It had seemed like a good idea at the time. "At the moment, we're focused on increasing the pressure of the engine. We've already succeeded in reducing her size."

"And this is what the contract's for? Is it safe?" Amelia yelled.

"Usually."

Her head spun toward him, her eyes wide. "*Usually?*"

"There were a few issues during the development phase, but she's been running for days this time. She's looking good, isn't she, Jeremy?"

The apprentice stoker didn't answer. Instead he gave Amelia a withering stare and continued shoveling coal. If she had noticed the slight, she didn't show it, thankfully. Benedict would speak with Jeremy later about his rudeness, when he wasn't introducing his wife to the thing that took up every moment of his time not spent at home.

"Upstairs is where I work mostly."

He took her back inside and up to the mezzanine that ran the perimeter of the room, lined with shelves stacked with books, paper, miniature prototypes, and curiosities he and his comrades had picked up over the years. A large office took up one corner.

John, his friend since the days of Eton and Oxford, was at a desk sketching with charcoal. He'd clearly been tackling a puzzle—his hair stuck up in a myriad of different angles. Benedict could always tell how far along his friend was in a project by the state of his hair.

John stood when they entered, fingers twitching at his side. Talking to people—particularly Amelia's type of people—was not something he was comfortable with.

Benedict put a reassuring smile on his face as he said, "Lady Amelia, Mr. John Barnesworth. You might know his mother, Lady Harrow."

Amelia proffered her hand. "Mr. Barnesworth, what a pleasure to meet you."

"The p...p...pleasure is mine." He bowed over Amelia's hand with a lithe fluidity and grace that contradicted his awkward appearance and speech.

Benedict had always envied John his ability to look the part of a gentleman, even if his speech faltered when he was anxious. Benedict could dress in the finest attire, take every damned dance class, and still never look anything but a lumbering footman's son.

Amelia stepped toward the desk and turned her focus to the sketches. "What are you working on?" she asked with the same easy grace as if she were asking about the weather.

"The thermal insulation properties of different lagging compounds. Nothing a lady would be interested in."

Amelia's polite smile tightened at the edges. "You could try me. I'm not entirely feather-headed."

John flushed. "I d-d-didn't mean...That is to say...I d-d-didn't—"

"Relax, John." Benedict sent Amelia a please-be-kind glare.

"Yes, well, I h-have to go." He grabbed a handful of papers, crumpling them in his fist as he left the room.

Amelia watched him leave with surprise. "Well, that was unexpected. Really, did he think I was going to bite?"

"You do have a reputation."

She smiled. "For devouring heads? My goodness. Tell me, am I the subject of bedtime stories?"

Benedict took a step closer, drawing her against his body. The sound of her breath, the warmth of her smile, the slight crinkle of her eyes as she looked up at him—it was all he could do not to throw her over his shoulder and take her home. "You're the subject of my bedtime stories."

Her mouth parted. "Benedict, I—" She put a hand on his chest, right over the increasing *thump, thump, thump* of his heart.

"Yes?"

"I think—that's the worst line you've fed me yet."

He grinned and dropped a kiss on her forehead. "It was worth trying."

"We're in public, Mr. Asterly. You must behave." She stepped out of his arms, reminding him how formal her lot were. "But truly, I'm surprised to see Mr. Barnesworth out here, given how much you can't stand the aristocracy. He's the second son of Viscount Harrow, is he not?"

"Yes. But he has even less to do with the *ton* than I do." Benedict went to the corner of the room where they'd set up a small stove and put the kettle on to boil. When he looked up, Amelia was still staring out the door John had just left through.

"A pity, he looked as if he'd be a magnificent dancer. How did you meet?" she asked, turning back to him.

Benedict stuffed his hands in his pockets, uncomfortable talking about his intensely private friend. "We were at Eton together and then Oxford. When I left, he chose to leave with me, and together we established Asterly & Barnesworth."

John had left Oxford because he couldn't bear the thought of facing his peers without Benedict's hulking frame behind him as protection. As bad as it had been for Benedict being the subject of scorn, John had had it worse. His speech impediment had made him the subject of extreme mockery—terms like *idiot*, *muttonhead*, and *simpleton* thrown around often. His father had all but disowned him. Despite his extraordinary intelligence, he'd come close to flunking out of school. It was no hard decision for him to leave.

Amelia cocked her head, as if she were about to launch into another thousand questions.

To distract her, he turned away and gestured to the room. "Well, what do you think?"

Hands on her hips, she did a full three-hundred-and-sixty-degree turn, taking in every single scribble, book, tool. Finally, she faced him. "Honestly? It's chaos."

As soon as the words were out of Amelia's mouth, Benedict's face fell, and she realized this might have been a good moment for some fortifying flattery. And if she were a better person, she would tell him how impressive it—*he*—was and leave it at that.

But she wasn't a better person, and a spade was a spade.

"It's utter chaos. How do you find anything?" She moved to the center table where Mr. Barnesworth had different sketches laid out. Some of them sat on top of a long tally of numbers. Others were stacked over a written document in completely different handwriting—Benedict's, by the look of it. Papers were held down by half-drunk cups of tea, a screw here, a lump of coal there.

"It may not look very organized—"

She raised both eyebrows with a don't-even-think-of-trying-it look. "This stack of papers, something to do with your engine, I'm assuming—" She grabbed the list of numbers.

"They're pressure test results."

"Yes, well, it's right next to a bottle of..." She sniffed it then held it as far away as she could.

He tried to grab the pressure tests out of her hands, but she pushed the bottle of foul-smelling liquid at him instead.

"That's Fiona's latest project. It's really quite interesting." He placed it back on the table with exaggerated care. "You should probably be careful with that. It's highly flammable."

The complete lack of organization boggled the mind. "Then it should be put to the side where it won't be knocked over. Nothing is labeled!"

He crossed his arms. "We know where everything is."

Before she could reply, they were interrupted by the entrance of a red-headed woman. In breeches. Who walked in without looking up from the notebook she was writing in. "Ben, have you seen my analysis of the latest incendiary tests? I'm trying to nail down the appropriate sulfur ratios."

Benedict rolled his eyes "Fi, your timing is dreadful."

Amelia couldn't help but smile in triumph. They clearly

didn't know where everything was, and she wanted to hug this new woman for handing her the proof.

But the woman did not look like she wanted to be hugged. In fact, the look she gave Amelia was highly suspicious.

"Lady Amelia, Miss Fiona McTavish. Fi, this is my wife. I was telling her that our filing system is more than adequate for our needs."

Fiona snorted. "Our filing system is a pig-wallow or worse, but none of us has the time to fix it."

It was the excuse given by everyone who lacked basic organizational skills. Amelia couldn't help but *tsk*. "It takes just a few minutes at the end of each day to put things back where they belong."

Benedict's eyes almost bulged out of his head. "This coming from the woman aghast at having to make her own bed?"

She sniffed. "I didn't say that *I* was doing the putting away. But I'm very good at making things happen."

"Hmph." Fiona put aside her notebook to really look at Amelia, who felt like a specimen under a glass. Which— given that Fiona was the one in men's clothing, her hair tied in a queue rather than put up, and clearly at work in a factory—seemed rather backward.

Eventually, Amelia passed muster. "It's an unexpected pleasure to meet you, my lady," Fiona said, with no real authenticity.

Hmmm.

"I'm not sure why it's unexpected, given my husband owns the business, but it's a pleasure to meet you too."

Fiona shrugged. "Unexpected because it's hardly a place for a woman like yourself."

Amelia wasn't entirely sure of her place these days, but

she did know that only she would determine where that was. "I'm heartily sick of being told what my place is. I would think a woman like yourself, who clearly forges her own path, would understand the sentiment."

Benedict moved to intervene, but Amelia shook her head. Needing rescue by her husband was not the ideal first impression. This woman needed to understand that, though they might be in a factory, if there was a pecking order, Amelia was still on top.

Fiona stared at her for a long minute before nodding curtly. "Thank you for your creative approach to mending Ben's shirts. Those flowers have been quite diverting."

If that was what acceptance looked like from this woman, she would take it. "You're welcome. It's nice to know the effort was appreciated."

"Before we give Amelia any more ideas, why don't we have some tea?" Benedict said. "Fiona, join us."

Fiona looked over her shoulder toward the exit. "I really need to find those reports."

"Please. Join us." He pulled out a stool and motioned for Fiona to sit, leaving Amelia to pull out her own stool. She couldn't help but throw him a look as she yanked it back.

"I think the two of you are going to be *great* friends." His tone was strained, as though he was struggling to convince himself of the fact.

They both stared at him, a synchronous roll of the eyes the only thing they shared.

"It would do you both good. Fi, you work too hard, and Amelia—"

"I what?"

"Never mind." He went to the stove and removed the kettle from the flame.

That small act made Amelia's heart thump. With the amount of loose paper around the stove and their obvious lack of care with flammable materials, it was a miracle the whole place hadn't gone up in flames.

"If you moved the bench with all those doodads to where the bookcase is, the room would feel more open, and there'd be less chance of papers falling out of your...immaculate...filing system and onto the stove." She turned to Fiona. "I don't know how this place hasn't burnt to cinders. I thought you scientists were supposed to have above average intelligence."

"Nothing has burnt down yet," Fiona said defensively. "We have everything in hand."

Benedict placed a chipped cup in front of Amelia. Without saucer or sugar or spoon. Amelia added a tea set to her mental list of things to purchase when she was next in London.

Fiona seemed unperturbed by the lack of basic provisions, lifting her tea and cupping it in her hands to inhale the steam. Her nails were cut short, and there was a long, thin scar that ran across the back of her hand. The smattering of freckles across them matched the freckles across her nose and cheeks. She was quite pretty, in a singular way. Odd, to be wearing a man's cuffed shirt and plain morning coat, but Amelia could imagine she'd be striking in a light blue dress with her hair pinned up.

Was she eccentric by choice or because life had left her few other options? If it were the latter, perhaps Amelia could help.

"Tell me more about what you do," Amelia asked. "Benedict says that your project is unrelated to his engine." Amelia picked up her cup, pretending its faults went unnoticed.

Benedict took the seat next to her. His shoulder brushed

against hers, creating a lovely friction that sent sparks twirling down her arm.

There was a long second of hesitation before Fiona answered. "I'm working on something that will make lighting fires easier. The latest prototype has been quite successful. It needs a few small modifications, but we hope to have further financial backing to mass produce it."

"Why outside backing?" As far as Amelia knew, Benedict had money to spare.

"A London backer will also come with London connections that he"—Fiona tilted her head toward Benedict—"refuses to make. The product is aimed at wealthier households so those connections could be useful."

That made sense. Amelia could think of several ways that a member of the *ton* could influence potential distributors. There were ways that *she* could influence distributors—assuming she could reestablish the significance she'd had prior to her marriage.

Had Benedict not considered her at all in his business planning?

"I'll try to look past your assumption that he hasn't just made a very strong London connection and instead simply ask if I can help."

Fiona finished off her tea in one swallow. "Can you make the Pearson Group respond to letters with less than a month's delay? They want us to hand over the designs so they can get cracking on development, but they have yet to hand over any money."

"The Pearson Group? The same Pearson Group that was selling shares in the Dallah Coffee Company last year?" Amelia asked.

Fiona looked at her, surprised. "The very one."

"Goodness, don't give them anything until you see the

cash. Lord Easton has no blunt. I removed him from the List of Eligible Bachelors last Season when it became apparent that he needed an heiress, any heiress. Even an American one." She shuddered.

"Why didn't you mention this before?" Benedict asked, as if Lord Easton had been a topic of breakfast conversation.

"Because you've shown such interest in the goings-on of society," she drawled. "In fact, I think your very words were *'Amelia, do you expect me to feign interest in this?'*"

Fiona scrambled for notepaper, grabbing a quill and ink. "Tell me more," she said. "Tell me everything you know."

Benedict held the door while the two women clasped hands. When Amelia suggested Fiona pay her a social call and his business associate agreed, he had a momentary sense that the world was tilting. Amelia seemed to be altering every aspect of his life.

"How does a woman get to be a chemist, inventor, what-ever she is?" Amelia asked as they descended the stairs.

"That's her story to tell, when she's ready." Fiona's past had been as difficult as his own—more so, potentially. It was no wonder she was determined to create independent wealth.

"Well, that sounds intriguing. But honestly, I had the best education a woman could have, and I don't understand a single thing in that chaotic stack of papers. How did she learn it?"

"Ah. She started here scrubbing the floors. John caught her reading one of his scientific treatises and decided that raw talent should be nurtured. Did you have fun today?" They reached the bottom of the stairs, and she looked up at him.

"You know, I really did. Thank you."

"You were very helpful up there."

"Truly?" she asked. "I'm so glad." She was more satisfied than he'd ever seen her. Even more than when she'd won last week's argument about buying a new piano.

"You know, you can visit here any time."

She ran a gloved finger down the banister, wrinkling her nose at the layer of soot against the satin. "I think I will. You clearly need someone in charge of cleaning and organization." She turned to him. "If you don't mind, that is."

The thought of anyone coming into the firm and making changes made him uncomfortable. But he had wanted to engage her with his life, and he could hardly back out now because it wasn't how he'd imagined.

"Of course. I can't promise there will be much for you to do, but I'll enjoy seeing you during the day."

Benedict nodded at the men they passed as they left the building.

"They enjoy working for you," Amelia murmured as the men nodded back. "And they're proud of what they do."

"They simply value hard work and know what they're doing makes a difference."

"I think you're underestimating your role in making their lives feel meaningful." Amelia put a hand on his arm, stilling them for a minute with a smile that was completely sincere. And it made his stomach flip flop.

He coughed to move the moment along. "Thank you."

But he couldn't help the giddy grin he wore all the way into town.

Chapter 13 ———————

Something was wrong. Amelia and Benedict had spent the better part of an hour looking at ribbons, fabrics, hats, and fake flowers. Normally this would not be an issue—she had been known to spend entire days shopping—but that was in London, where she'd had a plethora of shops at her disposal. Abingdale had one dressmaker and a general store, manned by a crotchety storekeeper who looked very suspicious at the amount of time they had spent pressing different colored ribbons against her hair.

And they had yet to argue.

Benedict just would not crack.

She had been pleasantly surprised to discover their day included a shopping trip. The slight flutter she felt at the thought of her husband courting her had mixed with amusement at the mental image of him engaging in such girlish activity. She'd guessed it would take ten minutes before he threw up his hands in disgust. Instead he nodded, feigned interest in the debate about pale blue or robin's egg blue, and even had an opinion about which colors best suited her complexion.

Insufferable man.

He stood there with a smile on his face, far too pleasant and too handsome for her liking. Gone was his usual day gear of dark, heavy woolen breeches, rough-spun shirt, and patched coat. Polished tan hessians replaced his usual scuffed and mud-covered boots. They were paired with stockings, breeches of a light cream, braces, a fine shirt, and a clean, well-made morning coat. His hair was brushed and neatly pulled back. In the shaft of afternoon sunlight that streamed through the dusty window, it looked like burnished gold.

"Shall we just take one of everything?" he said. "Except for that puce-colored ribbon. That's horrid."

She blew a small strand of hair from her face. "I suppose so."

As Benedict piled the ribbons into the basket, Amelia strolled to the shelf of books, tucking three under her arm. She didn't stop to look at the titles, just moved quickly. She'd read all of four novels. It would be deuced bad luck for one of these three to be the same.

She shifted to the side and pretended to browse.

"Find anything that caught your eye?" His breath was hot on her neck. He stood so close that she could feel the heat of him through her pelisse. She looked at the storekeeper. Thankfully his attention was elsewhere.

She turned, keen to keep the books out of sight.

He raised an eyebrow.

"Just this." She grabbed the nearest thing off the shelf and dropped it into the basket he was carrying. Heavens, a musket. What would he think of that?

"Nothing to add to the reading material under your bed?"

Amelia flushed. "That's an absurd accusation."

Benedict winked and took the books from her. "Relax, princess. Your secret is safe with me."

Shopping gave way to luncheon. Amelia stood at the steps of the Bull and Whistle with Benedict at her back. "Ladies don't go to places like this." Indeed, they didn't get within ten feet of one on purpose.

"This lady will. Courage."

The teasing needled. No one had dared call her lily-livered before. Squaring her shoulders, she nodded her head. "Fine, let's go."

The pub's small windows let very little light through, so despite the early day, it was dark but for the fireplaces at both ends and the thick, stub-like candles burning behind the bar and on every other table, giving off a stream of black soot.

She stopped dead in the doorway. The men inside were grizzled with unkempt whiskers, their hair long and greasy, their clothes wrinkled and sporting a myriad of stains.

Benedict nudged her forward. She kept her head held high as they walked the length of the room to the chairs closest to the fireplace. With a critical stare at the cushion, she sniffed and perched on the very edge. Heaven knew what grime she was sitting on.

A buxom barmaid with an obscenely low-cut dress came over to them. She lavished Benedict with a sickly-sweet smile, leaning over to brush non-existent dirt from his shoulder, her bosoms practically falling into his lap as she did so.

With the girl's fleshy bottom in her face, Amelia rolled her eyes.

Benedict caught the look and grinned.

"Marriage has made you a busy man," the barmaid said. "We never see you anymore." The girl pouted, her bottom lip sticking out like the nouveau riche at Almack's.

"Well, you're seeing me now. Lady Amelia, may I present Edwina Merryman. Edwina, my wife, Lady Amelia."

The buxom girl turned and ran a slow gaze over Amelia, from her fur-trimmed slippers, up her heavily embroidered brocade pelisse, to the gold-shot ribbon at her throat.

When she reached Amelia's eyes, she flinched. There was a reason Amelia had been the second most terrifying unmarried lady of the *ton*. A simple arched brow could be more cutting than a dozen words if one practiced. Even a cow herder from the back end of nowhere knew what that look meant.

Benedict cleared his throat. "Two ales and the usual for lunch please, Winny."

With a small sniff, the barmaid left, but her walk back to the bar was at a much faster clip than her earlier saunter over.

"Ale?" Surely he was teasing her. He might not move in her circles, but everyone knew that ladies drank orgeat. Madeira if they needed something stronger. Port only if the men weren't home and wouldn't notice.

Benedict's smile held a deliberate challenge. "There's a first time for everything. Be brave." He lounged back in his chair, as if he were perfectly at home in this den of tawdriness.

Amelia remained upright with as little contact with the furnishings as possible. "I hardly see how drinking requires courage."

"Then there shouldn't be any problem, should there?"

"Hmph." More and more people were entering the bar— a surprisingly diverse array. Some were dirt-stained and clearly just in from the fields. Others wore simple but clean attire that marked them as men of business of some sort. In the corner of the room were a handful of women yabbering away as they mended clothing.

"So this is where you go when you're not at work and not at home."

"Yes."

Edwina returned to put two large mugs of a dark-looking liquid in front of them. There was no flirting this time. In fact, the girl looked like she couldn't get away fast enough.

"I can see the appeal," Amelia muttered as the girl tripped away, her hips swinging.

"Jealous?" Benedict grinned.

"Should I be?"

"Not in the least." There was fire in his eyes, and wherever he looked, her skin burned. He didn't say anything, but it was clear he was thinking about the previous night, the things he'd done to her in the bath. She grabbed the mug in two hands, grateful for any distraction, and took a big mouthful.

Good grief.

She forced herself to swallow it and pushed the mug away, her eyes burning. "Ugh. That is horrid."

Benedict laughed. "It's not that bad."

"Not that bad? It's like I knelt down and licked a London sidewalk."

Benedict laughed, a deep throaty chuckle that vibrated through her chest. He signaled for some water, which she gulped down thankfully.

In the corner, a fiddler took the stage and began to play a tune.

"What's this?" she asked. "I feel like I've heard it before."

"Haydn. Sun Quartet," Benedict said. "One of my mother's favorites."

"I've never heard it played like this. Are all pub musicians so talented?" The tiny man on the stool had as much focus as some of the greatest musicians she'd seen at Hanover

Square. He played with his whole body, from feet firmly planted on the floor as if he'd take flight if he moved them, to the dip and turn of his torso. He was magnificent.

"Would it shock you if they were all talented?"

"A little," she replied dryly.

Benedict frowned. "When one's life is dirt and sweat, you could argue that beauty is far more appreciated than it is by someone who is surrounded by it all the time."

"But beauty is often the product of time and training, things the lower classes have much less of."

"And whose fault is that?" he said.

"Not mine, if that's what you're implying."

Benedict opened his mouth to respond but clamped it shut. His whole body stiffened as he focused on something over her shoulder.

"Benedict, me lad. What a surprise to see ye here." The heavy Scottish drawl was infused with sarcasm. She craned her neck to see who was speaking. The Scotsman was nearly a foot shorter than Benedict. His grey beard didn't fully hide his sagging jowls or the yellow tinge to his face. His eyes were small and mean and firmly fixed on her husband.

Behind him stood two others, a short barrel of a man and the gangly lad who'd refused to speak with her earlier in the day. The scowl on his face was even more fierce than it had been at Benedict's factory. *What is his problem?*

This was another reason ladies didn't belong in a place like this. She took a fortifying breath. Men could sense unease.

Benedict stood, crossing the distance between his chair and hers, effectively blocking her view as he shook the Scot's hand. "Alistair." His tone was a warning if she'd ever heard one. He put a hand on her shoulder, preventing her from standing.

"Good to see ye, lad. Ye haven't dropped by for a drink with us common folk in weeks."

The stranger stepped past Benedict, taking the seat Benedict had just left. He spread his legs wide, his elbows resting on the arms of the chair, fingers drumming, and turned his intent stare to her. It was full of dislike and derision.

"We've yet to be introduced, lass." His tone was familiar—the derogatory drawl of a man who thought women vacant, vapid fripperies. A type of man that existed across all social classes, apparently.

It was a tone she was glad to hear because it told her exactly how she needed to respond. If he thought to intimidate her, he was grossly out of his depth.

She gave him the same long, judgmental perusal the impertinent barmaid had given her and then wrinkled her nose and turned away, as if he were as inconsequential as a bad smell.

The drumming of his fingertips ceased.

Behind her, Benedict gave her shoulder a light squeeze. "Lady Amelia, may I introduce Mr. Alastair McTavish. Alastair, Lady Amelia Asterly."

The young boy snorted and crossed his arms. "Lady Asterly. Don't that sound fancy."

"It's nice to see you again, Jeremy," she said. Sometimes kindness was the most effective weapon.

His lips thinned, and he turned his face away, suddenly fascinated by a spider busily spinning its web in the rafters.

"I apologize," Benedict said. "He's generally better behaved than this."

The boy's ears turned crimson, and the look he threw in Benedict's direction was furious.

"No need to apologize," the third man said, clapping a hand on the lad's shoulder. "Jeremy's just exercising his God-given right to converse when and with whom he chooses. With your permission, of course. Charles Tucker, at your service." He gave a mocking bow.

"Charles Tucker? The same Charles Tucker whose gang threw rotten cabbages at Lord and Lady Darnmouth last Season as they left the theater? I thought you'd been arrested."

He smiled. "I'm too quick for that, m'lady."

Before Amelia could respond, Benedict took her elbow, firmly dragging her from the chair. "And on that note, we must take our leave."

"Go back to yer love nest then. 'Twas a pleasure to meet ye, m'lady. Ye both look very happy. I guess your marriage cannae be the flaming disaster Benny said 'twas."

Benedict's hand gripped tighter on her elbow, but no tighter than the grip those words had on her heart. She wasn't foolish enough to think he'd been thrilled at their marriage, but she also hadn't expected that he'd shared his horror with men like this.

That he would discuss her in any way was humiliating. Her ears burned, and she ground her teeth to keep from lashing out.

"We're leaving." He was angry. She could hear it in his voice, but there was no way he could be angrier than she was.

~⁓

Cassandra was sitting at the bottom of the stairs leaning against the banister when they got home, her hair in the ridiculous curls Amelia kept insisting she wear, a book in her lap. Her look of boredom transformed into excitement the moment she set eyes on the basket of shopping his wife gripped tightly. She jumped up and hop-skipped across the foyer to them.

"How was your day?" she asked Amelia. He had resigned himself to the fact that, for now at least, Amelia held his sister's attention more than he did.

"It was fine, poppet. These are for you." Amelia placed the bag of a thousand and one ribbons in Cassandra's arms and turned to Tom, who had his arms out ready to take her coat. "I'm going upstairs. This will need to be cleaned." Each word was short and clipped and perfectly moderate. She handed over her pelisse. "As will my dress and my shoes. Please send Daisy up to help me change."

And without looking at him, she left.

"What did you do?" Cassandra hissed.

"I didn't do anything," he hissed back. Which technically he hadn't. Not today, anyway. He probably shouldn't have told Alastair his marriage was a catastrophe, but that had been weeks ago.

Benedict looked to where Amelia's skirts were swishing out of view. Today she had been warm and funny and— relatable. But there was nothing warm about her now.

He had made such strides in bringing her into his world today. All ruined by a petty Scotsman who couldn't resist throwing a punch. God only knew when he'd be able to get her back into the pub.

"I'm going upstairs," his sister said pointedly and made ready to follow Amelia like a lovestruck puppy.

He held her back with a hand on her shoulder. "Best you give her some space, poppet."

"Why? She's not angry with me. She *loves* me."

The words caused a wave of fear and jealousy to run through him. Fear that Cassandra was going to get her heart broken when Amelia inevitably left, just as his mother had. Jealousy that his sister could make Amelia happier than he could.

Cassandra gave him a consoling pat on the arm. "She might love you too if you stop making her angry."

Benedict's heart flip-flopped in his chest. He wanted his wife to love him. He wanted the warmth and playfulness she shared with his sister to be shared with him.

At first, he'd never understood the ice princess's appeal. Now he wondered how many London men had been on the receiving end of her warmth. He felt sick at the thought of her lavishing her wit on others—the foppish men from town who were more her type than a big lummox from the country.

He was going to have to woo her. To show her a life so unlike her past yet rich and gratifying. To convince her to leave her life in London behind. And maybe his sister was the first step in that.

"Fine, head upstairs. But if she doesn't answer her door, you'll need to find something else to do."

Tom approached. "Letters, sir." From a silver platter—one Benedict had never seen before—he handed over three envelopes.

The first was for Amelia, from a Lord Hemshire. He'd be best off letting Daisy deliver that one.

The second was a bill for the new curtains his wife had ordered—for the entire house, not just his mother's wing. He made a mental note to ensure the old curtains were distributed among those in the village who needed some.

Benedict ripped the third envelope open. Competing feelings of relief and trepidation settled over him. The Americans were coming to visit. He would have a chance to plead his case, to convince them he could work well with the British. But to do that, he needed the help of his not-currently-speaking-to-him wife.

Damn it.

Chapter 14

And turn, turn, take his hand and curtsey." The book slid off Cassandra's head and onto the carpet. Amelia winced as it thumped. For the fortieth time.

Cassandra threw her head back, groaning at the ceiling. "I am never going to get this right."

Amelia *tsk*ed. "Of course you are. You've made excellent strides since this morning. I've never had a student with such potential."

"Really?" Cassandra's eyes brightened.

Well no, not really. But the truth wasn't going to be much use. "Absolutely. Now back to the beginning, please."

Training had begun at the bright and early hour of ten in the breakfast room. A full tea set, which had been discovered in the attic, was now cleaned, polished, and laid out, ready for its first use in decades.

Horrifyingly, Cassandra had no idea what half the items were, let alone how to use them. Once they'd reached the point where she knew all the steps to a perfect cup of tea, even if she was somewhat sloppy on the execution, they'd moved on to dancing.

And that's where they'd been for the past hour. Cassandra moved with the grace of a dozen children storming a sweet stall in Hyde Park. Not that she could be blamed for it. Poise took practice, and most females began when they were still in the nursery. Assuming there was an adult with some sense there to teach them.

Which just made Amelia more determined. The greater the challenge, the more she relished the success. A lesser tutor would have given up well before now.

"Having a dance partner will help. Not that you want to rely on him to keep you steady. Half the men at a ball are either too old or too soused to stand steady."

"But who can I dance with? Ben is at work."

And there was the conundrum. It wouldn't be appropriate for Cassandra to dance with any of the manservants. Generally, one would have a sister, a cousin, or dancing master. At the very least a—

Perfect.

"Daisy can help. She's practically a lady's maid now. Not a spectacular one, but certainly adequate for this." She pulled the rope by the doorway.

Within a few seconds, Daisy appeared. Gone was the drab brown dress and serviceable grey smock Amelia was so familiar with. Instead, Daisy wore a simple floral day dress that was only a few years out of fashion, and her hair was up, only slightly askew, in the new style they'd been practicing.

"Daisy, you look quite pretty," Amelia said. "Green suits you."

"Th-thank you, m'lady." She flushed as she curtseyed.

"We're practicing the cotillion, and Cassandra needs

someone to partner with." She pointed to a spot in the middle of the room. "Just over there, if you please."

"I...uh..." Daisy looked over her shoulder toward the door.

"What is the difficulty?" Today was becoming increasingly frustrating, and Amelia couldn't help the tap, tap, tap of her foot on the floor.

"I think it's her afternoon off," Cassandra whispered.

Daisy nodded.

Honestly.

"I'm not asking her to dust the cornicing, although it needs it. It's dancing. Everyone loves dancing. You don't mind, do you, Daisy? What could you possibly have planned that's more diverting than a cotillion?"

Daisy swallowed, her eyes trained on the tips of her toes. "Nothing, m'lady."

"See." Amelia turned to Cassandra. "She wants to help. And it's not every day a maid gets dancing lessons from an expert."

Cassandra rolled her eyes. "That wasn't very nice."

"What do you mean? That was just a fact. I can't help what the facts are." The words came out quick and terse, off her tongue before she'd even thought them. Cassandra's accusation stung, whiplike, and only years of training allowed her to keep her poise.

She was perfectly nice, thank you very much. And it was frustrating when her comments were willfully misinterpreted.

"Perhaps we should start the dancing, m'lady." Daisy stood next to Cassandra. "What would you have me do?"

The altercation soured all of their moods, a feeling that was not improved a quarter hour later when Benedict bellowed from the foyer. "Cassandra!"

"In heeee—errr."

Amelia rolled her eyes. An entire day spent discussing how to conduct oneself in a ladylike manner and still this.

Benedict walked into the drawing room and sketched a quick bow, one hand kept behind his back. Amelia nodded in his direction, her movements feeling stiff and awkward. He'd apologized for yesterday's argument, but their interactions were still strained.

"You found us," Amelia said. "What a relief. Why, if it hadn't been for all the yelling, you might have been wandering for days. Quelle horreur."

"Lady Amelia, I come in peace." He produced a single Christmas rose, a faint blush of pink touching each of the perfect white petals. The apprehensive look on his face turned quickly into a smile as she accepted it.

"Thank you," she murmured.

The scoundrel winked and turned to his sister. "Cassandra, you have a book on your head."

Giving him an I'm-not-an-idiot stare, Cassandra curtseyed, slowly and with precision, her back ramrod straight. As she rose, she wobbled, and the book slid off.

"Darn." She caught it before it hit the floor.

"That was close," Amelia said. "You were very nearly up."

"Daisy is helping us get ready for London," Cassandra said.

Benedict cocked his head. "Isn't it your afternoon off? I'm sure I saw Marcus shuffling his feet by the back door."

"It is, m'lord."

"Then off you go. Don't keep the lad waiting."

Daisy looked to Amelia, a question written across her face.

Amelia waved her hand. "Very well. Benedict can fill in for you."

The speed at which Daisy disappeared lodged a kernel of unease in Amelia. She stomped on it. "She *wanted* to help."

Did she need to protest so loudly? Probably not. But the words were out.

Benedict shook his head. "I'm not entirely sure she realized there was another option," he said gently. "You can be...inconsiderate."

The kernel of unease grew.

"Churlish?" Cassandra interjected.

And it sprouted thorns.

"Charmingly self-focused?"

And now it had drawn blood. Amelia stood and tugged the cuff of her sleeve until the muslin was crease-free. "Well, after that rousing assessment of my character, I bid you good day."

Benedict intercepted her, his hand reaching out and coming to rest against her waist. "I'm sorry. Don't let me run you off. I interrupted your fun with my unvarnished judgment. Tell me what you were doing."

Well, fine. If he wasn't going to let her politely escape, then he could help her with the training, whether he liked it or not.

"We were dancing."

"Oh." He took a step back.

"And you've arrived at the perfect time to help."

Hands raised, slight panic on his face, he said, "I don't know if I can be of help."

"Your mother taught you how to dance a cotillion, surely?"

He shook his head, another step back bringing him almost to the door he seemed intent on escaping through. "That was a *long* time ago."

She took his hand and dragged him into the center of the room, trying hard not to notice that the touch of his bare skin on hers caused her heart to beat a little harder. "I'm sure it will come back to you."

"My mother likened me to a bull stuffed into tails trying to walk on two legs," he blurted out.

Her first instinct was to reply with a quip, but he had folded in on himself—his shoulders caving, his head bowed.

Her husband was a strong, successful, annoyingly self-assured man. What cruelty had his mother inflicted that was now turning him into a frightened child?

"I don't believe that can be the truth. But show me. Cassandra, clap a beat please."

He inhaled sharply as Amelia slipped her hand into his, the best sign she had that he felt the same energy between them.

She gave his hand a reassuring squeeze. "Step and step. Turn one. Turn two." As she curtseyed, she looked up at him, fluttering her lashes. "Why Mr. Asterly, I do believe you're better at this than you think."

She turned toward him and placed a hand on his shoulder. They moved around the room with just the barest falter. After a handful of turns, his shoulders relaxed, and his face lost the grimace that had been plastered onto it.

Clearing his throat, he asked, "It's not too awful, is it?"

She stepped closer than propriety truly allowed and whispered, "I like the way you move."

His arm tightened around her.

"That was an awful thing for your mother to say. She should have kept those thoughts in her head."

"Not 'she should never have considered such a thing'?" His tone was back to the confident drawl she was used to. It was comforting.

"Well, you can't criticize what people say in their heads. Goodness, if I was held accountable for my every thought, I'd have no one willing to talk to me."

He shook his head. "You are a singular woman of many contradictions."

"Inconsiderate, too, apparently," she said, still smarting at his earlier words.

"And yet sometimes the sweetest woman I know," he murmured. "Wanting you makes no sense. But God help me, I do."

His words made her feel giddy. And safe enough to ask the question that had been niggling at her these past ten minutes. "Did Daisy truly have a caller waiting to take her out?"

"Is that such a surprise?"

"I just... It never occurred to me."

"That she might have a life outside of waiting on you?"

"No." *Darn it.* "Well, yes. I suppose." It's not that she actively thought Daisy had no life outside service. She just hadn't thought about it at all. Had given it no consideration.

Making her inconsiderate and self-absorbed.

Just like he'd said.

Disappointment hung heavy—a giant cloak of failure. And she hated failing.

Benedict tipped her face toward his. His look was kinder than she deserved. "Princess, you've spent your entire life seeking the esteem of others... but they aren't here. So maybe it's time to put that energy into the people who *are* here."

"I wouldn't know where to start. I have nothing in common with anyone here."

Benedict chuckled and tugged at her earlobe. "Start with these. Listen, and you might find you have more in common than you think."

"I just..." She took a deep breath and looked toward the door that Daisy had exited through so quickly. "I just worry that I'm too late. What must she think of me?"

⤜⤚

That night, as Daisy pulled the pins from Amelia's hair, Amelia stared at her lady's maid in the glass. Amelia did not, as a rule, apologize. So she had no idea where to start.

But their conversation so far this evening had been stilted. And on purpose or not, Amelia had clearly hurt Daisy's feelings.

"Daisy," she started. "I am…" And she faltered.

"Yes, m'lady?"

"I am…wondering how your afternoon with Marcus went."

Daisy's hands stilled. No doubt she shared Amelia's surprise at the content of this discussion.

"It was brief, m'lady." She put down the last of the pins and picked up the brush. "He only gets Thursday morning off, and I only get the afternoon. We make do with an hour together at lunch."

"Oh. I see." How could she not? The determined yank of the brush through her knotted hair made it plain.

Regardless, this would be the appropriate time to apologize. She had, after all, robbed the couple of a quarter of their time together.

"Daisy, I'm quite s…" The word just stuck there. Fast. "What I mean to say is, I'm very s…"

Ack.

"M'lady?"

"S…certain. I'm very *certain* that I want you to swap your afternoon off for the morning. If that's what you want. It's not an order. I just thought you might like to. And perhaps take another morning off, once I'm dressed and if one of the new housemaids can pick up the slack."

Daisy caught her eye in the mirror, and in a look, Amelia tried to convey what her mouth just would not communicate.

"Thank you, m'lady."

Chapter 15 ————————

"Up you get, princess." Benedict wrenched the curtains—new curtains—open. While he hated the fact that the old ones had been replaced, he had to admit her room looked cheerier with the bold yellow velvet.

Yellow was not the color of a London lady wasting away in the country. It was the color of a woman making sunshine out of daisies, or whatever the ridiculous saying was.

Which was good. Amelia was going to need that attitude today.

"You are the worst sort of cad." Amelia pulled the blankets up over her head.

"I brought breakfast..." He dragged a chair to her bedside and took the cover off the plates he'd placed on her bedside table when he'd snuck in.

Breakfast was hot and delicious.

She flipped over a corner of the quilt—not enough for her to emerge, but enough that she could smell the food. "Is aaac acon?" The thick bedcovers muffled her words.

"I can't hear you," he said. He picked up a rasher and began to munch on it. "But your bacon tastes delicious."

She flung the quilt all the way back and sat up, the sheets pulled over her chest. "You wouldn't." Her scowl turned into a perplexed smile when she saw the two plates on the tray.

"What? Can a man not eat breakfast with his wife?" He sat back, his ankle crossed over his knee as he balanced a plate on his thigh.

"This is very familiar of you." She looked longingly at the food but clearly did not want to release the sheets in order to eat, despite the fact that her nightgown reached right to her chin and down to her wrists, with ridiculous little ruffles on the neckline and sleeves.

"You are trussed up like a lamb for sale. I see more of you when we breakfast at the table." He waved the fork in front of her, her nose following in its wake.

"Fine." She dropped the sheets and reached for the plate. The nunlike outfit, so prim and proper a minute ago, shifted as she moved, pulling against her breasts, her nipples outlined.

It showed nothing but suggested everything. He shifted the plate from his thigh to his lap.

"Is this a special occasion?" she asked, oblivious to his distress.

"More an apology in advance."

She raised an eyebrow as she cut her food. "I'm listening."

He took a deep breath. Hopefully he wasn't pushing too far too fast. "The winter festival starts in the village today."

"Cassandra mentioned it. I believe she's planning on bobbing for apples." The tips of her ears turned red, as if she suddenly remembered the insult she'd thrown at him that night in Edward's study, when her father had bartered her away.

He swallowed back the memory of that day. "Yes...there's that." He paused. He'd planned breakfast, he'd planned his entrance, but he'd not actually planned how he was going to break the news.

Amelia took his silence as the end of his point and huffed. "Goodness, you sound like you're about to be sentenced to the prison hulls. I'm not a total ogre. I have been to a fair before. I've even somewhat enjoyed one..." She bit the end off her croissant.

He was just going to have to dive in. "There's also the town bandy match."

"Bandy?" She was so focused on her breakfast, she didn't seem to pick up on the tension that he couldn't keep from his voice.

"It's a sporting game, played on the ice."

"Oh?" She took another bite.

"And you'll need to play."

Amelia began to choke, crumbs spewing onto her quilt.

He poured her some tea and waited as she gulped it down.

"I don't play sports," she said once she'd recovered. "I don't know the first thing about them."

He patted her on the knee. "Don't worry. They'll put you at the back. You won't have to do anything."

"Then why even take part? Surely we've a footman or groom who would do a better job." Her eyebrows were knitted in a picture of complete disbelief, as if it were the most absurd request that had ever been made of her.

"It's tradition, the local women versus the local men."

"And why am I playing?"

This was the challenge because he'd brainstormed a dozen different reasons that he could give her that might inspire her to take part. Nothing seemed believable, which meant he was forced to go with the truth. "It would be good for you. It's time you made some friends in Abingdale."

Surprisingly, instead of a rolling of the eyes or a sarcastic quip, the comment was met with startled silence.

"You do know what friends are, yes?" he continued. "People you talk to, laugh with, visit."

That provoked the eyeroll he'd been expecting. "I know what friends are," she said. "I have plenty. I've just never particularly *liked* any of them."

He shook his head. Every day there was some offhand comment that demonstrated how twisted her understanding of human relationships was. Her father, and the society that had made her, had a lot to answer for.

"I'm kidding," she said. "Obviously, there are some people I'm looking forward to seeing again. There are a handful that are more than tolerable."

"You'll like the people you meet today."

"Truly?" Sarcasm dripped off the word.

"Probably not, but I need you to pretend that you do, at least. And while you're at it, maybe have a go at being a little less...Lady Amelia Asterly."

She set aside the plate from her lap. "And who should I be, if not myself?"

He was walking a fine line. He should probably have stopped with the request to join the bandy game, but he was in too deep now. "Just be Amelia....Amy? The townspeople need to see the warm, human side I know is in you."

She frowned. "As opposed to..."

"Lady Amelia the perfect, bloodless porcelain doll. Not porcelain, though. That's too fragile. Copper princess? Iron lady?" He shrugged.

She regarded him with deep suspicion. "Benedict Asterly, that almost felt like a compliment."

He grinned. "It would just be nice if the locals could see an aristocrat that was nice. Friendly."

She threw a pillow at his head. "Get out, Benedict." He stood to leave. "Leave the bacon!"

The local fair was colorful and boisterous, rollicking and carefree—everything that had been drilled out of Amelia since she was a little girl. Children whirled past, chasing each other with sticks tied to colorful flags and shrieking with laughter.

Two months ago, the sight would have spurred feelings of disapproval. But today it left a different feeling in her chest. Something she couldn't quite identify but which made her feel...lost.

Becoming separated from Benedict early had not helped. He'd given her a quick kiss on the lips, leaving her all fluttery and off-kilter, and then left with barely a backward glance.

Cassandra, at least, had stayed by her side.

"We're going to beat them this year," Cassandra said. "I just know it."

She grabbed Amelia's hand and towed her toward the group of women huddled under a marquee that had been set up alongside a clear patch of ice.

Fiona was the only woman she recognized. They exchanged brief smiles. Since Amelia's initial visit to the firm a week ago, they'd established a tentative friendship. At the very least, they were two colleagues working together to use Amelia's knowledge of London's elite to establish a business plan Fiona could take to town. It was not dissimilar to working with new debutantes to identify potential husbands, but it was infinitely more satisfying.

"I owe Benedict a ha'penny," Fiona said. "I never thought he'd get you here."

"I'll give you two ha'pennies to get me out of this."

Fiona laughed. "And deprive myself of the entertainment of seeing Lady Amelia Asterly compete on the ice? Never."

Amelia looked around. The rest of the women ranged in age. Two girls were clearly in their teens, and yet another was an older woman with solid grey hair wrapped into a wispy bun. The only thing the motley crew had in common was the look of determination on their faces.

"Lady Amelia," Cassandra said very properly, "this is the women's bandy team. Ladies"—she hesitated for a second, presumably realizing that none of the women were actual ladies—"this is Lady Amelia Asterly."

A couple of the younger girls curtseyed. More exchanged skeptical looks.

Amelia countered with the smile she reserved for those her father really wanted her to impress. She would show Benedict how charming she could be. "It is a pleasure to meet you all."

"Do you know how to play?" the older woman asked.

"I can skate, but no, I've never seen a bandy match before. I'm looking forward to learning." She wasn't sure she was looking forward to it at all, but she'd be run over by an out-of-control curricle before she let the women see that.

"You'll pick it up quickly," Fiona said.

"Or you'll break something. This isn't really a game for your kind." The comment came from a dumpy woman about Amelia's age. Her clothes were thin and patched in places. Her hands were rough and cracked, and her face was mean.

A couple of the other girls sniggered.

"Goodness, you speak as though I'm a completely

different species. I assure you, my limbs function exactly the same."

Fiona gave her a tiny shake of the head, indicating there was no point trying to reason with the woman. "Just try to get that ball"—she pointed to a fist-sized knotted ball in the center of the circle—"into that net with this." She handed Amelia a wooden stick with a curved end.

It was awkward to maneuver. Amelia swung it from side to side and almost dropped it. She tried hard to ignore the condescending glances shared between the rest of the team. Who were they to judge her anyway?

"Don't pick the ball up with your hands," Cassandra said. "And don't you use your head either."

"I think I can manage that," Amelia said.

"The winner is the team with the most points."

The grey-haired lady shook her head. "It's been four years since the women have won."

"Pardon? Four years and the men haven't let you win? That's not particularly gentlemanly."

The glowering faces around her made it clear her opinion was not popular. Even Cassandra looked unimpressed.

"We prefer to work for what we have, *my lady*," the grey-haired woman said. "No one gives us nothing because we happened to be born a girl."

"Or rich," another muttered.

Benedict had explained the political situation in the village, but she hadn't really understood until now. All these looks, these snide comments—the aristocracy was obviously despised in this part of the country.

He'd said much of it was due to mistreatment by the Karstarks, but if that were the sole cause, they wouldn't be so hostile toward her.

Fiona kept talking, defusing the situation. "Remember,

they'll skate at you and expect you to move because they'll think you don't want to get knocked down."

"Well, they'd be right. I don't want to get knocked down." What sort of barbarianism had Benedict gotten her into?

"Which is why they're going to target you. You need to stand your ground. They'll never expect that kind of gumption from someone...who hasn't played before."

Hmph.

Surprisingly, it was one of the youngest that had the women huddle round and started giving instructions.

"Her older brother plays for the Bury Fens. She's seen more bandy matches than Maggie," Cassandra whispered, nodding toward the grey-haired woman.

The next hour was pure hell. Amelia quickly forgot about the indecency of a dress short enough to display her ankles and concentrated solely on dragging enough air into her lungs in order not to die right there on the field.

Skating up and back, up and back, occasionally hitting out at a ball with the stick, sometimes connecting, sometimes not.

The rest of her team didn't send the ball her way unless they had to, not after the first time she'd promptly skated to the side as three burly-looking men charged right at her.

With only a few centimeters of candle left in the game— and goodness was she watching that, begging it to burn faster—the scores were tied, four all.

She stood with her hands on her hips, bent nearly double, halfway behind the line of woman attackers and the net, when somehow the men got the ball. Benedict charged down the center of the ice. Her teammates screamed her name.

Oh no. There was no one else. How was she supposed to stop him?

Benedict was skating on an angle that would see him run straight past her.

She skated right and then left, unsure of what to do and praying he'd give her the ball—he was her husband, after all.

His wicked smile was not a good omen. He was taunting her.

She bent her knees and launched herself into his path.

It was like hitting a solid brick wall.

She went down, and down hard.

Her back hit the ground, her head thwacked into the ice, and as he landed on top of her, all the air whooshed out of her lungs.

She tried to suck in breath but couldn't move under his weight. She pushed at him.

"Bloody hell." He propped himself up on his elbows, removing his crushing weight from her chest. "What the devil did you do that for?"

Breathe. She couldn't breathe. She clawed at her throat.

He rolled over and dragged her into his lap. "It's okay, princess," he murmured, brushing hair from her forehead. "You've just had the wind knocked out of you. You'll be okay."

Amelia finally dragged in a small, tiny thread of air. And then another. And another. The blackness that was crowding the edges of her vision receded.

Benedict ran his fingers gently over her scalp.

She winced.

"You've a lump. It'll be there for a day or so." He gently set her back on the ice—the wet and cold seeping through her skirts—and turned her face to his. He looked into her eyes. Really looked, as though he were examining them.

"What's your name?"

"Amelia."

"Where are you?"

"The back end of nowhere."

His lips twitched. "Why are we sitting on the ice?"

"Because you slammed into me, you giant oaf." She shoved him in the chest. He should have just given her the darned ball.

He chuckled. "You'll be okay. Let me know if you start to feel nauseous."

"I will not. That's not appropriate conversation."

He grabbed her chin so she couldn't look away. "You tell me if you start to get nauseous."

She swallowed and nodded.

"Now we should probably get up." He pushed himself to his feet and helped her up, holding an arm around her waist until she was steady on her skates.

Cheering erupted. She looked up to see Cassandra tearing down the ice toward her.

"We tied! We tied!" She went to throw herself at Amelia but was stopped by Benedict's outstretched hand. "You were amazing," she said.

The rest of her team joined them. "You were rather impressive," the grey-haired woman said, reaching out a hand. "I can't say I thought you had it in you."

The celebration lasted the rest of the afternoon. Food was set up on makeshift tables, and the townsfolk sat on logs, wagon carts, barrels, and the small handful of chairs that had been brought down for the event.

Benedict stayed by her side the whole time, despite the steady stream of people who came to talk to him, to ask him for advice or help.

Whether it was questions about crops, or repairing a roof,

or dealing with a customer who couldn't pay their account, Benedict had a solution for everything—a solution that usually involved his assistance.

By the time the sun started to go down, he'd committed to helping Farmer John fix the fence along the southern border of his property, going through Widow Bancroft's accounts, and showing Little Peter Podney how to parry an opponent's lunge.

For all of his protestations that he was neither lord nor leader, it was clear the people of Abingdale saw him as such. He commanded respect, and it fit him well—far more so than the popinjays of the *ton* who preened and prissed under the admiration of those around them.

"Having a good time?" he asked as they stopped at a sweet stall.

"I am actually," she said, accepting a piece of crystallized lemon from him.

"Good. You've got some sugar just..." He brushed the corner of her lips with his thumb, sending a shiver coursing through her. Without thinking, she stepped closer to him and his hand moved to caress her cheek.

Desire washed through her. Except it wasn't desire. It wasn't just a fluttering in the stomach and sudden goose bumps. This was something that wrapped itself around her heart and put down roots. It blossomed in all the lonely, empty corners inside her. Where she'd built a brittle shell of propriety and perfection, it filled her with color and flaws and other people.

It was the most pure moment of her life.

Every minute of the day had revealed something new about him. Something she'd thought could be found only among society's upper crust. Respect. Influence. Duty.

She reached for his hand, and he interlaced his fingers

in hers, squeezing gently. "I'm glad you came into my life, princess."

The roots around her heart tightened. To hell with propriety and all the people around them. Rising to her tiptoes, she kissed him gently. She wanted so much more, and the tightening of his hand in hers suggested he did too.

But he pulled away and, judging by the very interested faces around them, it was a good thing he did.

One of the local women approached them, curtseying briefly. Benedict's throat bobbed. He did not like the deference shown to him. "Good afternoon, Mrs. Bleufleur. How are you today?"

The woman, surely not more than forty, smiled when he did, the faint lines around her eyes crinkling. Despite the smile, she was tense. Her left hand was clenched in her skirts.

"I'm well, thank you, Mr. Asterly. I was wondering though..." She stopped, suddenly losing her nerve.

Benedict let go of Amelia's hand and leaned forward, giving the woman his complete attention. "Is there something I can help you with?" he asked. "Because after the tarts you sent for Cassandra's birthday, I owe you a favor."

"Well, actually...I need some advice. About Bessie. And London. You're the only person I know who has been there."

Benedict pursed his lips for a moment and then put a hand on the small of Amelia's back. "Have you met my wife, Mrs. Bleufleur? Lady Amelia is far more qualified to discuss women and London than I am."

Amelia almost put her neck out turning to face him so quickly. What was he doing? She was supremely *unqualified* to be giving any kind of advice to villagers.

Mrs. Bleufleur hesitated. It was not unexpected. The locals

had given her either looks of suspicion or shy acceptance—but none had directed more than a quick salutation her way.

"I truly feel you'll get better insight from her." He bent to kiss Amelia's cheek and muttered softly in her ear. "Listen. Be curious." He then not so subtly pushed her forward.

Left without another option, Amelia took the woman's arm in hers and began to walk. It was not unlike what she'd done countless times along the edge of a ballroom with new debutantes, so she would simply pretend that's where they were. "How can I help, Mrs. Bleufleur?"

The woman hesitated for a moment, chewing on her lower lip. "It's my eldest, Bessie, m'lady. I've always had hopes of her marrying the Pickens boy. That lad will own his father's farm one day, and they breed prize-winning heifers. It's a good match."

"I take it from your need to discuss it that your daughter doesn't share the same dream?"

The woman shook her head. "She wants to go to London to be a seamstress. I've told her time and time again that London's no place for a young woman on her own, but she won't listen to a word I say."

It was on the tip of her tongue to agree with Mrs. Bleufleur immediately. After all, if Bessie could secure a nice life with a reasonably successful man of her station, that was the sensible thing to do. But she held off. Be curious, Benedict had said. Listen.

"What is he like? The Pickens boy?"

Mrs. Bleufleur snorted. "He's like all nineteen-year-old boys, m'lady. More interested in farts and pigs and the barmaid's bosoms than anything else. But what he's like isn't as important as what he can offer. A home here, close to her family."

Not a scant month ago, Amelia would have agreed with

every syllable of that sentiment, but she looked over at her husband. What a man was like was more important in a marriage than she had ever previously credited.

"Does she have much talent as a seamstress, do you think?"

"Blimey if I know. She can mend a tear in five seconds, and you'd never know it was there, but the clothes she makes don't have any real place around here in Abingdale. Too fancy. They're good for a wedding dress but that's about it."

Benedict had had a solution for every problem presented to him today, and the people here admired him for it. Perhaps he was right. Perhaps she could build that same level of esteem if she put the effort into getting to know these people.

"You're right, Mrs. Bleufleur. London is no place for a girl on her own. But if the Pickens boy is only nineteen, he needs a few years to ripen before he'll make any woman a decent husband. Bessie could go to London and see what she can make of herself in a year or two."

The woman's frown deepened, and she crushed her reticule in her hand. "But isn't it awfully dangerous, m'lady? She's my little girl."

Amelia put a reassuring hand on Mrs. Bleufleur's shoulder. "Send her to me, with her best creations and her sketchbook. If she's any good, I'll give her the reference she needs to join a respectable household or an established business. She'll be safe and somewhere we can keep an eye on her. We may just give her dreams wings yet."

"She looks happy," Benedict said when Amelia returned.

"I think I actually managed to help." She couldn't hide her smile.

He brushed a strand of hair away from her eyes. The feeling of his thumb on her skin made her shiver, but the look he gave her was so full of heat she thought she'd melt from it.

"And are you happy? Here? Helping?"

She wrapped a hand into the lapels of his coat, edging closer to him. His nearness made her dizzy, giddy. Her cheeks flushed hot, and as she looked up at him, her gaze could go no farther than his lips.

"I am," she whispered.

Chapter 16 ———————————

I feel so ill." Cassandra collapsed on the chaise in a dramatic manner.

"You shouldn't have eaten so many sweets." It was the proper thing for Amelia to say but hypocritical in the extreme given she had also overindulged in wrapped peppermints.

"It might be best for you to sleep it off, little sister," Benedict said. "It's well past your bedtime." He leaned in close to Amelia. "Yours too."

She yawned. "I think you might be right." In London, she could dance until dawn, but after just a few weeks of country hours, she simply wasn't up to it. She held her hand out to Cassandra. "Let's go to bed, little one."

The house was empty. All the servants had been given the day off to enjoy the fair, and although it was nearing midnight, none had yet returned. Only the pad of their feet on the carpet broke the silence.

"Good night, poppet. Sleep tight." Amelia kissed

Cassandra on the forehead and walked down the hall to her room, leaning on Benedict all the way.

Inside, the fire had gone out.

Drat.

In her first week—back before they'd hired help—Amelia had learned the art of making a fire. But it was difficult, and it was too late for her to be bothered tonight. It was also too cold for her not to bother.

"Dash it."

"I'll get it." Benedict crossed to the fireplace and began to empty the ash into a bucket.

Exhausted, Amelia sat on the edge of the bed and unlaced her boots, tugging them off and arranging them at the end of the mattress.

Her husband was a very useful man. She couldn't imagine any of her London beaus knowing how to light a fire.

He was a very nice man too. And handsome. With broad shoulders and muscular arms that felt lovely to hold.

"Pardon?" he asked. Still kneeling before the fireplace, he twisted to face her.

"Excuse me?"

"You said something."

She shook her head. "No, not at all. I wasn't thinking— saying—anything." Heat crept up her neck. The late hour and her woolgathering were going to get her into trouble.

The flames held, and he stood, rubbing the back of his neck. "Well, I guess that's good night then." He made no move to leave though. And she didn't want him to. They'd been dancing around it for days, this attraction.

But he was her husband.

There was no one around.

And really, there was no reason not to kiss him again. And whatever came next.

"I can't get out of my dress." She stood and took two steps toward him, her pulse thrumming through her veins.

"You can't get out of your dress?" She couldn't tell if the flames from the fireplace were dancing in his eyes or if he was as scorching as she was.

"My lady's maid is out."

He crossed the space between them in three quick strides, coming to stop just inches from her. Close enough that she could feel the warmth of his breath. He rested a hand on her waist. His fingers flexed and pressed into her, but he left those few darned inches between them.

"Then can I be of assistance?" he asked.

She inhaled. This was her chance to change her mind. But that breath was potent. The smell of him made the room tilt. It swirled through her, turning her blood hot.

She leaned forward, turning those few inches into just a finger-width.

"Yes," she whispered.

"Thank God." He pulled her tight against his body, the long hard breadth of him setting fire to the deepest parts of her.

He sank his hand into the back of her chignon, sending pins flying. Tipping her face toward his, he touched his lips to hers.

This kiss. It was a new silk dress, a perfectly chalked ballroom, and meeting the queen all in one.

It was both familiar and an epiphany.

It was heaven.

"Amelia," he murmured. "My God, Amelia."

The strength of his sex pulsated against her, igniting the same primal throb in her.

His lips moved to her earlobe, the sound and heat of his breath making her shiver. He trailed a line of soft kisses to the edge of her dress.

"Oh." Her knees buckled, and only his arm around her stopped her from falling to the ground.

"You're perfect," he whispered, the words brushing against her skin, causing goose bumps to form. He ran his hand down the small of her back and cupped her backside, squeezing it gently.

Her fingers gripped his shoulders. "I thought I was an idle, pompous aristocrat."

"You're strong." Without raising his head from her chest, he started to free the buttons along the back of her dress.

"Are you sure you don't mean stubborn?" she asked, flinching at the sudden exposure to the cool air as her dress pooled around her waist.

"You're witty." He pushed her dress over her hips, and suddenly she was standing in front of him in nothing but her underclothes. She was tempted to cover herself with her hands, but he shook his head.

His stare was thirsty, roving, yet full of wonder.

"You said I was sarcastic," she whispered.

"You're intelligent." The words came out half-strangled— the effect she was having on him that pointed.

"Not calculating?" she asked.

He shook his head, untied the laces of her stays and removed them.

Tentatively, she took a step toward him and undid the knot at his throat.

"Amelia," he groaned. He swept her into his arms and settled her on the bed. He shrugged off his jacket and waistcoat, tossing them in a heap, and pulled his shirt over his head.

The first time she'd seen him half naked, she'd been barely conscious.

The second time she'd been curious, her body alert and tingling.

This time, the sight of his tanned skin, the ropes of muscle, the smattering of dark blond hair across his chest whipped up a blazing heat inside that writhed across her body, settling between her legs. Her body arched toward him. She wanted him here. With her. Now.

"Easy, princess," he said as her fingers brushed his thigh. He tugged off his boots and flung them across the room where they hit the door to his bedroom with a thud. He undid the laces at his waist and pushed down his breeches in one move.

"Heavens."

She wasn't a complete innocent. She had seen some Greek statues. But *this*? This was something else entirely.

She swallowed, unsure how it would work. "I…uh…"

Her uncertainty must have been plain across her face because his manner shifted. Gone was the intense urgency, the wild abandon. What was fierce became gentle.

He climbed into bed next to her, tipping her chin so she was forced to meet his gaze. "Trust me."

He curled his fingers around the hem of her shift, drawing it up, gradually exposing her. He bit his lip as he lifted it past her breasts and over her head.

The heady thrill of his expression overwhelmed any sense of shyness she felt.

He grazed his palm across the side of her rib cage and up. Up until his hand cupped her breast and his thumb circled her nipple, drawing a sharp gasp from her. It was the lightest, softest of movements, yet it rocked through her.

He bent his head and wrapped his mouth around her nipple, sucking gently, causing her feet to stretch and flex and her whole body to go taut.

"You're so beautiful."

What did one say to a man who was trailing his tongue down one's bare chest? *Thank you?*

That felt overly formal.

He slipped his hand to the curls between her legs, and all thought of responding vanished. A pleasure drove through her, and she gasped, pulling away.

With a satisfied chuckle, he stretched out beside her, propped up on one elbow, a maddening smile on his face. "Trust me." His fingers returned to her curls and found the soft, sensitive core of her. He stroked it, over and over. Each time pushing her higher and higher, though where they were going, she didn't know.

As the tension built, all reason and inhibitions fled. She grabbed his wrist, pressing his fingers harder against her as she thrust her hips forward.

A tiny corner of her was mortified. The rest was enraptured.

"Oh my god. Oh my god. Oh my god."

This. *This.* She couldn't breathe. She couldn't hear. Stars shone in her vision as the whole world dropped away.

This was why foolish girls risked their reputation, why married women sent satisfied, cryptic glances. Why Helen had left a king for a mere prince.

It built and built and built with each stroke.

And then she tipped over the edge of the precipice she hadn't seen.

She bit the back of her hand to keep from crying out as her body took on a life of its own, straining and twisting in pleasure, lifting from the bed before collapsing in a sated, languid heap.

He cupped her face in his hands, coarse and rough with calluses. Hands that had never known softening crèmes but had built things, tamed things. Might be taming her.

"I…" There weren't words to describe it.

No wonder this was kept from unmarried girls. Society would fall. There wouldn't be enough dark corners or locked rooms at any gathering.

She looked at him. The heat in his eyes hadn't banked. If anything, her—incident—had increased his desire. His cock was still hard against her thigh, and a muscle along his jaw ticced.

Where she was spent, he was coiled tight. She didn't have to be a genius engineer to know there was still more to come.

She stroked the rough stubble on his cheek, and he leaned into her hand, placing a hot kiss on her palm.

"What next?" she whispered.

He growled, a guttural, animal sound that formed no words yet spoke reams, and pressed into her with a desperate kiss.

In that ephemeral state between asleep and awake, there was no sight, just the light of the dawn inside him, even though a corner of his rational brain knew it was still dark outside.

This was a different kind of dawn, beyond the breaking of a new day. The smooth, soft pink of Amelia's skin, the slow rhythmic *whoosh* of her breath, and the enveloping smell of jasmine all heralded a different kind of beginning.

He curled his arm around her, pulling her close to him, content just to listen to her breathe. She shivered, goose bumps prickling across her arms—disappearing as he ran a hand over them in big, slow circles.

Why had luck favored him in this way? He had failed one woman so completely. How could the universe have sent another in his direction? Particularly one as perfect as her.

He nestled his cheek into her hair, his thumb drawing gentle patterns on her side.

Once the light flowed through the uncovered window, her sleep became lighter, more restless. She shifted, each move pressing her closer to him, brushing against his cock and flooding his mind with carnal thoughts.

She stiffened beneath his touch when she woke and then relaxed, sinking into his embrace. "Good morning," she said as she rolled to face him. Her chest and neck had flushed a delightful, self-conscious shade of red.

He reached down and grabbed the bedsheet, pulling it over them. "Good morning." He kissed her, soft, quick— like a habit they'd have for the rest of their lives. "Last night was—"

"Educational?" She didn't meet his eyes, instead focused on the hair on his chest, running her fingers through it in small, whirling patterns.

"Perfect."

She gave a satisfied little *hmph*. "So what next?"

Benedict stretched out, his feet hanging over the edge of the bed. "We ring for breakfast and spend the rest of the day in bed."

Amelia propped herself up on her elbow. "Tell me about your mother."

"You want to talk about my mother? Now?" When he imagined a perfect morning lying in bed with his perfect wife, his mother was decidedly not part of that picture.

"I feel like I know everything else about you now. I want to know this."

He shifted to face her. Her brow was furrowed, and her kissable lips were stubbornly pursed. There was no escaping this conversation.

"She was beautiful. Almost as beautiful as you."

Amelia colored, and the seriousness of her expression softened.

"She'd tell me stories of her life in London, of how she had dozens of different beaus and how even Prince Henry read her poetry. She promised we would travel there for the Season. One day. We would have an orangery and greenhouse and garden maze. One day. She would introduce us to the king. One day. There were a lot of 'one days' in my childhood."

It had been almost thirteen years since his mother had died. Two decades since she'd left. The twisting in his gut never went away.

"She sounds—"

"Unhappy," he interrupted. "You can't be happy while you're wishing you were somewhere else."

"Why didn't she move back to London?"

"My grandfather wouldn't allow it." Because the marquess was an unfeeling bastard.

"Short of hiring a thug to tie her to the furniture, I don't see how he could have stopped it."

"She went. For a few weeks. No one would see her—not her friends, not her mother. What little money she'd scraped together wasn't accepted anywhere. She'd been blackballed. At his request, I'm sure of it."

"And so she went to France."

"No. She wasted away here until she was barely a shadow. Then she moved to France."

A crease formed between her eyebrows. She tapped on his chest distractedly, her nail stabbing at his skin just a little.

He caught her hand with his and eased it away.

"I'm not the most sentimental person, but it does seem rather cold, even to me, to abandon your child."

He released her hand, preferring the pain of her prodding

to this. He turned his attention to a crack in the wall in the corner of the room.

"I was a disappointment. She wanted a son like her— fine, graceful, and well-spoken. I was big, gangly, could barely move without knocking something over. 'My son, the gigantic clod,' she said. I just...wasn't what she wanted."

Amelia cupped his cheek with her hand, gently turning him to face her. "That must have been very painful."

"When I was younger, I thought that if I could just be less oafish then she'd get well. Once she left, I thought that if I could just make my fortune in time, she'd come home."

"But you didn't."

"No. They gave me my first patent a year after she died."

She brushed a lock of hair from his eyes. "I'm not your mother. I like...this." She ran her hand across his chest, her cheeks flushing as she did. "And I'm not wasting away."

"I know that."

"Do you?" she whispered. "Because I promise you, I'm not going anywhere."

Chapter 17 ———————

As far as Amelia was concerned, the firm was running with authoritarian precision—the kind usually achieved only by His Majesty's army, navy, and any household she ran. Benedict had given her free rein to contribute to his business however she saw fit, and in the space of two weeks, she'd used a lifetime's experience managing a large household to increase efficiencies in the firm's operations—from adjusting the workers' timetables, to overhauling their inventory processes, to implementing a filing system so he could actually find his test results.

Now she leaned against the mezzanine railing and watched the workers do their jobs.

"You haven't moved for an hour," Benedict said, coming up behind her. He encircled her within his arms, nuzzling into her neck.

"I'm learning," she said. "And you're distracting." The scent of him played with her focus, interrupting the mental paths of workers' movements she'd been drawing in her mind, smudging the lines and rerouting the grooves.

"Maybe you need a break. Fiona and John aren't here. We have the office to ourselves." He pulled a lock of hair out of her chignon, sending a shiver right through her and causing her knees to go weak. His arms tightened around her in response, keeping her upright.

"We are supposed to be working," she hissed, but she couldn't keep her eyes on the factory floor beneath her. Instead she closed them, focusing her senses on the hot press of his chest against her back.

"Since when are you so dedicated to work?" he asked, leaving a trail of kisses from her nape to the collar of her dress. "It's such a common endeavor."

"Since I discovered that I'm rather good at it."

And she was.

And it meant something.

Her entire life she'd been told that her only worth was the title she would marry, so she'd become excellent at everything a duchess should excel in—embroidery, watercolor, piano, polite conversation. All pointless activities which she didn't particularly enjoy that served no purpose other than to generate praise and prestige.

But this past fortnight, she had made a real, useful difference.

According to Oliver, productivity was up by half a percent—not much in the grand scheme of things but a solid indicator of what was possible if she really applied herself. And while some of the workers were less than impressed at her "interfering" with their schedules, John and Fiona had been very clear. Her skills were wanted and appreciated.

And Benedict? He treated her like a partner rather than an accessory. After dinner they'd retire to his library, pour two glasses of brandy, and discuss the day.

A discussion usually followed by passionate lovemaking.

Benedict traced patterns across her ribs with his fingers. Each touch left traces of pure joy. She was happy. Against all expectations, she was happy.

⁓

"For an aristocrat, you have a good head for business," Benedict said. "The place has never run more smoothly."

His wife gave a satisfied little *hmph*—a sound he doubted she even noticed making. The same smug *hmph* that had infuriated him so many times. Her I'm-right-and-I-know-it *hmph* that had made his teeth grind only weeks earlier now ignited a little ball of pride inside him. That small sound felt like a whole different thing when they were working on the same team.

"Who needs society when you fit in here so perfectly?" he said as he pulled her closer. He rested his chin on the top of her head, fingers brushing against her hips, and looked out at the bustle of activity beneath him. This was his life's work, and he'd never enjoyed it as much as he did now, with her beside him.

"He-hem." Oliver cleared his throat. Somehow neither Benedict nor Amelia had heard him come up the stairs.

Amelia sidestepped out of Benedict's arms. As much as the ice princess had warmed up in private, she was a stickler for propriety when others were around.

"I'm going to inspect the builders at the house," she said. "They're clearing out the old orangery, and I want to see the progress." She gave an embarrassed little nod to Oliver and left.

"She runs a tight ship, that one. Wouldn't have thought her so at home in a place like this."

Neither had Benedict. That Amelia had not only accepted

his line of business but worked to be part of it had shocked him. Where his mother would have been horrified, Amelia was determined. Where his mother would have cried and then pretended it didn't exist, Amelia had balked, considered, embraced.

Everything his mother had taught him to be ashamed of felt normal—desirable even—around his wife.

She'd never shied away from his bulk or turned her face away in disgust when he'd lifted something heavy. She didn't want him to be delicate or dainty. She would run her fingers through the hair on his chest like she was reveling in his size.

He wasn't the fine and graceful gentleman his mother had wanted, or that Amelia was used to, but that was fine. She liked him just the way he was.

And that unexpected acceptance had begun to heal wounds he hadn't cared to admit he had.

The fact that she was happy, here, with him and without the trappings of London society was more than he could ever have asked for.

And once the contract was signed, the firm in full production, life would be complete.

Chapter 18 ─────────────

As Amelia was handed down from the carriage by one of the new footmen, she couldn't help but wish there was a little more gilding on the door frames, that the wood had been a little more polished, that the wheels were a little less mud-covered.

There was little chance that Lady Karstark was at this moment looking out from one of the many windows that faced the drive, but it was possible. And what Amelia wanted, more than anything, was to ensure one foot was firmly planted in the world of the *ton*.

She'd enjoyed her work at the firm, more than she expected to. And she had every intention of continuing with it. But Benedict's comment yesterday about leaving behind society had been the reminder she needed that she had two lives—there were two different parts to her—and the key to happiness was not leaving one behind but finding a way to be true to both.

A relationship with Lady Karstark, regardless of how Benedict felt about it, was essential to keeping the former part of her alive. It was the proof Amelia needed of her place in society.

She smoothed the folds in her dress, tugged on the fur edge of her kidskin gloves, and squared her shoulders.

There was no reason for the squirming in her midsection. Her father's country homes had been as large as Karstark Place by half again. She was born to be mistress of a home like the one in front of her. She certainly was good enough to be a guest.

Swallowing, she glided forward. The door was open before she'd reached the landing. The butler bowed but didn't move aside.

"Lady Amelia Asterly. Here to pay a call to Lady Karstark." She handed across her card.

The butler's face didn't change, but the wait was overlong as he stared at it.

She was already drawn tight—the implied censure from a servant brought her close to the breaking point. "I am recently married. I haven't yet had the opportunity for new cards," she said sharply.

She was a fool of a woman. She didn't need to explain herself to a butler.

"Is Lady Karstark at home?"

Surely the woman had to be "at home." Where else was she supposed to be out here? God knew there was no other society nearby.

"I shall enquire." He motioned for Amelia to enter and guided her to a small sitting room off the parlor.

Her dratted nerves began to work at her again. There was no reason why Lady Karstark shouldn't see her. In fact, the woman would no doubt be thrilled to see her given the lack of good society in the area. She was doing the woman a favor by calling.

To distract herself, she began to make mental note of her surroundings. The styling was a little outdated, but that was the norm in households run by the older generation. Yet it was impeccable. The curtains were not faded; the carpet showed no wear. The brass doorknob was polished to perfection; the glass window was clean despite the recent rain and mud.

Several of the rooms in the newly opened wings of her home showed signs of previous vermin infestation. Rugs and skirting boards had been eaten away at, and the air was pungent. There would be no chance of that happening here. This was how a country home was supposed to look. It was how her home would look now that she was in charge.

"Ahem."

Amelia stood as she turned toward the door. Lady Karstark was exactly as she had pictured. Pin-thin in heavy violet silks and brocade, a tall powdered wig atop her head. Most of society had moved past the heavy, itchy wigs, but some bastions of the old ways clung fast to the fashions of their youth. Judging by the heavy wrinkles and paper-thin skin, the woman looked a hundred.

"Lady Karstark." Amelia sank into a deep, perfect curtsey, the kind she reserved for the king and queen.

The older woman inclined her head and moved to the armchair opposite the settee, her cane thudding with each step. It was a long journey. Truly, Amelia aged a year in the time Lady Karstark took to sit.

It was only once the older woman was seated that Amelia followed suit.

"This is quite peculiar," Lady Karstark said. "To pay a call on a complete stranger. We have yet to be introduced."

Amelia flushed a little at the censure in the comment.

No one understood propriety like Amelia did, but desperate times called for desperate measures. And this was such a minor breach of protocol.

"Forgive my impudence. But I've only recently moved to the area, and I wanted to pay my respects. I believe you knew my grandmother, Lady Crofton. She spoke very fondly of you when she was alive."

It was a wild guess, but the two women were of an age, and grandmamma had known *everyone*. Everyone who had spent time in London, that is.

Lady Karstark's expression was skeptical. "I'm surprised. Both that Augustina had anything fond to say about anyone and that you would remember after all these years. She passed away almost fifteen years ago, did she not?"

Clearly the woman was going to make things as difficult as she could.

"You married the Asterly boy."

Boy was hardly the word Amelia would use to describe him, but perhaps Lady Karstark hadn't seen him recently.

"I did. We were married several weeks ago."

"I thought you were marrying Wildeforde." The woman squinted as she studied Amelia, who refused to flinch under the gaze. She'd been at the center of London's social scene for years and was well used to being judged.

"Lord Wildeforde and I made a mutual decision to dissolve our engagement."

"My husband said he dropped you like a hot brick after finding you in flagrante with his friend."

Every muscle within her tightened at the insult, but outwardly she kept the same pleasant smile on her face. "That isn't an accurate representation of the events, so either your husband needs his vision checked or he's being somewhat elastic with the truth in order to manufacture some gossip."

The woman recoiled at Amelia's rebuke, but really what did she expect? Amelia was *haute ton*. The woman was a ghost. One tends to lose one's standing when one decides to molder away in the country.

Which was why she needed to talk to Benedict about a London house. The Season was fast approaching, and after further thinking, she'd realized that they really should attend.

"So you plan to sell it as what? A love match? Some princess and the pauper fairytale story?"

"Hardly a pauper. My husband's richer than half of society."

Lady Karstark thumped her cane. "But an overgrown ass with no manners from what I can recall."

The words stung mostly because she'd uttered something so similar not long ago, when she hadn't known any better.

"Manners can be learned," she said. It took every ounce of effort to respond calmly and not to put the crusty old woman in her place, but Amelia had her eyes on the end goal. Establish appropriate connections in the area. Maintain her status as a popular lady of the *ton*. "It is not my intention to argue, Lady Karstark. I came to pay my respects with the hope of establishing a friendship."

Lady Karstark sniffed. "Life in the country must be somewhat duller than you're used to."

Amelia thought back to the past weeks spent sparring with her husband and lending her talents to the firm. Nothing about it was dull. "It is not quite how I used to spend my time."

"His mother found the same thing."

"Benedict's mother?" Amelia's ears perked up instantly. He'd refused to give Amelia any more information than he had that morning, and she hadn't pressed him because it was clearly too painful to talk about. But that hadn't stopped her curiosity. "All I know is that she wasn't happy."

"Fool of a girl eloped with a footman. Marcus Asterly. She thought she could have it all—an inappropriate love match and her old life in society. That notion soon wore off though, once she realized people weren't visiting, letters weren't arriving, and her friends were never 'at home' when she went to London."

"That was poorly done of them." Amelia's voice didn't falter, but in her head, she was tallying up the number of letters she'd written, the days since she'd written them, and the lack of replies.

Lady Karstark smirked, as if she could sense Amelia's rising concern.

"I'm not worried," Amelia said, as much to convince herself as anyone else. "I'm a very influential person."

"No doubt."

"I'm not his mother." The words came out more forcefully than she intended. "I didn't marry a footman; I married the grandson of a marquess. I'm perfectly capable of maintaining one life in London and another out here."

"Perhaps. Or perhaps history will repeat itself. I hear Paris is lovely this time of year."

You devil woman. Agatha Karstark was every bit as cruel as her husband. No wonder the local villagers couldn't stand them. They were evil incarnate. "I am not abandoning anyone."

Lady Karstark sniggered. "We'll see how you feel about it when you've been stuck in the country for a few years. When the papers have forgotten you and you miss London so much even its rotten smell of refuse would be welcome."

Amelia tried to tell herself that this was different. Benedict wasn't a footman. He was a descendant of the Marquess of Harrington. Yes, he was in trade, but he was wealthy. Wealthier, probably, than the blasted woman in front of her. And if anyone had the clout to make this situation work, it was her.

But all the reasoning in the world couldn't quell her sudden unease.

Chapter 19 ———

Host a hunt? Are you mad?" Amelia had lost her bloody mind. The thought of a horde of toffs descending on their home sent shivers crawling up Benedict's spine.

Questioning her sanity had the very effect he should have anticipated. She straightened and tilted her chin defiantly. "Yes, I panicked. Yes, I concocted a cock-and-bull story to save face in front of that cursed woman. And yes, telling her that she's wrong and we have plenty of influential people coming to visit was probably an error of judgment. But we can't go back from it now."

What the devil had happened? Yesterday they'd been all warm and cozy inside their little bubble of home and work. Now she wanted London to come slaughter animals. "I suppose that explains this?" He indicated the mountain of fabric samples that had taken over their drawing room and the neatly stacked pile of fashion plates she'd forced him to look through.

"Your new wardrobe was already in the works. Our house party has simply increased the urgency for it."

"And what exactly does one wear to send a pack of frothing dogs after a fox? Yellow?" He took a piece of buttery fabric from her hand. "Is this a happy enough color for such festivities?"

"Benedict."

He heard the warning in her voice as she snatched at the swatch in his hand but didn't heed it. He was so damned frustrated. He crushed the fabric; it wasn't remotely satisfying. "Only pompous, useless, entitled aristocrats think foxhunting is a worthwhile way to spend an afternoon."

She took in a deep breath. He could practically see the ticking down of numbers in her brain. "Careful. These are my friends you're talking about. Show some respect."

Respect? *Respect?* For noblemen who chose barbarous entertainment to fill their empty days?

He didn't even need to say the words out loud. She threw the remaining fabric in his direction. It fluttered to the floor before it could hit his chest. "Respect for *me*, you bonehead."

A headache was forming behind his right eye. He rubbed his temples in an attempt to keep it from settling in. His wife was an incredibly intelligent woman. She had to understand that a relationship between him and her old chums was not on the cards. "I've spent my life working against the absolute rule of these wastrels. I have no interest in entertaining a group of them."

"I have no delusions of your being *entertaining*. I swear, Benedict. You are every bit as narrow-minded as you accuse others of being. If you would just take a moment to hear me out, you'll see that what I'm suggesting is actually a very good idea."

"A hunt in order to prove to the Karstarks that London still cares for you? Amelia, it's understandable that you would want to carry on with life as you'd planned it, but it's not possible." And it hurt that she would still want to. The past few weeks had been glorious. All his fears and trepidations surrounding their marriage had seemed unfounded. Until now.

And since his distaste for the idea didn't seem to matter, he turned to logic. "The house isn't prepared to host a large gathering, for starters."

Her obstinate look turned pleading. She put her hands on his chest, her fingers curling into his shirt, and looked up at him. "I could make us prepared. It's what I do. I organize dinners and balls and house parties. I was born for this."

It was painful to hear the timbre of hope because at some point the desire to make her happy had become a major priority. But it wasn't his only priority, and he couldn't give this to her.

"You can't get *me* prepared. I've no intention of wearing yellows or greens when my current wardrobe suffices. I won't learn to engage in inane conversation with men I don't respect. It may seem a great idea to you, but it won't go the way you think it will. Oil and water don't mix. Put me in a room with those people and something bad will happen. I know it. This hunt is not happening."

"You're not even going to listen to me, are you? You won't hear me out?" She stepped back, crossing her arms. At first glance, she was angry. Then he noted the way she wrapped her arms around her chest, as though she were hugging herself. How often in her childhood had she had no one else to console her?

He was denying her the company of her friends, and he felt like a cad for doing so. "I'm sorry. I'm sorry I can't be what you need in this situation. But you've married a businessman, not a duke."

"Wildeforde is not the issue here."

"Is he not? If you had married him, you could have had as many house parties as you liked. He might be a deceitful arse, but he rubs elbows with the best of them." Benedict tried to keep the bitterness from his voice but couldn't keep his contempt from showing.

"What happened between the two of you?" Amelia asked. "Sometimes I get the impression that you were friends, but at times like this, you seem to despise him."

Benedict rubbed at the spot between his eyes. "We were close. Hell, at school we were inseparable. There's a certain safety in numbers when you're outcasts."

She wrinkled her nose and cocked her head to the side as she absorbed the information. "It's hard to think of Edward as an outcast," she finally said. "He's so well-admired."

"When we met—it wasn't long after his father had died— the other students at Eton had stripped him naked and shoved him into a trunk. So no, he was not exactly admired. He was bearing the brunt of his father's scandal. John and I heard him yelling and went to help. I was big, even then, so there was no fight. The curs only ever came for me when I was alone. From that day forward, our continued proximity to each other was the only thing that kept the three of us from being thrashed daily."

Amelia brushed her fingers across his cheek. "That doesn't sound like a bond one grows out of."

He caught her hand. He didn't want her sympathy. His school years had been hard, but they'd taught him better lessons than Latin and algebra. They'd taught him that the upper classes looked on everyone else as no better than dogs, and smart men kept as far away from them as possible.

"Wilde is no better than the rest of them. He'll use people—a woman even—and discard them without thought. He caused a lot of hurt for someone I care for, and I don't know if I can forgive him."

She dropped his hand and stood back. "*Someone.* A woman. While he was engaged to me, I'm presuming, since we were betrothed since childhood. Goodness, for a man who prides himself on propriety, he manages to make shocking choices." She brushed her skirts with force enough to dent steel.

"You care," he said flatly. Of course she did. She'd said she'd never loved Wildeforde, but he'd been everything she had ever wanted. Benedict had been a fool to think she could ever have valued him more than a duke.

"Well, it's not quite flattering to know your fiancé was off cavorting with other women."

"And that hurts."

She noticed something crushed in his expression or tone because she sighed and took his face in both hands, forcing him to look at her. "It hurts my pride, you dummy. That's all. And if you were to choose a darned color, it might not even hurt that."

⸺

"Easy now," Amelia said as the men lifted the giant anvil used to shape the steam chest. The weight of the thing was immense, and everyone gasped as one of the blacksmiths' knees buckled under the pressure. Oliver, who was bearing the bulk of the load, exhaled sharply, his eyes widening from the unexpected strain. Two others rushed forward to shore up support in that corner.

Amelia's heart thudded as she waited for each man to

confirm that they were right to keep moving. After a moment, they all nodded at her. "Everyone to my left in three, two, one," she said.

Slowly, inch by inch, the men began to move the anvil toward the trolly, which would be used to reposition it to the other side of the room. As they set it down with a satisfying *thud*, Amelia wiped her slightly sweating hands on the pair of breeches Fiona had given to her. That had been a touch more trying than she had anticipated. If the anvil had fallen on any of the men as they moved it, the injury would have been severe.

She was so preoccupied with the progress of the transfer that she didn't notice Benedict's approach until he was right beside her. "What are we doing?" he asked.

"Well," she said, eager to show off her idea, "Oliver and I are rearranging the workstations. It'll be about a three-day delay in production while we do so, but the time saved ongoing will be roughly twenty hours per month. It takes far too long for items to be transferred from one bench to another when the benches are on opposing sides of the factory. By ordering the workstations in a line from one production step to another, we should be able to increase production speeds." She offered him the planned layout Oliver had signed off on.

"Huh." Benedict studied her sketch, nodding as he did. "I'm impressed. This is why you've been standing on the mezzanine watching?"

Initially, she'd been standing there just to take it all in; this environment that was so different from anything she'd seen before. But as she'd stood there, she'd noticed patterns in the way the men moved—tangled patterns like embroidery threads that had been carelessly tossed in a bag—and she'd needed to neaten them.

"This is remarkable," he continued. "But I'd actually come to ask if you'd seen the invoice for the latest coal shipment. I need to get that paid as soon as possible."

"It's in the new filing cabinet on the right of the door. Second drawer down under the letter *C*."

"Thank you." Ben hooked a finger into her waistband. "I don't suppose you want to come upstairs and help me find it?"

"Of course not," she hissed and batted his hand away. They were working, and there were people around. Honestly, her husband could be so inappropriate at times.

"I know, but these breeches…"

A flush of embarrassment crawled up her face. "They are a necessary requirement when working on the factory floor. My skirts literally caught fire yesterday when I walked too close to the forge." Normally, she'd be horrified to have a bucket of dirty water thrown at her, but had been grateful for the blacksmith's quick thinking. Her dress was ruined beyond repair, but she hadn't been injured.

Benedict frowned. "You didn't tell me you were almost hurt."

"It was my own fault for not paying attention. And the issue is resolved. Fiona lent these to me, and Bessie is sewing me a set of my own. And if you're very good, I'll model them for you when they come in. At home. When we're alone."

Benedict leaned close, his breath sending shivers through her. "I'll be good." The words ignited a warmth between her legs. She swallowed and was almost ready to suggest they head home now when one of the floor assemblers approached them, scratching his head.

"Excuse me, m'lady. Pardon the interruption but we've had a delivery arrive. It must be some kind of mistake. There's a cart chock-full of bed linens, towels, and tablecloths."

Oh, good heavens. "Thank you, Paul. They should be sent

to the house. I'll be up to deal with it in a minute." Maybe, if she was lucky, Benedict's lusty thoughts would prevent him from putting two and two together. She'd had every intention of telling him about her plans to continue with the house party. She just hadn't yet. Things had been so nice between them, and she hadn't wanted to ruin it with an argument, so she'd put it off.

She turned to him, as businesslike as possible. "As I said, on the right, second drawer down. I'll see you at home." She spun, and for a moment thought she'd gotten away with it, but at the last second, he grasped her elbow.

"Chock-full of linens?" he asked. "Why would we need more linens?"

"Well…" She couldn't think fast enough, and with her moment's hesitation, his face darkened.

"Shall we go to the office for a moment?" He gestured to the stairs.

She could protest. She could insist on seeing to the man with the linens. But this argument was going to come sooner or later, and Mrs. Greenhill was more than capable of managing a delivery.

As she climbed the stairs, she laid out her case in her head, the way she had every night for a week now. Once they'd entered his office, she leapt into it before he could take control of the conversation and she ended up on defense rather than offense.

"I've already sent out the invitations. They were dispatched yesterday to a select group of influential members of the *ton*, comprised of friends I desperately want to see again and men whose interests likely align with those of the Americans. And the Americans themselves, obviously."

"Without my permission?" He was as furious as she'd ever seen him. He glared at her, his arms crossed, practically looming like an angry cloud over her. And while it might have been sensible to talk to him soothingly, to placate him, she was also madder than she'd realized.

"You were being irrational on this issue."

"Amelia, we discussed this." He rubbed at his temples. Good. He deserved whatever headache was coming.

"We did not discuss this. You spoke, loudly and at length, and then refused to hear a word I had to say. And if you weren't going to be reasonable, then why should I?" Hands on hips, she stepped closer to show him that, while he might intimidate others, she was unfazed.

He cursed under his breath. "Fine. Convince me. But if you can't, then you're going to have to write to every one of those people and rescind the invitations."

Perfect. Time to explain her thinking was all she needed. "You said the Americans were concerned that there was bad blood between you and their English investors."

"Yes, but—"

"And you said they were planning to visit soon—"

"Yes, however—"

"And is there a better way to show them how well you get along with the English than to have everyone together in a convivial house party?"

"That's not enough." He took a seat by the table and folded his hands in his lap. It was like a criminal trial, and he was positioning himself as the judge. Very well. She was more than capable of playing the part of barrister.

"You claim to have had your business reputation ruined, something that could negatively impact not just our family, but the future of all of those that work in your factory."

Benedict grunted but said nothing.

Gathering steam, she swept her arms wide, as though addressing a room full of critics. "You cannot rescue your own reputation. It's a task that can only be accomplished by people of influence, which includes those that I have invited. Together, we will show them that you are a gentleman and the allegations against you are false."

"Hmmm."

It was time for her most salient point. She moved closer to him, crouching until her gaze was level with his, her hands pressed against each other like a church steeple. "I've been reading up where I can on these Americans, and Mr. Grunt has brought his two daughters to England with him. If we make some exceptional introductions, potentially facilitate an engagement with a lord, the Americans will give you anything you want. And in turn, you can provide those that work for you with everything they need."

It was the best argument she could make. This hunt would get him the contract he so desperately wanted. And she could tell that it landed because he rubbed the back of his neck.

"We can't. The villagers wouldn't like it. Anti-aristocratic sentiment runs deep."

"They will like the extra work, and the money it brings."

He sighed. "Can't we just have a dinner? You can ask Wildeforde to come, the devil knows he owes us a favor, and won't that be enough to show the Americans that we can all play nicely?" His face was so hopeful that she was tempted to acquiesce, but it wouldn't be enough. Not for him and not for her, so she kept silent.

"Fine," he said. "But the Karstarks are not welcome. Invite whoever else you please, but not them."

It was a reasonable compromise. The benefits of pursuing a relationship with Lady Karstark probably weren't worth actually having to spend time with her anyway. "It's a deal."

"But, Amelia. If this goes bad, it will be on you."

Chapter 20 ————————

The morning started like every morning in the fortnight before it. They woke in his bed. They made love. They dressed. They breakfasted. He went to work, where she planned to join him for a few hours in the afternoon.

It was all decidedly civilized. Homey. Close to a perfection she'd never known she wanted.

Amelia sank farther into the cushions on the chaise longue. This sitting room had been the first room of the closed wing to be opened, aired out, and refurbished. She could see why Benedict's mother had loved it. The windows were wide and looked out onto the gardens. They were expertly planted and maintained—with winter jasmine forming graceful, pale yellow arches. The sun streamed in from late morning until mid-afternoon. It was the perfect place to curl up with a novel.

Across the room, Cassandra had her feet on the lounge, her own nose also deep in a book. They had spent the past three hours in complete silence—a silence filled with fictional voices and sounds and images. Amelia could read for days. She'd missed a whole lifetime of novel reading so far, and now she planned to dedicate serious hours to catching up.

Greenhill entered. He'd yet to master the expressionless façade of a true butler, and the concern on his face had her sitting up quickly.

"Greenhill, what's wrong?"

"Lady Karstark is here to see you, my lady."

Amelia's heart thudded. It was the first time she'd been paid a call since she left London. Clearly, she was making progress. Not progress Benedict would be happy with or that she was particularly looking forward to, but progress nonetheless.

She shoved the book under the cushion and straightened, neatening her hair as she did so.

"Cassandra, book away. Come sit by me."

The young girl's face screwed up in protest, but she carefully placed her bookmark and crossed the room.

Amelia yanked the hem of Cassandra's dress. How reading caused so many wrinkles she had no idea.

Grabbing the embroidery that had gone untouched by the chaise for the past few weeks, she tossed a piece onto Cassandra's lap. What she couldn't fix she would hide.

"Show her in, Greenhill," she said. "And please ask Mrs. Greenhill to bring some tea."

"As you wish, my lady." He wasn't happy—obviously—but he knew well enough to leave it alone.

As he exited, Amelia allowed herself a small smile. She might have taken a step backward in her quest for social domination, but like Wellington, she could not be put down for long.

"Benedict doesn't like Lady Karstark," Cassandra whispered.

"Well, I doubt he's spent much time in her company. Learn to judge for yourself, poppet."

They were prevented from saying any more by the woman's appearance in the doorway. Amelia stood, followed a half second later by Cassandra.

"Lady Karstark. What a pleasant surprise."

The smile she got in return was cold. "I was in the neighborhood," Agatha said.

"Lucky us."

They'd been making strained conversation for thirty minutes by the time Benedict barged in. By the looks of him, their groom had ridden down to the firm, and Benedict had run back.

"Lady Karstark." His voice was cold, clipped, his expression closed as he walked to the chaise longue and put a hand on Amelia's shoulder. He didn't sit. Either he didn't plan on staying long or he was about to boot Agatha from his house—a distinct possibility given his recent decree that "that woman will never be welcome. Ever."

The old woman's face barely changed. Her lips remained pursed as if current company left a bad taste in her mouth, but her eyes took on a nasty gleam. "Benedict. You continue to grow. It's quite unseemly."

He didn't respond, but Cassandra flinched. "That is very rude. You shouldn't say mean things."

Whether the shock on Agatha's face was due to the censure or simply because a child was talking, Amelia couldn't tell.

"It's all right, poppet. Why don't you head to the kitchens? I smelled pastries." Benedict shooed her out gently.

"What are you doing here?" he asked bluntly once Cassandra was out of earshot.

Amelia sighed and made a mental note to chastise whoever

had decided to fetch the master of the house. "Lady Karstark is paying a social call," she said.

Be nice, she wanted to yell.

"Your house looks adequate. I suppose that's her doing." Agatha squinted at the furnishings as though she had just walked in.

"What are you doing here?" he repeated.

Agatha took a sip of tea. "I wanted to express my sympathies. I was so sorry to hear that no one was coming to your hunt. I was quite looking forward to some proper society."

As the meaning of Lady Karstark's words sank in, Amelia clenched her stomach and calves and thighs and jaw—everything she could clench to avoid tightening her fists and giving that woman any satisfaction in her distress.

"I'm not sure what you mean," she managed to say evenly. "I've had an excellent response. I'm afraid I've invited far too many people and am trying to work out how to house them."

It was a lie. Agatha knew it.

She gave a horrid, knowing smile over the rim of her tea-cup. "What a relief. How mortifying it would have been to host your first event as a married woman and to have no one attend. I shall have to inform my sister that her information is faulty."

Agatha's sister was Lady Merwick—the biggest gossip London had ever seen—and her information was always annoyingly accurate.

She'd received one reply—a polite decline from the Duke of Camden—but he had always been fastidious in his correspondence. Most of the *ton* took longer to respond to an invitation.

That was why she'd not received any other responses. Because her friends were fashionably late in all things. Surely. And if they were running a little bit later than fashionable?

Amelia felt as though the laces of her corset had taken on a life of their own and were squeezing every ounce of breath and hope out of her.

She had worked so *hard*. Harder than she'd worked at anything.

It was no mean feat training an entire staff from scratch. Redecorating the entire house—from carpet to ceiling frescos—was the largest project she'd ever taken on. And she was doing all of this while helping Benedict with the firm. She had put in more work over the past month than she had in the past five years.

And all of it for naught. It was almost enough to make her cry.

Agatha remained silent, waiting for Amelia's reaction. No doubt in breathless anticipation, the wretched creature.

For a brief moment, it was all Amelia could do not to let her anguish show. But then she felt Benedict squeeze her shoulder. Just a light touch, a you're-not-in-it-alone gesture.

It was all she needed.

She lifted her chin and met the old crone's stare. "Please inform Lady Merwick that I'm so sorry I was unable to include her on the guest list. When Prinny attends a hunt, so does every other reputable gentleman, and there really wasn't room to spare."

Agatha's fingers tightened on her saucer just a smidgen.

Satisfaction pooled in Amelia's gut at the older lady's surprise. How she would manage to wrangle Prince George into attending was a matter for later, not now.

"Do tell me," Benedict drawled, "must I serve De Luze cognac to our beloved regent? I much prefer a Scottish whiskey."

Amelia looked at him, surprised. He did not remotely

approve of this hunt. She hadn't expected him to willingly defend it.

Agatha cleared her throat. "Well, I do hope you're correct. But at any rate, there will be plenty of opportunities for society to visit next year once we've cleared the land to the south of the Peach Tree River for a proper hunting ground."

It set Amelia back a minute because, surely, she couldn't have heard what she thought she had. Benedict suddenly dropped to the arm of the chair next to her, suggesting her ears were working just fine.

Good grief.

In a second, saving her hunt had become a trivial matter.

"Did you say you're clearing the land to the south of the river? How much of it?" she demanded.

"You bitch," Benedict said under his breath, but Agatha still heard it and her face paled.

Her mulish look of determination didn't change though. "I don't know the details. That's Lord Karstark's domain. But by next autumn, the woods will be stocked, a trail will be built, and Abingdale will be able to hold a proper hunt."

A swirling, seething unease settled into the pit of Amelia's stomach. There were so many farms south of the river. So many families. Children she'd seen running in the village square. Mothers she'd played with on the bandy field. Men that worked hard at the firm.

"But the farms. The Joneses and Pattinsons and Mc-Tavishes. Where will they go?" Her tone betrayed her fear, but she didn't care.

"I suppose they can go to the colonies."

"The Americas," Amelia ground out.

"Whichever. That's not our problem." Lady Karstark sniffed.

Benedict's anger was palpable. He stood, fists clenched. He seemed twice his normal size—a furious leviathan.

He loomed over Lady Karstark, his face as close to violence as Amelia had ever seen it. "They have worked those farms for generations."

Amelia jumped up, putting herself between her husband and the woman who had clearly come here just to wound him.

Had anyone asked ten minutes ago, she'd have said he'd never hit a woman—let alone an old, frail one. But at this moment, she wasn't going to risk it.

And there was nothing frail about this witch.

She pushed Benedict into a chair and then rounded on her guest. "Surely you owe them some loyalty. You profit from their hard work."

Lady Karstark's complete lack of visible reaction was damnable. She was discussing people's livelihoods as though it were a debate about pineapples versus peonies for table centerpieces.

"We owe them?" the woman asked. "Don't tell me you're becoming one of those subversive frogs. Surely Lady Amelia Crofton, daughter of Lord Crofton, once-fiancée of the Duke of Wildeforde, isn't suggesting that private property become public?"

"Of course not," Amelia said through gritted teeth.

"And if the property belongs to us, should we not use it as we see fit?"

"No!" Benedict bellowed. "You have a duty."

"Young man, my duty is to the king and the country." She thumped her cane. The first sign of any real emotion.

"Are your tenants not the country?" Amelia asked quietly. "You are in a position of deep privilege, entrusted with the care of your estate—which is more than just the buildings and rose gardens and gold in the bank."

"I wouldn't expect you to understand, child. Nor do you need to. It's an issue that only needs to be dealt with by those who actually *own* an estate, not just a couple of cottages and dilapidated house—no matter how hard you try to polish it." She rose and brushed her hands against her faultless skirt. "It has been a pleasure."

Lady Karstark left the room with decidedly more speed and less reliance on her cane than when she had walked in.

Benedict sank into the chair, head in his hands. "What are we going to do?" In those few words, she heard the weight of years of responsibility, of the people who couldn't rely on their lords so relied on him instead.

She stretched an arm across his shoulders, leaning into him. "We'll think of something, love."

Chapter 21 ————————————————

Breakfast the following day was a somber affair. Lady Karstark had left, and Amelia had started spurting out ideas—one of which was the suggestion that Benedict approach his grandfather for help.

It had been a mistake.

His reaction to the words "Marquess Harrington" rivaled his reaction to the news of the Karstark clearances.

After a series of colorful curse words, he'd stormed out of the room. For the first time that month, Benedict hadn't come to her room at night. And when she'd knocked on the connecting door, he didn't answer.

This morning when he walked into the dining room, there was a bluish tinge beneath his eyes, and his jaw sported blondish-red stubble. His hair was more disheveled than usual, as though he'd spent the entire night running his hands through it.

"Good morning," Amelia said cautiously.

"Morning." It was a grunt more than a greeting, and he barely looked at her as he moved to the sideboard.

Tentatively, she continued. "I was thinking that we should hold a meeting—a war council if you will—to come up with a response to Karstark's plans." He wasn't the only person who had spent the night thinking about the disaster.

He didn't respond, instead dumping food onto his plate, sauce splattering everywhere.

She tried again. "We need to find jobs and housing. That's the priority. The rest can follow."

Again, no response.

"I've heard that many Scots who have been asked to leave their farms have found new lives in America."

He slammed his plate down on the far end of the table. Short of taking his breakfast out of the room, he couldn't have put more distance between them if he'd tried. "Asked to leave? That's how you're describing the highland clearances? What a civilized term."

She sighed, biting back a sharp retort. "Please don't snap at me. I'm just trying to help."

"By suggesting they leave their lives for a new country?" He pointed his fork at her, the sausage on the end wavering with his anger.

Ten, neuf, eight, sept, six, cinq, four, trois, two, un.

She smoothed her napkin on her lap before meeting his gaze. "It's an option, and I just thought that you may have some business connections that could be useful." He could likely open up a whole range of opportunities in the cities and on the frontier where new communities were being built. It wasn't a dreadful idea.

"What would be useful, princess, is a law against this practice. Or systems in place that allow people to work their way into independence rather than remain in effective slavery."

She took a deep breath. "Of course, but those systems and laws are not in place, and we need to deal with the problem in front of us."

"What do you think I've spent all night trying to do?" She hadn't heard that tone of voice from him since he'd argued with her father—that frustrated, scornful accusation.

"Just tell me how I can help," she said quietly.

"You can't," he said. "This isn't something you can fix by rearranging furniture and making things look pretty."

Oh.

"Well, thank you for clarifying our roles. From business partner to bauble in a day—what an exhausting transformation."

Thankfully Cassandra entered, effectively ending their argument before it could truly develop. She and Benedict had agreed to keep the news away from his sister for as long as possible.

"Good morning, poppet," Amelia said. There was heavy silence while Cassandra filled her plate. Benedict refused to look at Amelia, which was perfectly fine. She didn't want to look at him either.

If Cassandra noticed the difference in their seating arrangements, she said nothing, instead turning to Amelia expectantly. "What do the papers say this morning?"

They had developed an enjoyable morning routine of social pages and gossip. It wasn't quite the same as morning calls following each ball, but it was as close as she was going to get out here.

And if it took her mind off her bear of a husband, then she'd be glad of the distraction.

Amelia unfolded the paper and scanned the first page of the society section. "Lord Gerton is apparently looking for a new wife. He's been seen at Almack's twice, and lord knows no man goes there unless he's on the hunt for a new 'Lady Whatever' or he's bullied by his wife, his mother, or his daughters. As he has no wife, nor mother, nor daughters, he's on the lookout for a new Lady Gerton."

"What happened to his last wife?" Cassandra asked as she shoveled eggs onto a fork.

"It's a mystery," Amelia whispered.

"Really?" The girl's eyes bugged open. As it turned out, a childhood full of novels turned one into a sucker for intrigue.

"It's a mystery why it took four years for him to bore her to death. I thought she'd perish in two." She waited for some sort of response from Benedict—his usual, self-righteous quip or a comment about how inappropriate gossip was. All she got was silence.

"You can be bored to death?" Cassandra asked.

Amelia shrugged. "Technically, she died of the ague, but no doubt she caught it deliberately—an unpleasant way to escape an unpleasant marriage." As she said the words, she recognized the cynicism. She was sliding back into her snide, spiteful past self. She could hear it happening; she just didn't feel like stopping it. It felt good to be snippy. Familiar.

"What else does the paper say?" Cassandra asked.

"Miss Margaret Farnsworth was spotted in a multi-hued dress at the Belford soiree. I've told the girl a dozen times that she looks like a peacock when she chooses her own clothes. Without me there, she'll likely become a laughingstock."

"Because life can't go on in society without you?" Benedict drawled.

Amelia shot him daggers, hoping they'd land somewhere

painful. "I'm sure life in London will go on. It will just be a little less well-dressed."

Completely oblivious to the maelstrom undercurrent, Cassandra said with confidence, "When we go to London, we'll be the best-dressed ladies there."

"Of course we will."

"And we'll take tea with Lady Belford, ride through Hyde Park, dance at Almack's, and be fine ladies of the *ton*."

Benedict flinched at each word Cassandra spoke. And Amelia relished it. "Precisely."

That was clearly his last straw.

"Cassandra, you weren't raised to be a lady. You have a brilliant mind, and I won't have you waste it on watercolor and flower arranging."

He could not have found words that hurt Amelia more. She couldn't help but look to the sideboard at the flower arrangement she'd spent the previous evening creating. She'd used snowdrops—because Benedict always commented on them and she'd wanted him to start an awful day with something beautiful.

Anger dissolved into humiliation, which dissolved into grief remarkably quickly. She picked up the paper to hide the tears in her eyes.

She'd worked hard to be the perfect lady her whole life. It was the reason she got up, the focus of her days. Whether it was conversation, piano, dancing, or arranging flowers, she'd striven to be the best at it.

Tens of thousands of hours wasted because apparently those skills held no value in her new life. It hurt to think about, so she focused on the newspaper.

Oh. My. Goodness.

There she was again. Yet unlike her previous appearances in *The Times*, the sketch was not one of a perfectly dressed future duchess. Her hair was unkempt, her clothes rags, and she was sprawled on the ground, skirts above her knees with a bandy stick on the ground next to her.

Curse Benedict for convincing her to play that stupid game. Curse whoever had passed along the news to the gossips in London, and curse the dashed cartoonist. She would wring his neck.

"What does it say?" Cassandra asked.

"It's none of anyone's business." She closed the paper. Then folded it, and folded it again, hammering on it with her fist to get it to sit flat.

Benedict raised one eyebrow before turning to his sister. "Cassandra, go take your breakfast in your bedroom."

"But only married ladies can take breakfast in bed. Amelia said so."

"Lady Amelia is not the head of this household. Off you go."

With a hop, Cassandra took her plate to the sideboard and started piling it high. Ridiculously high. Enough food for three breakfasts high.

"You'll make yourself sick," Benedict said.

"I'm taking my book. Bed, breakfast, and a book. I'm never going to leave." She gave a wide grin before she danced out of the room.

Amelia couldn't wait to see her shiny, happy bubbly-ness leave. This was as awful a morning as could be had, and there was no room in it for hope or innocence.

Benedict glowered. "Whatever disagreement *we* may be having, you will not take it out on a child."

"Oh, loosen your breeches. Remarkably, not everything is about you."

He rolled his eyes. "I don't have the energy for this."
Seriously?

He wasn't the one who'd had his life turned upside down. He wasn't the one who'd gone from having everything to nothing, and he wasn't the one who'd just been disgraced in a newspaper read by all of England.

"This is all your fault. You convinced me to take part in that stupid bandy match with all your talk of 'being a human being.' Jackass."

"Princess, I don't know what you're talking about, but I have the small matter of half my friends losing their homes to deal with."

"This is what I'm talking about." She threw the paper in his direction. "You've made me a laughingstock."

She couldn't help the tears that assailed her. She drew in a ragged breath. It was one thing for society to think her trapped in a common life. It was another for them to think *her* common.

Benedict unfolded the paper. "This? Really? For heaven's sake, it's an idiot cartoon, drawn by an idiot, for other idiots to read."

"And that's what you really think of me, isn't it? Just some cotton-headed aristocrat."

"No, that's not what I said."

"I read that paper. Am I an idiot? With all my flower arranging and watercolors?"

He exhaled loudly. "I don't always understand your priorities."

She stood, tossing her napkin onto the table. "I do know that there are worse things happening in the world. There are worse things happening right here. But that doesn't mean I can't care about being made a mockery of. These are the people I grew up with. I used to have value. Except apparently now I don't."

Her father had always told her that she was only worth the

title she could marry. Over the past few weeks, she'd thought maybe he was wrong. He wasn't. Even her contributions to the firm had been sidelined in a night.

"It was one silly cartoon. It doesn't define you."

"Except apparently it does. Lady Karstark is right. No responses to our invitation were lost in the mail. I've been cut." The tears rolled down her face freely, and rather than have him see them, she walked toward the door.

Before she could exit, he grabbed her hand.

"Useless buggers, the lot of them," he murmured into her ear. Guiding her back to the table by the waist, he pulled her into his lap and hung his chin on her shoulder. "They'll regret it when they're old and grey and friendless."

"In their hundred-room Mayfair houses surrounded by help and enjoying the finest dresses?" She wiped at her cheeks.

"Big houses are lonely. And you're better surrounded by people who *want* you rather than people paid to wait on you."

She turned and sobbed into his neck. His arms wrapped around her like they were the only thing anchoring her in a storm of sorrow. The gentle stroke of his fingers in her hair just made her cry harder.

"There is so much more to you than the dresses you wear and the people you have to tea. I just wish you'd see it. Isn't it enough that the people in this house think the world of you?"

It caught at Amelia's heart to hear it. He thought the world of her. And he was quickly becoming her world. But could she be happy here? To never dance at another ball, smell the soot of London, feel the buzz of the opera? She was born to that life, raised to it, loved it. Could she ever be happy tucked away in the country?

"No," she whispered. "It's not enough."

Chapter 22 ————

It was barely noon, and the day had been bloody awful. Benedict shook his head, trying to clear some of the fog that came from a night without sleep. His eyes hurt, strained by hours of running numbers by candlelight. Numbers that didn't add up, no matter how he tried.

And now, while his focus should be entirely on how to save the livelihoods of half the village, he couldn't get four words out of his head.

No. It's not enough.

He dropped his head into his hands. He'd been a fool for thinking that he could make her happy. If he hadn't been enough for his mother, who by law of nature was supposed to love him, how could he ever have been enough for a woman who'd detested him from the beginning?

Despite all his efforts not to care, his heart was crumbling like high ash coal.

"You look like shite," Oliver said from the doorway.

Benedict looked up. "You're late."

Oliver shrugged and leaned against the doorway. "Not as late as the others."

It was true. Benedict had sent a runner for Fiona and John a full half hour ago. They might not typically be at his beck and call, but if he'd sent for them, they should damned well assume it was important.

"What's got such a bee in your bonnet that you're sending orders like a bleeding general?"

Benedict shook his head. "We'll wait for the others."

He stood and walked to the cabinet—newly dusted and neatened and catalogued like the rest of the office. The brandy sat next to the cognac, which sat next to the gin. It was early in the day, but to hell with it. He opened the cabinet door and grabbed two glasses, offering one to Oliver, who crossed his giant, ex-blacksmith arms over his barrel of a chest.

"No alcohol in the workshop during working hours, lad. Put it away."

Benedict raised an eyebrow. "I am your boss."

"And you're the one that made the bleedin' safety rules. You can damn well stick by them."

Devil save him from overly efficient foremen. "You're fired."

"Not today, lad. Maybe tomorrow." He took the bottle from Benedict's hand and steered him toward the center bench. "Now why don't you tell me what's wrong? Whatever it is, there'll be a solution."

What's wrong.

Benedict should start with the bloody upcoming clearances—that was what was important—but it was Amelia on the tip of his tongue. Amelia, who had his insides twisted in convoluted knots and his heart feeling like lead in his chest.

He was on the verge of telling Oliver how much it hurt to

be married to a woman he could never truly have. A woman whose heart would always be elsewhere. But before he could say anything, a terse female voice came from the doorway.

"Yes, Ben. Tell me exactly why you dragged me away from home on my day off."

Fiona stood with her hands on her hips, a particularly annoyed look on her face. John stood beside her, his expression equally perplexed. He raised his eyebrows slightly as he took in Benedict's ragged appearance but kept quiet.

"Karstark is planning to clear out all farms south of the river."

"What?" The single word came from three different people, their faces mirrored images of shock.

"How do you kn-kn-know this?"

"Lady Karstark visited Amelia yesterday."

"Has it been confirmed?" Fiona's grip on the doorframe tightened, her knuckles white. The news would hit her hardest. Her father's farm was on Karstark land. South of the river.

"I wrote to Lord Karstark immediately to ask if it was true. He responded this morning." Benedict tossed a crumpled ball of paper into the middle of the table. Oliver opened it and read the scrawled text aloud.

"*It's not your business, but yes.*" He flipped the paper over, and then over again. "The bloody bastard." He turned to the cabinet and grabbed the bottle of brandy he'd confiscated from Benedict and took a long swig. He held out the bottle to John, who joined them at the bench and then took his own mouthful.

Fiona stalked over to them and snatched the paper. "That's it? That's all he said?"

"D-d-did Lady K-k-arstark say when?" Anxiety always made John's stutter worse.

"All she said was that the area would be ready for deer hunting next autumn."

"Christ," said Fiona, sinking to a stool. "They'd need to evict us soon to make that happen." She took the bottle from John.

"By my count," Benedict said, "we have three months, maybe four. Then half of Abingdale is without a home."

All three stared vacantly ahead of them as the magnitude of the disaster sank in. He gave them a moment. Devil knew he'd needed it when he had heard.

"What do we do?" Fiona asked.

"I've been looking at the numbers." Benedict spread some sheets out over the table. "A third of the affected farms have someone employed with us already. Another fifteen percent have a son who could join us in the next week, and most of the others could join us once they're evicted."

"They'd need training. They're farmhands. They sow and plow and raise sheep, not shape steel into parts," said Oliver.

"Then we'll train them. You d-d-did it with the men we've g-got."

It had taken time to get his people trained well enough that the firm ran as smoothly as it did. And it had been done in increments. They'd hired staff as the company had grown. Such a sudden intake of novices would present a challenge they hadn't faced before. A potentially dangerous one in an environment like theirs.

"So we can provide work for what, ninety percent o' them?" Fiona asked.

Chains tightened around Benedict's chest, like they were being pulled by engines traveling in opposite directions. "If we have the work to give them."

Because while his gut wanted him to support the whole

village and promise them a roof and income regardless of the situation, his head knew it wasn't sustainable. To make this work for the long term, they needed money coming in to support the money going out.

"We need the Americans." Fiona's hand was to her mouth. "We'll never negotiate another contract in time."

Benedict grimaced. "And we need to convince them to move the timeframe up so that we receive the funds months earlier than planned. The prototype needs to be fully functional in the next fortnight. And we'd need another three ready to ship within a year."

"Impossible." Oliver shook his head. "Not with new workers that don't know what they're doing. The current workers would need to do double the hours they're currently working to make up for it."

"Then that's what they're going to have to do." Benedict's tone of voice was harsher than intended, but he'd been up all night, and he couldn't think of another way out of the situation.

"They're not going to like it."

"I'm sure their friends will like being homeless less," Fiona said. Her face was hard as stone, but her eyes were bright with tears.

"We can p-p-provide jobs, but what about h-housing?"

Benedict exhaled sharply. This was what had kept him awake when he'd finally put away the ledgers. Because all the money in the world wasn't going to keep families warm at night or dry in the rain. Employment was only part of the problem.

"The only suitable land I have for building on was earmarked for extending the firm, which we're going to bloody well need to expand so quickly. The rest is wooded. It will take months to clear it."

Oliver polished off the last of the brandy. John was drumming his fingers on his forehead—something he only did when the numbers weren't what he expected, and he didn't know why. "Wilde," he said finally.

"What about him?" Benedict asked, a knot immediately forming in his gut.

"He has all that land north of the g-granary."

"No." Fiona and Benedict spoke as one. Turning to his wife's ex-fiancé was not an option he wanted to consider.

Oliver, however, was nodding. "Aye, he may have the country's largest stick up his arse, but he's got a soul. He won't let the village down."

"It's worth asking," John said.

"I don't want to go begging to Wildeforde for help." The thought made his stomach roil. "Besides, I stole his bloody fiancée. I can't imagine he'd be keen to accept an audience with me."

"He won't say no to Fi," Oliver said. "Not when it's her he'd be saving."

Fiona paled. "Nae. I cannot." It was a sign of just how rattled she was that she lapsed into her father's Scottish accent. "I can't ask him for this. Not after everything. I cannae go to him for rescue."

John took her hand and gave it a small squeeze. "You've the best shot of saving every tenant south of the river."

Fiona's eyes filled with tears, but she gave a curt nod. "Then I guess I'm going to London." She looked at the empty brandy bottle in front of Oliver and then crossed to the liquor cabinet and grabbed the gin.

Benedict gladly took the bottle when she was done. Wildeforde coming to the bloody rescue. Wildeforde, who would have no doubt "been enough" when Benedict wasn't. How could it get worse?

"There's something else we need to consider," Oliver said, his tone darker than it had been. "The village. They're already fired up. Tucker's been preaching revolution to them every other night. And when he's not addressing a crowd, he's whispering in ears. This news could turn things even worse."

Benedict blew out a long breath. Bringing Tucker to town was proving to be a mistake. He was a variable they didn't need.

"I'll talk to him. Ask him to temper his tone some-what. Surely, he can be forced to see sense. No one wants violence."

"And if he won't see sense?" Fiona asked quietly.

"Then the Karstarks are on their own."

⁓

Acceptance of her undeniable fall from grace was gradual. Amelia had cried in Benedict's lap that morning, the first time she'd ever been held while crying, and then she'd run a hot bath and cried in there too. It hurt to see her downfall so plainly illustrated—literally in black and white, complete with captions. The printer's ink smudged, and the paper wrinkled from a combination of steam, tears, and bathwater.

She'd had dinner in her room and cried herself to sleep before Benedict had even returned home.

The next day she'd woken, energized, and fired off two dozen furious letters—to the printer, the publisher, the illus-trator, the condescending patronesses of Almack's, and the whiny snot-nosed debutantes who owed her more loyalty. Hell, she'd even sent one to Prinny to demand an inquiry into publishing standards.

The next day she didn't leave her bed.

Or the day after that.

Both mornings, Benedict brought her breakfast and flowers. He gave her sweet and gentle encouragement. Both nights he'd held her and talked her through all the progress the team had made toward solving the Karstark situation.

The next morning, he'd stripped her of her quilt and quite literally dumped her on the floor. *Get up, get dressed, and get something done*, he'd said. *Find a damn project. I will not watch another woman waste away in this room.*

And he'd stormed out, flinging the door into the wall as he did.

So she got up, got dressed, and found a project.

That was three days ago, and since then, the morning room had become a refuse site. Dozens of the trunks her father had sent were still in the lumber room where they'd been since they were delivered. With no house party to prepare for, Amelia had made the goal of sorting through at least one trunk a day. That should see her occupied until summer.

"Should we finish sorting yesterday's trunk?" Cassandra asked, gesturing to the piles of hats and gloves and shoes that littered the room.

"No. One trunk a day. That's what we said."

"But we still haven't worked out what to do with this stuff." Cassandra held up a Russian beaver hat and stroked it against her face. "This is soft." She put it on her head and did a twirl.

She looked adorable, but Amelia would not be swayed. "It has a tail. Wear that and the village boys will be yanking it every two seconds."

"We could cut the tail off..." Her face was sweet, hopeful—just as it had been every quarter hour since the project began.

"Cassandra, the point of sorting through all of this is so that I can get rid of my old life, not transfer it to you."

"I'll put it in the maybe pile." Cassandra's maybe-I'll-keep-it pile had started on the couch and had now overtaken half the room. She picked up a single white glove from the floor. "Oooh, pretty!"

"Impractical. And it has a tear at the wrist."

"Tears can be mended."

"Its partner is probably lost."

"But it might not be." The glove got tossed on top of the beaver hat.

Amelia shook her head and turned to today's trunk. A thin film of dust covered it. Had it been that long since this all began? She'd have to remind the maids that, even if it wasn't overly attended, they would need to clean the lumber room.

She undid the leather straps. Cassandra skipped over, leaning over her shoulder. This was Christmas to her, hell to Amelia.

The leather edges stuck together for a moment before they pulled apart.

"Ugh."

"Ugh indeed." Amelia picked up one of the dozens of embroidered cloths from the pile. It was a king-fisher. Objectively speaking, it was lovely with exceptional detail. Excellent work. It should be—she'd spent a week on it.

"Why would you keep so many?"

"Why did I make them in the first place is a better question."

"The toss-it pile," Cassandra said.

"The burn-it pile."

The grin on Cassandra's face lit up so quickly Amelia

worried she'd unlocked an inner pyromaniac. But as quickly as it appeared, it vanished. "The fireplace isn't big enough."

"Perhaps I could donate them?" They were exceptional embroideries. Worthy of a gallery wall, she'd been told.

Cassandra drew in a swift breath, grasping Amelia by the shoulders and shaking. "The firm!"

Amelia caught the girl's wrists before her head was shaken off. "I'm not confident a building full of men want walls decorated with peonies and poppies."

"No, silly." Cassandra rolled her eyes. "There is *a big* fireplace at the firm."

For a split second, stomach-clenching, breath-catching euphoria flared inside her. A lifetime of propriety snuffed it quickly. "Cassandra Asterly, we are not dragging a trunkload of embroidery that I spent years of my life creating down to a factory just so we can watch it burn."

Except wouldn't that be amazing? She'd hated every minute spent embroidering those useless, ridiculous cushion covers and wall hangings. But she'd done it because she was a lady of the *ton*, and that's what ladies do.

The past week and the obvious lack of response to her house party had made it clear that she was no longer a lady of the *ton*. That life was done now. She would have to forge another. And what better way than setting fire to this trunk full of wasted dreams?

Cassandra gave her a sly smile, as if she could read every thought Amelia had.

"Fine. Let's get our coats."

Cassandra was out of the room before Amelia could even stand. She brushed the grey dust from her hands. "Green-hill?" she called as she entered the hallway. "Could you ask Charlie to bring around the cart?"

She stopped at the sight of her butler talking with a stranger at the front door. He was a long, lanky man in a well-fitting but dull outfit, with a bowler hat pressed to his chest.

"Mr. Asterly is not at home," Greenhill said with a level of exasperation that suggested it was not for the first time.

The stranger didn't budge. "Then I will wait for him," the man said in a voice as dull as his outfit. "It is of great importance."

Well, this is interesting.

"Greenhill, can I be of assistance?" she asked, walking toward them.

The butler turned to her. "He's from London, my lady. He wants to see Mr. Asterly."

She turned to the stranger, who kept his eyes on his shoes. "I'm Lady Amelia Asterly, his wife."

The stranger gave a short, perfunctory bow. When he rose, he fixed his gaze just over her shoulder. "Mr. Andrew Coventry, my lady. Of Coventry & Co. I'm a solicitor. I am here on a matter of great urgency."

The only great urgency Amelia could think of was the Americans and the contract that needed to be signed. A tiny trickle of anxiety crawled down her spine. Either this was good news—the contract was signed—or it was bad. And given they'd yet to visit the firm and see Tessie in action, there was a high chance it was bad.

She fixed a smile on her face. "Greenhill, please send Charlie down to the firm to fetch Mr. Asterly. Mr. Coventry, would you like tea while you wait?"

She guided him toward the sitting room just as Cassandra thundered down the stairs with the grace of a thousand elephants, two coats in her arms. She skidded to a stop when she reached the landing.

Mr. Coventry blanched.

Amelia cringed. She'd been lax on Cassandra's training in

the past few days, and that short loosening of the reins had allowed her to slip back into unladylike behaviors.

"Cassandra. There's been a change of plans, I'm afraid. Why don't you go do your lessons, and we'll go for our walk later?"

"She is an...energetic...creature," Mr. Coventry said when Cassandra had left.

"Youth has its advantages," she replied, leading him through the door.

"She might as well enjoy the freedom now. Things are about to change for her."

It was an offhand comment. He didn't elaborate. But the trickle of anxiety became a deluge. It soaked under her dress, filled her slippers, and made her shiver to the bone. Maybe it was just her recent foray into novel reading, but for the first time in her life, she felt a sense of impending doom.

Something was very, very wrong.

Chapter 23 ————————

Benedict strode into the morning room with sharp steps that echoed his frustration at having to leave work. The pressure was on. Once the contract was signed, they'd need to launch straight into a production schedule twice as fast as originally planned—and now Tessie had developed a problem. It needed solving fast, and he couldn't do it from the sitting room.

That said, if the lawyer Charlie mentioned was from the Americans . . . God, what if he was there to say the contract had been given to someone else? What the devil would happen then?

He entered the sitting room where his wife had a teacup in hand while the lawyer—a reedy-looking man if he'd ever seen one—was laughing.

Thank God for Amelia. Benedict was too rough and too straight-talking to deal comfortably with London folk. Amelia was smooth as cream and could put anyone at ease. She was an element of his business negotiations that he hadn't known he needed.

The thin fellow stood when he saw Benedict enter. He gave a deep bow. This man was definitely not from the Americans.

Benedict held out his hand. "Mr. Coventry, I presume."

The lawyer hesitated a moment before clasping it. His handshake was like a wet fish—clammy and soft.

"What can I do for you?" Perhaps he was too direct, but he didn't have time fit for wasting.

The man flicked his eyes to Amelia and back to Benedict. "Perhaps it would be best if we spoke in private?"

Muscles tightened around Amelia's jaw. Her lips thinned almost imperceptibly. Nothing annoyed her like being left out of gossip.

"This sounds serious. Perhaps we should relocate to the study."

The look Amelia shot him was furious and gave Benedict the distinct feeling that, if he wanted to be welcome in her bed any time soon, having this conversation without her was not an option.

"Darling, will you join us?" He held his arm out.

The lawyer made a gulping noise, like he'd gone to breathe but had inhaled his ego instead. "I'm not sure that's appropriate."

"My wife is…" He hadn't put any thought into what exactly she was, just that things worked better with her around. "…part of my business advisory council. And a board member of Asterly, Barnesworth & Co."

Her eyes widened in a transparent and utterly-unlike-her manner. But why not? The advice she'd given him so far was excellent, she was clearly invested, and perhaps an official role might go some way to repairing the damage he'd done the other morning acting like a complete ass.

"I'm not here about any firm. This is not a *business*

matter." The distaste on the man's face was plain. Bloody hell. Even lawyers were stratified.

"Then what is this about?" Benedict asked. His patience— what little of it he had—was wearing thin indeed.

"If we could just go into your study." A twinge of urgency entered the man's voice. This conversation was clearly not playing out the way the grasshopper had intended.

"Spit it out, man."

Mr. Coventry wiped his brow. "This is highly unusual. To have this conversation in a lady's room…"

Benedict ran a hand through his hair. Whatever this was, it wasn't good. And he didn't want to waste another five minutes changing rooms and making small talk.

As if sensing his looming outburst, Amelia placed a firm hand on his arm, stepping in front of him. Probably trying to put the insufferable lawyer at ease.

"I apologize if my husband seems abrupt. He is simply a very busy man and has never been one to stand on ceremony. If you could just tell us who sent you and what for, we can get this all fixed up so he can go back to his office."

She was sweet and reasonable and oh-so polite, even though he was sure she wanted to wring the grasshopper's neck as much as he did. It was a level of poise he didn't possess.

Mr. Coventry swallowed. "I was sent by your grandfather. There has been an accident. Your cousin has passed, and you are the new heir to the Marquess of Harrington."

Chapter 24

Benedict was vaguely aware of Amelia leaving the room with the damned lawyer. She would show him to the front door. She was the perfect hostess, even at a time like this.

Benedict still sat on the edge of the spindly, flowery seat that, by all standards, should have collapsed under his weight a long time ago. This room, with its patterned wallpaper and abundance of small, useless cushions—this very feminine room—was exactly what the lawyer had said. Completely unsuitable for news like this.

There wasn't a brandy glass in the place.

He squeezed his head between his hands, as if he could push out the words he'd heard over the past hour. *Cousin. Carriage accident. Grandfather. Heir. Grandfather. Duty. Grandfather. Letter. Grandfather. New heir. Grandfather.*

He stared at the leather-bound package on the table in front of him. It was all the necessary paperwork for a new estate in Hemshire. According to the lawyer, his grandfather had bequeathed it to him. A training estate to prepare him for the eventual inheritance of a half dozen others. A letter from his grandfather lay on top.

He didn't want it.

He didn't want any of it.

Amelia entered, tucking away a handkerchief and refusing to meet his gaze.

"I don't understand." He'd said it a dozen times to the lawyer, and all he'd heard back was a whole lot of legal vernacular that his overwhelmed brain couldn't deal with.

"Why am I the future Earl of Hemshire? My mother was female. Obviously. What I mean is, why am I the heir? There are laws against this sort of thing."

There was a smallness to her voice when she replied. Pity that made him feel powerless. "Some peerages can go through the female line if there's no direct heir. Not many, but Hemshire is one of them. Most of your grandfather's titles will revert back to the crown—including Harrington. But the earldom will pass on to you. Your mother would have been the Countess of Hemshire in her own right if she'd outlived her brother and nephew."

His mother. Countess in her own right? She would have been euphoric. It might even have been enough to keep her from leaving, if she'd known this was in her future.

But she'd left and taken with her any reason for him to accept the position.

He shook his head. "I don't want it. He can give it to someone else. I'm not interested."

Amelia held him to her side and stroked his hair. "It doesn't work that way," she said gently. "It's not something you get to choose."

"I don't want to be the bloody earl!"

As he leapt out of the chair, she stepped backward, tripping over a side table and falling.

He would have helped her up, but the livid look on her face made him hesitate.

"Well, you're not the earl," she spat. "Not yet, anyway. And the last time I saw your grandfather, he was fighting fit. You have at least a decade…unless he does something foolish, which I highly doubt, given you're completely unsuited to the role and he's bound to want to keep it out of your hands for as long as humanly possible. He'll likely live to a thousand."

She untangled her skirts from her legs and pushed herself to standing.

"This is unfair." He slammed his hand into the wall, the plaster cracking under the impact. The pain in his hand was a welcome distraction from the nausea in his stomach.

Amelia's expression was pure scorn. "This is a rather extraordinary display of emotion, isn't it? Even from you."

"I just—" He couldn't put into words just how furious he was. Instead he thumped his bruised and bleeding fist into his palm over and over.

"Given you've never met your cousin, your grief seems a little extreme." Her voice was sharp and full of edges. Was she angry with him?

What the hell did she have to be angry about? It was his life being ruined.

But of course, if he was the future Earl of Hemshire, she was the future countess. No doubt the chance that he might turn down the title had her in her own panic.

"This is exactly what you wanted," he said. "Don't pretend that you're not ecstatic right now."

Her face went slack, as if she'd copped a blow to her midsection. Then it firmed into the brittle mask he'd not seen in weeks. "Actually, the plan was to marry a duke," she said quietly. She moved to the window, turning her back on him. "But I suppose an earl will do."

Finally the truth, out there for him to smack straight into. Whatever she'd said over these past weeks, whatever she'd done, she hadn't been one-hundred-percent happy. There was still that part of her that found him lacking, just a little bit.

Until now.

Until a title he didn't want was forced on him.

Until responsibilities he didn't want and had no idea how to live up to were made his. As if he didn't have enough burdens as it was.

But she didn't care. As long as she was the future countess. "You are a cold one. So caught up in your titles you can't see how much I don't want this."

She whirled around. "I'm cold? You're so caught up in how awful it is to be handed something people dream of, you can't see *anything*. You poor darling. How dreadful Ducky's death must be for *you*." She grabbed a vase from the still-standing side table and threw it at his head.

It wasn't her loss of control that sucked the air from his lungs. It was the grief etched into all her features. The way she bit her lip hard. The tears running down her face. The lines around her eyes that made her look older than she was.

He was more than an ass. Of course she'd known his cousin. Amelia knew everyone.

"Sweetheart, I'm sorry."

If she heard him, she showed no sign of it. "Forget those of us that knew and liked him. Our grief pales in comparison to that of Mr. Benedict Asterly, who has been granted a future title, estate, vote in the House of Lords, political influence. What a poor wretch. My heart bleeds for you."

"That's not…I didn't mean that. Obviously, I am sad for his loss." Even to him, the words sounded like insincere platitudes.

"Why? You never met him. He was nothing but a parasite to you. Another great example of injustice and oppression."

He closed the gap between them and tried to wrap her in his arms, but she pulled out of his embrace and shoved him in the chest.

"Well, we were of similar age. To me he was a sweet, kind boy who told terrible jokes and always saved a quadrille for me. He cared about the people of his estate. He showed up to every parliamentary session. He fought for his country even when your grandfather forbade it."

She put the couch between them.

"Amelia."

She untucked her handkerchief from her sleeve and wiped it across her face. "Did you know he was the only person to write to me after our marriage? He hoped that it might signal the healing of your family rift. For you to think that I would be happy that my friend has died so that I could have a bloody title shows that you don't know me at all."

Amelia stuffed her feet into walking boots and grabbed a coat. Normally she would change into a walking dress before leaving the house, but right now she just needed to get out—away from her boneheaded husband, away from the house and all its reminders of what she'd lost. She just needed a moment to grieve.

Ducky.

There were so many vile people in this world. It wasn't fair that someone sweet and kind should be taken so soon. Ducky was one of the few people she *liked*. He and Benedict might have actually gotten along if they'd managed to set aside the conflict their parents had created. They both had a similar sense of humor. They both liked the work of Voltaire. Ducky was softer, though—more willing to shift and ebb with the plans of others than Benedict was.

The last she'd heard, he'd been courting Josephine Livingston. She should send some flowers.

She kicked a pebble out of her way. It bounced and rolled on the drive. She kicked it again, thoughts tumbling through her head.

Benedict's accusations had hurt. To call her heartless? To suggest she'd choose a title over a person? It was cruel, and she didn't deserve such treatment. She almost wished her aim with that vase had been a little better.

But as hurt as she was, it made sense that he'd lash out at her. He had just found out that his life was not going to turn out as planned—in fact, the very opposite. If anyone knew the kaleidoscope of anger, grief, and fear that rolled through you when your life upended unexpectedly, she did.

The pebble rolled and bounced again, lodging at the base of new shoots sprouting through hard dirt.

Winter was beginning to lose its grip. She wasn't an avid enough gardener to tell what the plant would be—tulips? Jonquils? Daffodils? But in a few more months, this path would be lined with color.

The irony didn't escape her. She was surrounded by new life but had no idea what it would be.

If Benedict truly refused to take on the title when his grandfather passed, who knew what would become of the people who lived there. There would be no guarantee those who relied on the Earl of Hemshire would be well taken care of.

So Benedict was going to need to take up the mantle,

whatever his personal opinions. And as much as he might wish to do so later rather than sooner, it wasn't possible. It was an immense task to manage an estate properly, to become acquainted with all the information necessary to help run the county. And given Benedict's blindness on so many aspects of a lord's life, he was going to need all the time and help he could get.

Sweat rolled down Benedict's neck as he put his weight into the crank of the slip roller. The sheet of steel between the rollers formed a wide curve as it wound out of the machine. The crank reached the bottom, and he shifted his grip, raising it up, his muscles straining.

"You know, we have people to do that," John said as he entered the empty workshop.

"I gave them the afternoon off." Benedict pushed on the crank again. His mind had been a chaotic jumble of thoughts from the moment the solicitor had left. Channeling them into hard labor was the only way he could get them under control.

"Want to talk about it?"

He didn't particularly, but he couldn't get his thoughts straight on his own, and of all the people he could turn to, John understood the machinations of the upper class the best.

Except for Amelia. But he was not sure she'd want to help given the way he'd just treated her.

"Alexander Douglass died in a racing accident last week." He grunted as he switched grips and leaned into the shaft again.

"Ducky?" John frowned. Benedict could almost see John

forming connecting lines in his mind until he reached the absurd conclusion. "You're the new heir."

Benedict exhaled in frustration. "How is that not a surprise to anyone else?"

John shrugged.

"Of course, I bolloxed things up by yelling at my wife. Who may or may not forgive me."

He heaved on the crank, his muscles burning.

"And I'm stuck with an estate I don't want, out in bloody nowheres-shire."

He huffed with the turn.

"And my damned grandfather has written to me."

John's eyes widened at the mention of the marquess. He'd been there when Benedict had received word that Lord Harrington refused to send help to Benedict's sick and impoverished mother. When the marquess had refused to attend her funeral.

"What did he want?"

"Don't know. Didn't read it. Here, help with this."

John grabbed the other side of the sheet and helped guide it off the machine. Together they carried it to the edge of the room and leaned it against the wall.

"It could be what we need?"

Benedict snapped his head around.

John put up his hands in defense. "The heirdom. Not the letter."

And there was half his bloody problem. The Americans still insisted on seeing him play nice with the English before they'd sign any contract. They needed to know that signing with him wouldn't jeopardize any of their other ventures. With no one coming to their ridiculous hunt, word of his sudden elevation to the one-day peerage might be all that saved the deal.

He grabbed a rag from the bench and wiped the sweat off his face. "I don't want anything from that man. Not his title, not his practice estate, not his damned letter."

He should have told the lawyer to go to buggery. Shouldn't have let the grasshopper leave without taking those damned papers with him.

But he hadn't. Now he either had to face his grandfather to hand them back or accept that he had new burdens to bear.

But first, he needed to make up with his wife.

Chapter 25

The letters started arriving thick and fast over the following days—belated acceptances to Amelia's house party. *The dog ate my invitation* or *So sorry, this fell behind the dresser. Or I asked my maid to answer for me, but she forgot. She's been fired.*

It would be amusing, really, the pathetic excuses for their previous silence, if it weren't so irritating. Because it wasn't Amelia that the *ton* was replying to.

Certainly, her name might be at the top of each page, but it wasn't until Benedict's elevation in status that London had cared about her. Her father was right—to them, she was only worth who she could marry.

She had known that her whole life, but it had only begun to grate in the past few months. It was Benedict's fault. For making her feel like she was so much more.

But after weeks of complaining that her party was over before it could start, she could hardly tell them all to go jump off a cliff. Besides, it was what they needed to get the contract signed, and it was important for Benedict to be introduced to the people he'd be associating with when he took up the title.

So it was all hands on deck. Every able body in the village had been employed to get the house up to snuff.

All day, Amelia was consumed by wallpaper samples, training her staff on the proper way to set a table, and helping Cassandra master the art of small talk.

The task was tremendous. Every inch of the house needed to be scrubbed and polished. The workmen who came through to fix cracks in the plaster, unstick old windows, and repaint the interiors tracked in mud and dirt that left the floors in the sorriest state Amelia could imagine. Thank goodness new carpets had been ordered.

Getting the house to rights in time to host a contingent of British *ton* required more manual labor than the small village of Abingdale was able to provide.

So with a grimace, Amelia rolled up her sleeves—Daisy's sleeves, to be exact—and got to work with an old cloth, polishing brush, and jar of beeswax.

Polishing was deathly dull. It ranked somewhat below embroidery—which at least had the joy of creating something pretty—and somewhat above spending an hour in the company of the Fairbrights, a family with more money than sense whose small talk was very small indeed.

First, she hummed, hoping to distract herself with a pretty tune. Then she turned to counting backward. By the time she reached zero, she should be done. Four hundred and sixty. Quartre cent cinquante-neuf. Fünfhundert achtundfünfzig. Four hundred and fifty-eight. Each number was accompanied by the sweep of her arm.

By four hundred, her arms hurt so much her strokes had sunk to half their original size. By three hundred, her knees hurt so badly they were bound to be bruised. By two hundred, the muscles in her hands had seized around the brush so tightly she might never be able to pry it from her fingers. She would be forced to go to bed with it. By one hundred, her entire back was in spasms.

Five, four, three, two, one.

She sat back. The floor looked spectacular. At least the twenty percent she'd managed to polish looked spectacular.

Grinding her teeth, she wiped sweat from her brow. She was sticky and grotesque and desperate for a bath. Writing to her "friends" and telling them to visit in a year was more and more appealing. To hell with the contract.

"Well, there's a sight I'll never forget." Benedict's voice was tinged with laughter.

For an engineer, he wasn't very smart. Anyone could see she was two brush strokes from murder.

She turned to him. "If that's the case, then the threshold for your amusement is pitiably low." She stood, leaning to the left, then right, forward and backward, trying to stretch out the kinks that had developed.

"The famous Lady Amelia Crofton on her knees with a scrubbing brush. I daresay that's a tidbit that would amuse the entire *ton*."

"I swear, Benedict. If you tell anyone about what you just saw, I will teach Cassandra the most annoying and banal piece of music I can find and insist she perform it for you. Nightly."

He grabbed the hand she had pointed at him and tugged her close. Her body melted at the feeling of him against her. In the week since their argument, they'd tried to move forward. But despite their efforts, interactions between them had felt formal, their conversation stilted, their kisses perfunctory, and their nights spent in separate bedrooms.

Apparently, all she'd needed to breach the wall between them was to be caught looking completely disheveled.

"Your utterly shameful secret is safe with me. No one will know how delightfully determined you really are." He ran a trail of kisses along her neck.

"Stop. I look horrid. I'm filthy." The dress was ill-fitting and now covered in grey marks. She had streaks of dust up her arms and, she suspected, everywhere else.

"Then perhaps you need a bath. And someone to help you with it." He ran his hand down her back and cupped her bottom, sending a line of heat coursing through her body.

"Now?" she asked.

"I've missed you," he murmured into the crevice of her throat.

She reached up greedily and drew his head to hers, desperate for a kiss.

He obliged, his tongue teasing against hers. She could feel his cock jutting against his breeches. She wriggled against it.

"We should stop." He dragged himself away from her.

"Why?" She didn't want to stop. She wanted him to take her upstairs and make love to her.

"It's ungentlemanly to consort with the help."

"You wretch." She batted him on the shoulder.

He laughed. "Well if the bounds of propriety aren't going to get in our way..." Scooping her into his arms, he carried her up to her bedroom, taking the steps two at a time.

Chapter 26 ———————

Coach is in the drive!" Cassandra said. She was as excited as Benedict had ever heard her.

She'd been glued to the sitting room window for the past hour waiting for the first of their guests to arrive. While she'd been buzzing with excitement, he'd been sitting in an armchair pretending to read through Fiona's latest report. In truth, he'd get to the end of a page without having taken in a single detail—his mind kept returning to the approaching hordes. And unlike his sister, he took no joy in their imminent arrival.

Amelia set down her needlework and stood, brushing away the slight wrinkles in her dress, smiling. She appeared genuinely happy, as though she was actually looking forward to having these people in their home.

He had to remind himself that these people were her friends, even if their behavior wasn't something he'd tolerate in a friendship.

He was nervous—both that their presence would make

her yearn for her old life and also that the event wasn't going to go the way she hoped.

The last thing he wanted was to see her crushed.

"Remember what I said?" she asked Cassandra.

"Curtsey to everyone including the Americans. Don't speak unless spoken to. Keep my hands clasped in front of me."

Amelia smiled. "Good. Then let's go." They held hands as they left the sitting room, Amelia shooting a demanding look over her shoulder when she realized Benedict wasn't following. He sighed and folded the paper before trailing after her.

The nervous energy in the house erupted into movement as they entered the hall. Tom handed Benedict a coat, and Daisy helped Amelia with her pelisse. Through the front windows, Benedict could see the rest of the staff marching out into a neat line by the entrance stairs. To their credit, with the exception of a few nervous shared glances, they looked completely unaffected by the arrival of the London crowd— the house's first visitors since most of them were hired.

"Benedict?" Amelia's concerned voice interrupted his drifting thoughts. She held out her hand, and he tucked it into the crook of his arm. Theoretically to support her, but they both knew the truth.

With a short nod at Tom to tell him to open the door, they walked out into the pale spring sunshine.

Next to him, Amelia stood calm, still, like a safe harbor. On the other side, Cassandra bounced on her toes, the jig, jig, jig making the curls in her hair dance. Daisy had spent all morning getting his sister's hair "just right"—more time than she'd spent even on Amelia's.

He could understand the milestone, Cassandra's first introduction to society, but it was one he'd hoped to avoid.

Thankfully, Amelia had said Cassandra was too young to join them for dinner and activities. While his sister had been crestfallen, she'd accepted it without an argument. Had it been his refusal to allow her to participate, it would have been a very different conversation.

"I hope they like me," his sister whispered, looking up at him. She was so vulnerable that all he wanted was to pick her up and carry her away, shutting the doors and keeping out all that might hurt her.

What kind of brother was he, risking her heart like this?

Instead, against all his better instincts, he nudged her gently under the chin. "How could anyone not like you, poppet?"

The giant grin she gave him sank his heart. He should be warning her. Helping her build a wall around her heart so she wouldn't feel the pain that had defined his childhood when these people did reject her.

But it was too late now. Excitement rippled off her in waves.

It was a long drive, and the horses were going slowly. The longer they took, the tighter his clothing felt. His cravat was like a noose around his neck, and the waistcoat and jacket—tightly fitted with unnecessary embroidery and ridiculous jeweled buttons—began to squeeze the life from him. He tried to take a deep, calming breath and failed.

"Quit fidgeting," Amelia murmured. "I wish you'd let me buy you something with color."

He looked down at his outfit of charcoal and grey and wished he was wearing anything that let him breathe. Waiting there at the foot of the stairs, flanked by childhood friends dressed like stuffed turkeys, he felt like the worst kind of imposter.

"This is a bloody nuisance."

She gave him a you-must-be-kidding look. "This 'bloody nuisance' is giving those ladder-climbing Americans the opportunity to rub shoulders with the cream of London society. You need this."

And he damn well knew it.

He grunted and fixed his eye on the coach that was nearing. "Who is this?" There was an elaborate coat of arms on the coach door, but he'd not had the time—or inclination—to bother learning insignias.

"Lord and Lady Bradenstock and their son Nathaniel. You might actually like him—Lord Bradenstock. You'll despise the boy."

"What am I going to like about him?" It was hard to imagine these people having any useful qualities he'd admire.

"Lord Bradenstock's quite progressive. He recently purchased a cast-iron plow."

That was something. The cast-iron plow was an exceptional leap forward in engineering, not that many estate owners had adopted it. There were too many fears that it would poison the earth. They were stuck in traditional ways of doing things, as if accepting the smallest change would start a cascade of dominoes that would overthrow life as they knew it.

"How do you know he has the plow?"

She smiled at him. "I make it my business to know everything, have you not noticed? Information is power, at least…" She trailed off, turning her focus back to their impending guests.

"At least what?"

She kept her gaze dead ahead, not looking at him. "In London. Information is power in London. It's hard to come by and fairly useless in Abingdale."

It was just a little criticism. But it was enough to remind

him that Abingdale was not her first choice. She seemed happy and enthusiastic, but if another opportunity arose, would she stay?

The coach pulled to a stop. The outriders, whose ridiculous costumes came with bloody two-foot wigs, opened the door.

Lady Bradenstock was a nondescript woman in what he was sure was a very fine dress. Not as fine as Amelia's, whose blue dress skimmed her curves, but nice enough. The man next to her was equally uninspiring, but the youth that trailed them looked like an overly prissy peacock in a cacophony of colors.

Amelia gave him a quick nudge in the ribs, and Benedict realized this was his part. He bent over the woman's hand. "A pleasure, Lady Bradenstock."

The woman took a long, unashamed look at him, from the tips of his perfectly polished hessians to his hair, which was pulled back in a way that Amelia insisted was de rigueur.

"I hear congratulations are in order," she said. "From footman's son to the future Lord Hemshire. That's quite a rise."

Only a member of the bloody aristocracy would congratulate someone on a man's death. He was just about to say as much when Amelia surreptitiously stepped on his foot.

Damnation.

He would play nice, or at least play politely. "The inheritance was a surprise. I'm sorry I didn't know my cousin before he passed. A dreadful waste of life so young."

Lady Bradenstock's eyes narrowed, fully aware of his censure.

Amelia interrupted. "May I introduce my sister, Miss Cassandra Asterly."

Cassandra sank into a deep curtsey, eyes downcast. There

was not a single falter where a month ago she would have looked like a wobbly spinning top.

"It's an honor to meet you, my lady." Her voice was steady, lower than normal, and lacking her girlish enthusiasm. It made him anxious. And the approving look from the over-powdered, overdressed woman in front of him nudged the anxiety into full-blown panic.

He clenched his hands to stop himself from dragging Cassandra behind his back, out of this woman's reach.

"You are delightful," Lady Bradenstock said to her. "I do hope to see you again before we leave."

His sister didn't grin or bounce or react in any way that he expected. She simply inclined her head graciously, looking like a tiny replica of Amelia.

Before Benedict could inform Lady Bradenstock that she was unlikely to be seeing his sister again, Lord Bradenstock grabbed his hand and pumped it forcefully.

"I hear you're an engineer," the older man said. "Fascinating. Just fascinating. I might have done the same if it were an acceptable profession when I was young." He seemed utterly oblivious to the insult he'd just given.

Benedict ground his teeth. "It's funny that scientists gave us bridges and roads and coaches and housing, yet are unacceptable."

Unlike his wife, Lord Bradenstock did not pick up on the undercurrent of criticism. He just smiled and said, "Perhaps an engineering earl might change all that, eh?"

The sniff that came from behind him was long and dismissive. "I doubt that. You don't see a dancing monkey and think it belongs in a ballroom."

It took every ounce of self-control for Benedict not to put his fist into Nathaniel Bradenstock's pale and limpid face.

And when the popinjay bent over Amelia's hand with a

sugary flourish, Benedict was consumed by a sudden, acrid dislike.

Not because of his insults, or the way his lips lingered on Amelia's fingers—although that was not an act Benedict wished to watch again—but because Nathaniel was fine-boned, delicate, with perfect curls and long lashes, pallid skin and long, delicate fingers. He wore color. Lots of colors. And fabrics that Benedict loved to tear off his wife but would never feel comfortable wearing.

Nathaniel was everything Benedict's mother had wished for in a son.

Throughout his childhood, Benedict had cursed his tall frame and shaggy hair that fell flat and limp to his shoulders when he tried to grow it into fashionably long curls. His skin had tanned at the very hint of sun, and though he spent months refusing to exercise at all, he was still lumbering.

He had tried hard to be Nathaniel and had never managed it. *To hell with him.*

"Welcome to my home," he ground out, crushing the popinjay's fingers.

Nathaniel's look morphed from condescension to apprehension. The boy wasn't as idiotic as he seemed.

Amelia frowned and took the pretty boy's arm. "You must want to freshen up from the journey. Let me show you to your room." She threw a pointed look at Benedict over her shoulder as she left.

Damn, it was going to be a difficult week.

It was as though Amelia had never left London. While the men played billiards and smoked cigars in the billiards room, Amelia spent the day with the women her own age and soaked up the *ton* gossip. Who had been in town for the little Season. Who had been courting whom. Who had been wearing what and when and how the rest of the *ton* had reacted.

It had been a shame that she'd missed out on so much, they said. Her absence had been mourned. Society hadn't been the same. How exciting it was that she'd returned to the fold. What a smashing week this would be.

There was no mention of the circumstances surrounding her marriage. Nor the cartoons in the gossip pages, nor the fact that her letters had gone unanswered, her invitations to visit ignored. In fact, it seemed as though the past three months had been entirely wiped from existence.

And if that needled a little, then she would just push the feeling aside and focus on the fact that, for the moment, she had achieved what she wanted. She was a full-fledged member of society once again.

Now she needed to greet her final guests because there was more than one mountain to climb over the next few days.

The coach that was coming to a stop was garishly appointed with complicated carvings covered in gold leaf. Amelia didn't recognize the coat of arms on the door. Recently created, clearly, given she knew every significant one by sight.

Even if they weren't the last guests to arrive, she would still have known that it was the Americans. No Englishman outside the royal family would cover their carriage in that much gilding.

Two men exited, both dressed alike in clothes the height of fashion, but in everything else they differed. The tall one—Grunt, Benedict said—was disproportionately wide and had a beard that fanned out like one of her parasols.

In contrast, Harcombe was thin and gangly—the kind of man who could be blown away by a stiff wind. Looks were deceiving, though. According to Benedict, he was by far the more ruthless of the two.

They each held out an arm for the remaining passengers.

"My goodness," Amelia said as the misses Grunt exited. It was an utterly inappropriate exclamation, but she had never seen such an entrance during daylight hours.

The girls were preened and primped as if ready for a ball. They even had pearls seeded through their black hair. Where most women would have simple jewelry—if any when traveling—the sisters wore ropes of pearls. Their white dresses were made of heavy silk, a fabric more suited to dancing than hours sitting in a carriage.

"Aren't they cold?" Cassandra whispered. "Why aren't they wearing cloaks?"

Benedict chuckled. "A cloak would ruin the effect."

Amelia nudged him in the ribs as discreetly as she could. The last thing they needed was to offend their guests of honor.

"Gentlemen." Benedict shook the men's hands. "May I present my wife, Lady Amelia Asterly."

She curtseyed and gave the men her most charming smile. Her goals this weekend were twofold. Ensure Benedict gained acceptance by the *ton* and that the firm gained the contract it needed.

For that reason, she would curtsey to the gauche Americans as if they were Prinny himself.

"It is a pleasure to meet you," she said. "Welcome to our home."

By the time Benedict had worked up the nerve to join his guests in the drawing room before dinner, all but Wildeforde and his mother had arrived.

Even from a distance, he could tell Amelia was annoyed at his tardiness—he'd said he'd be down directly, and that had been more than a half hour ago.

Trying to hide his discomfort, he strode toward her in long, confident steps, acknowledging those he passed with a quick nod.

They were staring at him. They might be trying to disguise it behind their fans, or a drink, or by looking into the long mirror against the wall, but he felt every glance burn through his jacket.

He'd been turned into a zoo animal. He could picture the sign: HALF-BRED BUSINESSMAN TURNED SOON-TO-BE PEER. NATURAL HABITAT: NOT A DAMNED DRAWING ROOM.

However annoyed Amelia was at his tardiness, she let it go as he neared, her brows furrowing in concern. She took his hand and pressed a quick kiss to his knuckles—a very forward gesture in front of guests, and exactly what he needed. His chest relaxed slightly.

"Mr. Asterly." The misses Grunt dipped into perfect curtseys, deep enough that light bounced off their diamond necklaces. In all other ways they were perfectly demure, but it was clear to anyone who looked what the two girls were offering. And what they were after in return.

Benedict executed a quick bow, and by the time he'd looked up, Amelia was well into her conquer-through-charm assault on Grunt and Harcombe, leaving him alone to deal with the two debutantes.

The eldest was exquisite. Her black hair against her pale skin gave her an almost otherworldly look. Her facial structure was perfectly symmetrical, her lips rosy—although he suspected not without the help of some paint—and her golden eyes arresting. And sharp. Taking in everything around her.

Her sister, Miss Eliza Grunt, was less—everything. Pretty but not striking. A participant, not predator.

The girls smiled at him expectantly, and he realized he had no idea how to talk to young women. Twelve-year-olds? Sure. His wife? Absolutely. A female engineer? One hundred percent. But debutantes?

"I, uh, I hope everything is to your liking." He looked around for someone to save him. Right now he'd even take one of the coxcombs Amelia had invited.

From the side of the room, he caught Peter smirking in his livery, clearly enjoying his employer's distress. What Benedict would give to be a footman and not a host this evening.

"Are you enjoying London?" he asked the girls.

"It's a lovely experience," Miss Grunt said. "But it's a pleasure to visit the country to spend time with such distinguished persons." Her smile was smooth, gentle, and as fake as the diamonds around her neck were real.

"It's a pleasure to be somewhere I can breathe," the younger Grunt muttered. Benedict decided that, if he had to sit next to either of them at dinner, he hoped it was her. He gave the girl an encouraging smile, which was met by an utterly bland one in response.

Devil help him. He'd give one hundred quid to whoever got him out of this conversation.

He looked over at his wife, who was smiling and laughing. She playfully batted Harcombe on the shoulder with her fan, and the man turned deep red.

Help was not coming from that quarter.

He turned back to the debutantes to find Miss Grunt's eyes alight and fixed at a point over his shoulder.

Behind him, Greenhill cleared his throat. "Their Graces the Duke and Duchess of Wildeforde and the right honorable Earl and Countess of Karstark."

The energy in the room shifted—not that his guests would notice. But his staff? They went tense. Peter didn't hide his anger, his lips pursed and jaw set.

Hairs stood up on the back of Benedict's neck, and the chatter in the room suddenly sounded much farther away. It took a second for him to remember to breathe.

What were the Karstarks doing here?

He turned to Amelia, who gave him a barely perceptible don't-ask-me shrug before going to greet the new arrivals.

Agatha Karstark looked even more ancient than she had a month ago. She wore a three-foot powdered wig—perhaps that was how she hid her horns—and a red, wide-skirted dress that looked more like a costume than a dress of today. The powder on her face had settled into the creases, creating a ghoulish effect.

Lord Karstark looked much the same as he had that night that he'd manipulated Benedict into this marriage—small and frail, but it was a façade. Karstark didn't need a physical advantage to take advantage of others. He had power and money, which was enough to cow the young women unfortunate enough to work for him. They never lasted in his employ long.

Benedict looked over at Peter, who was tracking Karstark's movements. His sister had worked for them a few months back, and it had not ended well. She was still reluctant to be alone and was skittish in the company of any man.

Peter needed watching tonight.

Benedict stretched his jaw. "Excuse me for a moment, ladies," he said to the Grunt sisters. Taking a deep breath, he stalked toward the foursome at the entryway.

He would tell them to leave. With any luck, they'd refuse. Then he would grab Karstark by his breeches and toss him out the door.

Except he couldn't, because Amelia got there before him, and instead of throwing them out, she curtseyed.

"Your Graces," Amelia said to Wildeforde and his mother.

Benedict wondered if he were the only one in the room that noticed the slight tightening of her lips as she paid deference to her ex-fiancé.

Turning to the Karstarks, she said, "It's a pleasure to see you both again."

All eyes turned to him.

He wouldn't bow. Not in his home. Not to these people.

It didn't go unnoticed. Lord Karstark smirked, as if Benedict had just proved him right on some front.

Lady Wildeforde *tut-tut*ted. "Benedict, stubborn boy. You're taller again. You're putting a crick in my neck."

It was the same welcome he'd received from her every time they'd met during his youth—always accompanied by a disapproving inspection. She'd made it repeatedly clear that he was not the friend she wanted for her son.

How he hated these people.

"Agatha, why are we here?" Karstark asked his wife loudly.

"I believe you're satisfying your wife's need to know everyone's business," Benedict said. A murmur rippled through the room.

Damn these people. If they weren't going to try for civility, neither would he. Who showed up to a dinner without an invitation?

"My love..." Amelia's tone was honeyed but her eyes flinty. Whatever their shared opinion of the Karstarks, it was clear they did not share a strategy for dealing with them. Her glare was as clear a warning as he was going to get.

"What a surprise to have you join us," his wife said to them. "I'll arrange some extra seating, though we may be a touch squashed."

Lady Karstark sniffed. "To save you the surprise, girl, we'll be here every night."

⁓

The only thing that got Benedict through a dinner having to watch the Karstarks eating and talking and laughing as if they were at home in his home was to focus on the plan. The reason he'd agreed to this bloody hunt in the first place.

This morning's tour. The contract that would be signed after.

He had laid it all out. He would wake at country hours, meet Harcombe and Grunt in the foyer, and the three of them would visit the firm, where he would show them firsthand why they should contract his team to produce the engines that would run the trains between the coal fields of western Virginia to the port at Alexandria.

By the time the rest of the guests woke, the deal would be done, and he'd be able to disappear into his study for the remainder of the week.

The first hitch began before the day even did. Nathaniel Bradenstock overheard him making plans with the Americans the night before and decided that it would be a smashing way to start the week. A real look at the other side of life.

He put the idea out to a group of puffed-up, pompous peacocks that had gathered in Benedict's drawing room. One unwanted tagalong quickly became three, and it was decided among the guests that eight in the morning was frightfully early, and why didn't they all leave at midday?

Which meant Benedict had all morning to work himself into a jumble of knots, questioning every part of the well-prepared presentation he needed to give. By the time the three coaches pulled up outside the workhouses, his hands were sweating and heart racing.

He fingered the ribbon in his waistcoat pocket. Amelia had given it to him that morning, along with a kiss full of confidence. Her absolute faith in him had the opposite effect to what she'd intended. It just added to the number of people he could let down today.

Oliver was standing outside. Benedict had sent Charlie to the firm in the morning to let them know of the change in time and the additional visitors.

Oliver had taken note and looked as clean as Benedict had ever seen him in a white shirt, brown breeches, and jacket. The foreman was usually covered in grease and soot—everything a shade of grey, regardless of what color it started out as. The fresh shirt showed how seriously he took this visit.

"Oliver." Benedict shook his hand, and then introduced him to the guests.

Lord Bradenstock was as curious and enthusiastic today as he'd been when he arrived. He'd come somewhat prepared, in a plain coat and old boots that had clearly known hard work. Amelia had said the earl was dedicated to his estates. The worn patches on the boots increased Benedict's opinion of the man.

The two popinjays that had joined him were another case altogether. They were dressed in colored silk tailcoats entirely unsuited to visiting a work site. They had pomade in their hair and sweet-smelling perfume on their elaborately tied cravats.

They shrank back when Oliver approached. Benedict

didn't blame them. Plenty of men shied away from Benedict's presence, and Oliver made Benedict feel diminutive.

"My lords." The foreman's tone was stiff and formal. "If you would come this way."

The two colorful lads held kerchiefs to their noses and exchanged nervous glances, as if realizing this might not be the lark they were expecting. Benedict couldn't help looking at their white pantaloons and grinning.

Grunt and Harcombe were unfazed by the firm or its foreman. They had worked their entire lives and were no doubt more comfortable here than back at the house.

The firm was a hive of activity as his team worked on what would be the second engine.

Nathaniel and his friend stood stock still near the entrance to the room, wincing at each clang of a hammer on metal. More than one worker went out of his way to jostle them as they walked past, leaving smears of dirt and sweat on their perfect jackets. There had been a different energy in the firm since the Karstarks had announced the clearances, and today it was palpable.

Jeremy, his recalcitrant stoker, spilled an entire barrow of coal at the boys' feet. "Sorry, m'lords," he said, sniggering as they jumped back, horrified.

"Move along, Jeremy." Oliver put himself between the coxcombs and those who were looking at the party with undisguised disdain. His opinion of the two might not have differed from everyone else's, but he knew what rested on today's visit and would keep the men in line.

Grunt returned from having done a quick solo inspection of the building. "Looks like a very well-oiled operation," he said. "Workspaces laid out for maximum efficiency. Clever."

"My wife," Benedict said. "She looks gentle but has the

organized ruthlessness of a general. She tends to make things run better."

"You're a lucky man then," Grunt said.

Jeremy snorted. "Sticks her bloody nose in," he said, not to anyone in particular but loud enough to be heard above the din of the machines.

"I said get gone, lad," Oliver barked. "Or you'll find yourself scrubbing the floors until the second coming."

Benedict could box Jeremy's ears for making such comments—particularly in front of their guests. He'd been meaning to have a conversation with the boy about the consequences of the path he was going down but hadn't had a spare moment in months.

"So where's the engine?" Nathaniel asked.

"This way." Benedict gestured to the rails that extended from the center of the building out through large wooden doors, which ran the width of the south wall. The test track ran in a three-mile circuit around the perimeter of Benedict's estate.

Tessie, the reason they were all here, glinted in the sun twenty feet away. She'd been washed and polished, ready for inspection. The light caught on her brass trimmings, and he'd never felt prouder.

"We call her Ten-Tonne Tessie," Benedict said as they walked toward it. "Although her actual weight with no additional wagons is closer to five tonnes."

"And what makes her special?" Lord Bradenstock asked. "No offense intended."

"She has a return flue boiler, and her cylinders concentrate on one drive shaft rather than two. Their vertical function makes it safer for the fireman. They don't need to duck the piston rod in order to shovel coal into the firebox."

His English guests looked at him blankly.

"More power and less chance of decapitation," he said.

The young ones sniggered. "Do you think their blood would be red or black?"

"I'd rather be decapitated than spend my life shoveling coal."

From the corner of his eye, Benedict saw the workers around them stiffen. A few shook their heads. One clenched his fists as if to take a swing.

The last thing he needed was an all-out brawl in front of the men they were hoping to be employed by. Oliver fixed each of his men with a glare and got them moving along with a small gesture.

"It's no laughing matter," Benedict said to his idiot guests. "Not to the families that have lost loved ones who were just trying to make a decent wage."

The popinjays didn't answer, just rolled their eyes.

"Flanged?" Grunt asked, bending over to run a finger over the cast-iron wheels. "We were planning to run a rack-and-pinion system. Can these be modified?"

"Yes, but I wouldn't recommend it. In theory, the rack provides grip between the track and wheels. But in practice, there's enough adhesion with smooth wheels—even in the wet—and it's cheaper to produce and causes less wear. I'd suggest taking another look at your plans for the track."

The Americans exchanged a glance Benedict couldn't quite identify. Had he ruined his chances by criticizing their plans?

"We were hoping to see something…interesting," Nathaniel said.

Benedict tried to ignore him and focus on the questions Harcombe was asking about the gear train and axle-load and the framing of the bogies. All things he knew like the back of his hand, but which he struggled to articulate with an audience of lords making snide remarks.

"Projected maintenance costs over a ten-year period?" Grunt asked as he examined the piston.

"Roughly one hundred—no, five hundred—pounds per annum using Trevithick's train as a base and considering the decreased grinding to the gear train. Having one shaft—"

"What kinds of speeds is she getting?" Harcombe had a notepad out and was jotting down figures.

"She is the premier engine. She could make the trip between Boston and New York in—"

"In miles per hour, man. Give me the figures, not the story."

Benedict struggled to get his thoughts to line up. He'd spent a week running through his pitch—the strengths and weaknesses, the financials, the social and economic benefits, his vision for the future. And now they were asking questions all out of order.

"The flue is smaller than others I've seen."

"The psi is higher. The additional pressure creates additional force."

Grunt nodded and continued his inspection, getting close up to every part of the engine, even getting onto his back and shuffling underneath. He fired question after question, barely stopping to hear the answer.

Harcombe was just as thorough, if less chatty.

It was a full half an hour before the two of them stood in front of Benedict, dusting off their hands.

"Well, let's see it work then."

Benedict nodded at Jeremy, who glowered at the visitors and then climbed onto the platform in front of the firebox. The glowing red of the smoldering coals reflected against his leather tunic. He transferred a shovel of black rock from the tender to the boiler.

Heat billowed out. He stoked the flame with an iron rod, the added oxygen causing the fire to expand with a pop and crackle.

Benedict held his breath and waited for the piston to start moving, for the wheels to start turning.

And he waited.

There should be motion by now. Something. His heart started to race. The past year had all been leading to this moment. The Americans. Their contract.

Jeremy looked at Benedict uncertainly. With a cough, Benedict gestured toward the pile of coal.

Another shovelful on the fire. Another billow of heat. Steam shot from the chimney, but the wheels remained where they were.

Goddamn it.

They waited there in awkward silence for a full three minutes. Almost silence. The muttered comments from Nathaniel and his friend turned into giggles, turned into laughter. Then they started with a slow clap.

Benedict was tempted to shove *them* in the damn boiler.

Grunt and Harcombe looked at each other and then turned to Benedict. "Well, thank you for your time." Harcombe slapped Benedict on the arm and turned away.

All the air rushed from his lungs, and the general noise of the firm disappeared behind a ringing in his ears. Benedict grabbed at Grunt's arm. "No. Wait," he choked.

Grunt's expression was kind, if somewhat pitying. "I've been in this business for many years, lad. You'll get there eventually. Progress is a succession of failures until it's not."

This couldn't be it. Not with everything that was riding on today, this decision. In one moment, he saw everything that would happen if he failed. Children without food, families split apart as husbands left their wives to look for work elsewhere. The village he'd grown up in turning into a ghost town of vacant homes.

"You don't understand. It worked fine yesterday."

Grunt shook his head. "We need something that works fine yesterday, today, and tomorrow. Perhaps in a few years when you've had time to refine it." He gave a firm, this-conversation-is-over nod and followed Harcombe.

The idiots snickered as they too made their way back to the waiting carriages. Lord Bradenstock paused. "Stay. Don't worry about seeing us to the house. I'll send the carriage back."

Benedict turned to Oliver, who kicked the bloody wheel with his barrow-sized foot.

"Find out what happened. They're here for two more days."

Chapter 27 ———————————

Benedict stood in the doorway that separated his room from Amelia's, watching her touch perfume to her wrists and behind her ear. He wanted to press his nose to the spot and inhale. The candlelight reflected off Amelia's dresser mirror, bathing her in a warm glow.

She caught his gaze in the reflection. "You look nice," she said, indicating his new evening kit. She tugged on her gloves, pulling them up over her elbow. "How did the tour go? Did they fall in love with Tessie?"

For a split second, he considered not telling her—casting a pall over her much-awaited evening felt cruel. But she needed to know now because Nathaniel likely wouldn't keep his mouth shut.

No doubt gossip was already traveling.

He dropped onto the bed, head in his hands. "It went about as badly as it could."

She turned, her full attention moving from the tiny silk buttons to him.

"What happened?"

"Nothing." He exhaled, a long *whoosh* of air and disappointment. "That was the damned problem. The bloody engine didn't move."

She leaned forward, a furrow of disbelief forming between her brows. "No." And then a heartbeat later, "Why?"

He shook his head, still in disbelief. "The chains coupling the cars together had been shortened, and there was a penny wedged in front of the wheel."

And there was no way that had been an accident.

He couldn't believe it was one of his own men, but the only alternative was that someone else had snuck down in the middle of the night to sabotage them. And they would have needed some understanding of how trains work to disable Tessie so effectively.

True to self, Amelia went straight into solution mode, the whys of the problem not mattering.

"Is it fixed? You could take the Americans back down there tomorrow."

"If I can convince them." He ran a hand through his hair. "I don't think I did a very good job at selling it. Nothing went to plan. My pitch was a mess. I forgot half of it, the other half was delivered in disjointed bursts."

She joined him on the bed and brushed a lock of hair from his forehead, giving him a gentle kiss.

"We have tonight. Between the two of us, we'll get them down there in the morning. I can be quite persuasive, you know."

"Oh, I know. It's one of your many talents."

The smile she gave bordered on wicked. She was scheming and manipulative and damned good at both. Funny how those were traits he'd come to admire in her.

"You haven't asked how my day was with Grunt's

daughters," she said, patting him briskly on the leg and returning to her dresser, where she picked up a necklace. "Help me with this."

He opened the clasp, lifting the chain over her head. "To be honest, I'd forgotten all about his daughters."

In the reflection, he caught the eye roll she didn't mean for him to see. "I do realize the idea of entertaining is a foreign concept to you, but it is expected to at least remember one has guests."

"Noted. What did the misses Grunt have to say? Were they shockingly American and appalling you with stories of cowboys and Indians? Or were they sufficiently demure and talking of weather and embroidery?"

Amelia shrugged. "Neither. I rather think they're as business-focused as their father."

"Really? They were talking about the new railways? What did they say?" Grunt and Harcombe had been transparent about their plans, but any additional information might be useful.

"The business of marriage, not transport. It seems the misses Grunt are doing their own prospecting this weekend."

Benedict couldn't help smiling. "Poor Wildeforde."

"Poor Wildeforde indeed."

By the time all the guests had arrived downstairs and they'd proceeded to the dining room, Amelia was once again questioning her decision to bring London's elite and Benedict's potential business partners into the same space.

It had seemed so simple at the time—the Americans would gain important connections and, in their gratitude, would sign whatever contract Benedict wished.

London society would see how polished her husband and her household were and would acknowledge their mistake in thinking her no longer part of the beau monde.

And Benedict would see that her ability to entertain was a real asset to his business.

She hadn't anticipated just how crass the Americans would be. Or how shamelessly they would throw themselves at every titled gentleman in the room. Or how the other females would consider Amelia responsible for introducing two pretty, wealthy heiresses to "their" men.

By the time the second course arrived, the atmosphere was that of circling sharks. Blood would be spilt.

And it seemed Lady Luella—Amelia's protégée and finest achievement—would be the first to sink her teeth in.

"Lord Wildeforde, it is such a surprise to see you here after…everything." She gave a pointed look toward Amelia, who clenched her teeth together in an effort not to interject. "I do hope you're not too heartbroken."

The table went silent.

The events surrounding Benedict and Amelia's marriage had gone unspoken for the better part of two days. No longer, apparently. It took every ounce of her self-restraint not to rake her nails down Luella's face.

She held her breath. *Stick to the script.*

Edward, to his credit, didn't skip a beat. "Through the grace of good brandy, my heart is on the mend. How can one stay angry in the face of true love?" He raised his glass in Amelia's direction with a smile that fooled almost everyone else.

"To true love." There was an undercurrent of speculation in the words as both tables raised their glasses in Amelia's direction.

She smiled tightly and pretended that yes, the story was just as it was told.

Desperate for a friendly face, she tried to catch Fiona's eye. Her friend's gaze was directed at her lap, her toast a half-hearted tip of her glass. She looked meek and miserable—the complete antithesis of the fiery and independent trailblazer Amelia snuck away with for tea every other afternoon.

Something was amiss, and Amelia would get to the bottom of it.

If she could get away from her guests. *Dash it.* Tuesday. When they were all gone, she would find out exactly what was wrong.

Lady Luella laughed—obnoxious and annoying. She was talking to Edward, leaning over further than necessary to give him a direct view down her neckline.

How pathetic.

The cackle had grabbed Fiona's attention. She flicked her gaze from her lap to Edward, and then Amelia and back to her lap. Her ears flushed red and jaw tensed. It might have been a trick of the light, but her eyes shone with unshed tears.

After dinner. Forget her guests. She'd make time for Fiona tonight.

Their newest footman cleared a soup dish from the head of the table, the plate quivering. A spoon dropped, the clatter of silver on china attracting the whole room's attention.

More than one person sniggered. The footman's ears turned bright red, but rather than simply pick up the spoon and move on, he attempted an odd synchronized bow/spoon-clearing maneuver and nearly clipped Lady Karstark in the ear with the dish.

Every inch of Amelia's body wanted to turn in on itself. This would never happen in a proper London household.

"You stupid fool," Lady Karstark hissed.

The footman swallowed, his face draining of color. "Apologies, m'lady."

He looked to Amelia for direction, panic in his eyes.

She jerked her head toward the door. With every intrusive rattle of china on silver, her reascent back into the *ton*'s ranks became that much harder.

Peter stepped in to clear the remainder of the table—his face stone, his lips pressed firmly together, his eyes flinty.

He was precise, perfect in his movements, the picture of an experienced footman, but the fury rolling off him gave away his lack of experience.

It was tempting to find a subtle way to dismiss him for the evening, but that would leave her with just butterfingers to serve the next course, and who knew what the consequences of that would be. Soup in Lady Wildeforde's lap?

She turned back to her guests. "Excuse the interruption. What were we discussing?"

"I was about to comment on the difficulty of finding good staff in the country," Lady Karstark said. "Your footman preempted my comment with a perfect demonstration."

"There is some training required," Amelia said, trying to remain neutral.

"You can give them all the training in the world, it doesn't help. Why, our maids barely last a month before they leave."

Lord Karstark smirked. At the other end of the table, Benedict made a half-strangled sound, which Amelia promptly ignored. "I do hope you have better luck with your next lot of maids."

She turned to Lady Luella, trying to put the current conversation in the past before it derailed the entire evening. "Is there any London gossip I can wrangle out of you?"

Wrong move. Wrong guest to ask that question of. She'd never have made that mistake three months ago.

"You've more gossip than I do. Tell me, how did you and

Mr. Asterly meet? I can't say that I've ever seen him in a London drawing room, and you so rarely venture out of the city, Amelia. Surely you didn't meet your current husband when you were visiting your former fiancé. That would be rather...scandalous."

Once again, the room quieted. Guests on the next table over found excuses to lean in her direction.

Amelia looked at Benedict, her heart pumping faster. They had absolutely planned to say they'd met in Abingdale during her last visit. How had she not thought that through?

Benedict stepped in. "We met a year ago. In a London bookstore. We've been exchanging letters ever since."

Lady Luella raised an eyebrow. "In a bookstore? I wasn't aware that Lady Amelia read. It's not really the done thing in our circles."

It was like being caught admiring a groom while he brushed down a horse. The only way through was to brazen it out.

"It might not have been the done thing two years ago, but a good novel is quite in vogue since Teresa Cummingsworth first published. Really, Lulu. You must keep up. I can lend you one before you leave."

Lady Luella ground her teeth but didn't issue a contradiction. Amelia had always known everything first. Heavens, she'd created half the recent fashions. And it was clear by the look in her protégé's eyes that she wasn't sure if Amelia was bluffing—and wasn't about to risk it.

Lord Karstark he-hemmed. "Novel reading is a frivolous pastime for frivolous females who ought to be focusing on more useful pursuits."

A good ten feet of table, china, and vases stood between Amelia and Lord Karstark. Lucky for him.

She took a sip of wine and gave him a saccharine smile. "And what, pray tell, would those be?"

"Learning how to properly manage a household is one. Something you should remember next time you choose to open a book rather than properly instruct your servants."

Every head in the room had been swiveling as each parry was thrust. Now all eyes were on her.

Serene. Unruffled. Unruffle-able.

"I—"

"Lady Amelia isn't frivolous," Peter called from the side of the room where he was waiting with a bottle of wine.

If her guests had been shocked at the conversation prior, it was nothing compared to the shock of hearing a footman contribute to the conversation.

"Thank you, Peter," Amelia said. "That's enough."

But the boy was not to be silenced. "She works hard, she does. Hard as anyone. Why, she polished the ballroom floor herself."

Her heart stopped. Her breath would not come. If ever the floor would just open up and swallow her, please God let it be now.

Snorts of laughter and giggling came at her from all directions—each sound a hot iron to the skin.

She twisted a napkin in her lap and smiled widely even though she could feel the cracks appearing all over her. "You're dismissed, Peter."

"But—"

"Out, before I reconsider your employment entirely."

Peter stiffened.

For a moment, she thought he was going to argue, to say something else that would make her a mockery in front of her guests. But he knocked his heels together and stalked down the length of the room toward the servants' entrance.

"You need a better class of footman," Luella said.

"Servants are not hired for their wits."

As soon as the words were out of her mouth, she regretted them. Not just because the hard slam of the door suggested Peter heard her or because Fiona was looking at her with such disappointment.

No, she regretted them because it was the cruel kind of thing she'd have said months ago, before she knew better. Was better.

Shame ate up every inch of her. Blinking back the tears before they could be seen, she looked to Benedict for support.

He looked back, his face set in an expression of absolute disgust.

Chapter 28

Servants are not hired for their wits.

Benedict had been a fool to think that the life he'd built had a foundation of anything but sand. For all that his wife had appeared happy and content, it had taken two short days back with her friends for all of that to shatter.

This Amelia wasn't the one he'd spent his days and nights with. This was the elitist aristocrat who'd been mortified at the prospect of a life with a working man. Iron walls began to shutter around his heart.

Benedict drained the glass of claret in one desperate swallow and motioned for it to be refilled. Anything to make the night easier.

Grunt, who should have been holding Benedict's undivided attention, was prattling on about the velocipede.

"…It's a darn sight more attractive than Karl Drais's version. Not a fan of the name 'hobby horse' but the wheels are bigger and it's significantly more efficient."

Amelia had turned to Wildeforde and was nodding, with that practiced smile that looked charming but hid any sign of what she was truly thinking. He hated that smile. He preferred her laughing or angry or bored—really any expression that showed the wife he'd fallen in love with.

"...don't you think?"

Benedict turned back to Grunt. "Absolutely." He had no idea what he'd just agreed to but given his desperation to get the Americans back to the firm the next day, he'd agree to almost anything.

He twisted the conversation back to where he needed it, giving Grunt the full force of his attention. "There are similarities between Johnson's hobby horse and our next incarnation of the steam train. Small refinements made that deliver significant boosts in efficiency."

Grunt pushed his food around with his fork, refusing to make eye contact. "Yes, yes. I'm sure." There was an uncomfortable edge to his voice, and for the umpteenth time that night, he changed the subject. "Tell me more about Lord Wildeforde. He seems like a sensible chap. A bit reserved, but all these English types are."

Benedict's inability to pin Grunt down into a serious conversation about the locomotive just put more coal in the furnace. The pressure was building, and every second that slipped away took the contract, the firm, and his people's security with it.

"Wildeforde's sensible enough, I suppose."

"What's his situation? Moved on from your wife yet?" Grunt asked, the same calculating look in his eye that Benedict had seen during their early business relationship.

"I wouldn't know. We haven't discussed it." Benedict finished his glass and motioned for it to be refilled again. Grunt couldn't dance around talk of the firm all night.

"I'd be interested to know what he's looking for in a wife. See how compatible he might be with my girls."

"Amelia. He's looking for someone like Amelia."

Because she was the perfect duchess. She'd spent her whole life training to be Wildeforde's bride. He'd been a fool to think a few months could change that.

"Hmmm." Grunt ran his fingers through his beard, more invested in Wildeforde's marital status than what he'd been brought out here to do.

"We sorted out the issue, today. Tessie is running as well as she ever has. It was a misunderstanding—some miscommunication in the team."

Grunt sighed. He shifted in his seat to face Benedict directly. "Lad, I appreciate your tenacity. It'll do you credit along your journey. Business is a tough game and needs a certain level of bullheadedness. But a real businessman also knows when to back away. Try me again in a few years."

Grunt turned in the opposite direction and started a conversation with one of Amelia's bloody friends.

Benedict's hand tightened around his glass. Pushing any further at dinner was just going to cause a spectacle—one that wouldn't help his case with the Americans at all.

He looked over to Amelia, who was deep in conversation with the young Bradenstock fop. His insides writhed to see her so in her element.

He'd failed again. He'd failed his mother, his firm, his village, and now his wife.

⁓

Standing at the foot of the servants' stairs, Amelia took a deep breath. She'd give anything not to go in. For some emergency upstairs to call her away so that she had a good excuse for not walking through that door.

But there was no emergency, and she had no excuse.

She took another deep breath. Her feet were leaden.

The sudden scrape of chairs and clatter of cutlery on china as the servants stood gave way to awkward silence.

More than one of them refused to look at her. The rest of them held expressions of disgust, disappointment, and suspicion. She didn't blame them.

She'd practiced this in her head a dozen times over while making vapid conversation upstairs. But not one variation of what she'd rehearsed felt like it was enough.

"I've come down to apologize—to you in particular, Peter—"

He held her gaze, clearly hurt but thankfully prepared to hear her out.

"—but to the rest of you as well."

Some of their faces softened, just a fraction, but enough to give her confidence moving forward.

"What I said was disrespectful and unkind. Truly unkind, and I am ashamed and embarrassed those words came out of my mouth. Particularly when you were defending me. I repaid kindness and loyalty with cruelty. I do hope you'll give me the opportunity to make it up to you."

There. The words were said.

Some of the weight lifted off her. Not all of it—she'd carry the shame around for a long time to come—but she'd started to repair the damage.

"Thank you for your apology, m'lady," Peter said. "Though I must say, I don't think much of your friends."

"An opinion we're beginning to share," Amelia said wryly. As desperate as she'd been to have all of these people visit, the reality was far from what she'd envisioned.

Tomorrow would be easier. She'd planned a day of parlor games—how wrong could that go? And the hunt was the following day. Assuming none of her guests shot each other, it should round out the visit in a way that made *The Times* for all the right reasons.

Crack. Amelia whirled around at the high-pitched sound of ceramic breaking. Benedict was sitting on the floor, one arm hugging an almost-empty bottle, the other wiping at his pants. A broken cup lay beside him. "Bloody hell," he muttered.

"What are you doing here?" she asked.

"We ran out of whiskey." He waved the bottle in his hand in the general direction of the men in the room. "I went to get some more."

Which explained where he'd disappeared to after dinner. She pressed her lips together and took a deep breath. If they hadn't been having this discussion in front of their entire staff, she'd strip his hide.

"Generally, one is expected to join one's guests after dinner rather than leaving them to their own devices."

"Generally, one expects their guests not to be jackasses."

Behind her, the servants sniggered.

She crossed her arms and glared at him. "You'll be pleased to know that, despite your lack of manners, I managed to convince Mr. Grunt and Mr. Harcombe to visit the firm again tomorrow."

He straightened quickly and then swayed as the movement set him off balance.

"So unless you want to botch this again, I suggest you leave the liquor here and go sleep it off."

Chapter 29 ─────────────

The aftereffects of his night spent drinking made what should have been an exuberant day painful. Tessie's high-pitched whistle as she chugged back to the warehouse after a successful run of the track almost split his head open. When Oliver patted him on the back in excitement, he almost cast up his accounts on the spot.

But despite him, Tessie had done what she needed to. When she'd finished, the two Americans had gone over every inch of her, asking questions about every design feature that differed from Trevithick's existing model. After that, they'd gone to the upstairs office and pored over every test record, every costing, every piece of thinking behind her design. They'd asked to see the letters of patent, and after four solid hours, they turned to him and offered him the contract.

To move to America.

They would buy the license to build three engines. But the parts would be built in America, and he would need to supervise.

Benedict gave the excuse that there was work still to be done when he saw Grunt and Harcombe into the wagon with a promise to give them his decision that night. In truth, he needed the long walk home to process their offer.

A cloud of fog marred his vision as he sighed into the night air. The licensing fee was better than expected. With it, he could turn the firm's focus to producing a prototype of Fiona's invention. The town would still have work, just not the work they were expecting. And diversifying their investments was a smart strategic move.

He could achieve what he'd set out to—bring enough industry into Abingdale that no one in his town would need to survive on the goodwill of the aristocracy if they didn't want to.

But it would come at a cost.

He felt nauseous—a roiling pit of fear and guilt and heart-break had settled into his core the second he'd realized he was considering the offer.

Perhaps Amelia would welcome a move to the Americas. Perhaps it would be the fresh start they needed. He tried to picture her—perfect Lady Amelia—in a country with no traditions, where wealth was no indication of breeding, and an Irish working man could have the same influence as a gently-born aristocrat.

He couldn't ask that of her.

Benedict kicked his boots against the wall by the servants' entrance, knocking off as much mud as possible. At least the kitchen was warm and bustling. Mrs. Duggan gave him a nod as he passed through, barely pausing in her direction of the staff around her.

He climbed up the back staircase. He needed to see her. He was hungry for the sight, the touch, of her. They'd barely exchanged more than a quick peck on the cheek since their guests had arrived.

When he found her, she was at the piano, friends crowded around as she sang.

She was beautiful. She was smiling. She was happy.

How could he think of taking her to America? She'd finally found her way back into the bosom of society.

Nathaniel joined her for the chorus, his voice smooth and polished. Every move of his slight form was graceful. His appearance perfect.

Benedict looked down at his mud-stained boots, the ends of his coat sodden where it had trailed through uncut grass. Amelia might be where she belonged in this company, but Benedict would never fit in here.

As the music trailed off, he ducked out of the doorway. A dead, numbing weight settled over him. The sound of her died away, and with it went what little spark of hope he'd had.

He knew what he needed to do.

～

"Hello, poppet," he said as he opened the door to Cassandra's room. She was sitting up against the bedhead, knees drawn, a book resting on them as usual.

She'd braided her hair before bed, the thick plait hanging over her shoulder. He preferred it like this, rather than the artificial tumble of curls Daisy had nearly perfected. The simple braid was a reminder that she was still the little girl he'd raised.

"Ben!" She put aside the book and patted the blanket beside her. "I'm so glad you're here."

He crossed the room and settled in on the bed next to her,

drawing her into a hug. "Sorry I haven't been in to see you today, poppet. I've been caught up."

She snuggled against him, the only person who'd ever just loved him with no conditions and no hesitation.

"Yes," she said. "Amelia mentioned you've been working with the Americans." There was a twang to her voice—a slight shudder at *the Americans*—and Benedict wondered if the less-than-desirable aspects of his ever-so-desirable wife were rubbing off.

"I think we got there. Tessie was brilliant today."

Benedict had no idea who had shortened the coupling chains, or why, but the Americans had believed his story that one of the newer workers had misheard an instruction.

The deal was ready to be signed, if he could bring himself to do it.

It wouldn't be forever—a couple of years at the most— but it was long enough that Amelia could really establish herself in London, unencumbered by a husband who simply couldn't be the perfect gentleman she needed.

Hopefully, two years would ease the agony he was already feeling. Because she was going to leave, sooner or later. These past few days had proved that.

The house would never go back to what it was before she arrived, and there were too many memories of her for him to stay once she'd gone.

So America it was.

"How do you feel about an adventure?" he asked Cassandra.

"Oooh, London? Amelia said Lord Roxburough was planning to sell his townhouse and that she wants to buy it."

The words hurt to hear, but if she was already talking of leaving for London, then he was making the right decision. "I was thinking a little farther than that. Maybe Boston."

Cassandra wrinkled up her nose, a crease forming between her brows. "Amelia would hate that. She says the Americas are full of people with too much money and not enough polish."

His wife at her finest, clearly.

"I think it best that you don't get too attached to Amelia, poppet. I don't think she'll be around much longer. We need to let her go back to where she belongs."

Cassandra pulled away. "But she's our family. She belongs here."

He rested his chin on her head, giving her a tight squeeze.

He wanted her words to be true, but after the past few days, he could no longer convince himself that Abingdale was where Amelia would be happy.

"I don't think that's the case, Cass. But we'll get by in America without her."

—

It was like a physical blow. Amelia struggled to breathe, sagging against the hallway wall next to Cassandra's room.

She'd thought she'd finally found The Place. The Person. After a lifetime of having no one who truly loved her, she'd found herself with a family.

Except that family didn't feel the same if they were planning to leave her here and go away.

After a long moment of not moving, not breathing, she quietly put down the tray with Cassandra's dessert and left.

She fished a handkerchief from her sleeve, wiping away the tracks her tears had made. She had ten minutes before she needed to be back downstairs. Ten minutes to put a smile on her face and be the perfect hostess once again, despite the world beneath her fracturing.

Chapter 30

Amelia had managed to keep a smile on her face right through dinner and dessert. Even when the Karstarks showed up uninvited once again. Even when Lady Wildeforde made sly comments as Peter served. Even when Mr. Grunt described all the things she'd love about Boston.

But inside, she was breaking.

Today had been a perfect day. Lady Luella had remained in her bedroom, Nathaniel Bradenstock had remained in the billiards room, and without their cutting influence, Amelia had been able to reconnect with her old friends like nothing had happened.

Yes, the conversation seemed rather pointless in comparison to her conversations with Fiona, but not every woman could be a chemist.

The truth was, she had managed to achieve everything she'd set out to. Her house party was a success, her friends had welcomed her back into the fold, and she'd managed to help save Benedict's business.

But despite all of that, she still was not enough. Not for him to take her with him.

Which killed her, because against all reason, he was enough for her.

She loved him. How had she not told him that yet?

Benedict stood by the piano, turning the pages for Miss Appleby as she played. It hadn't escaped Amelia's notice that, despite how uncomfortable he was entertaining, he paid special attention to the debutantes clinging to the fringes of the room each night.

He was a kind man. Kinder than she deserved, if she were to be honest.

Looking at him—in his stark black and white evening clothes, his hair perfectly done—he looked every part the heir. He would make an excellent earl when the time came, one who would care for his tenants, ensure their health and well-being, and argue for their rights in the House of Lords.

In a room full of men with their bright, fashionable clothes, elegant manners, and lofty titles, Benedict stood above them all.

She was embarrassed, really, to remember how she'd once thought him beneath her.

The music ended, and he looked up from the piano. Their gazes collided, and with it, she tried to convey everything she was too proud to say in person.

I love you. Don't leave. Please.

She could have sworn his look said all the same things. He opened his mouth as if to speak, taking a step toward her, and her pulse thrummed. But something caught his attention. He turned his head just a fraction, and their connection was lost.

And with it, her hope.

She looked to the door to see what had distracted him. Greenhill had entered. There was a sense of urgency to his movements as he strode toward Benedict. He didn't skirt around the sides of the room trying to stay inconspicuous. He walked right through the guests to the piano and whispered into Benedict's ear.

Benedict paled. Something was wrong.

She followed them into the foyer where Fiona stood, drumming her fingers impatiently against her skirts. Her hair was windswept, as if she'd ridden hard to get here. Her face was drawn, and she had the aura of a tightly coiled spring, ready to unleash.

"What's wrong?" Amelia asked.

Fiona swallowed. Her hands twisted in her skirts. "Trouble in the village. Charles Tucker has them riled up."

"Damn, damn, damn." Benedict rubbed his jaw.

"I don't understand," Amelia said. "What do you mean when you say trouble?"

Fiona bit her lip. "He told them you've invited the Karstarks here again. They're planning to march on the house in protest."

The hair on the back of Amelia's neck lifted. She grabbed Benedict's hand, gripping it until her knuckles went white.

"This house? Our house?" She couldn't keep the shrill pitch from her voice.

"They've lit torches and are carrying pitchforks." Fiona's voice wavered, as if it were buckling under the weight of her words. "I think you need to get everyone out of here."

Benedict yanked at his cravat. "We can't send everyone away. If the mood has run in this direction, they'll be in more danger on the roads. I'll go. I'll talk some sense into them."

Amelia's stomach churned. If it was too dangerous for

her guests on the road, it was too dangerous for Benedict to walk into the maw directly.

"You can't." She clutched his lapels, not caring how strangled or desperate she sounded as she begged. This was her family. She'd finally understood what that meant, and there was no way she was going to let it be taken from her.

He cradled her face in his hands. The rough caress of his callused fingers sent shivers of longing through her— longing for a life, a full and long life. Not one cut short by a pack of angry men.

"I don't have a choice," he whispered, drawing her closer to him, kissing her gently on the forehead.

"Then I'm coming with you." She tugged hard at her sleeves. She was Lady Amelia Asterly, and she could manage any situation.

He caught her hands, trapping them between his. "Like hell you are. You stay here. Keep Cassandra safe." The urgency in his tone, the fear in his eyes—he wasn't trying to push her aside. He was entrusting the person most dear to him to her charge.

She nodded. Instinct fought against reason, but he was right. Cassandra came first.

She raised onto her toes and gently touched her lips to his. "I'll look after her. Be safe." Her voice broke on those last two words, and her control was not far off.

Benedict turned to Greenhill, who was standing nearby, waiting for orders. He'd heard the conversation. His weathered face was grim, but he stood to attention, ready to take on whatever might be needed.

"Find Wildeforde," Benedict said. "Tell him what's happened but don't let anyone hear you. I'll meet him in the stables."

"Yes, sir."

Benedict turned to Fiona, placing a hand on each of her shoulders. "You should stay too."

Fiona shook her head. "My father is one of the instigators. You'll never talk him down, but I might."

He hesitated. Amelia knew that exposing a woman to danger went completely against everything he was. But she also knew he was a pragmatist. He nodded curtly. "Let's go."

He gave Amelia a long look, heavy with all of the things they had not said to each other. And then he strode through the door.

~

By the time Benedict arrived at the village green, almost every man in Abingdale—and a few of the boys—was deep in his cups. A bonfire had been set up with men sitting on logs, crates, and makeshift benches all around it.

Above the roar and crackle of the flame was shouting and swearing. Men staggered. Some engaged in mock fights. Others leaned on scythes and pitchforks, all kinds of everyday working tools turned potential weapons.

Tucker—that bastard—had built a makeshift stage and was bellowing to the audience in front of him. Alastair walked through the crowd, acknowledging the men and turning their attention toward the revolutionary.

"Oh my lord," Fiona breathed. "It wasn't half this bad when I left."

"Hell," Wildeforde said. He turned to Fiona, grabbing her roughly by the arms. "You go home, now. Stay out of sight and lock the door behind you."

"But my father—" She strained to see around him, but he held her fast. In all their years together, Benedict had never seen this level of fear on Wildeforde's face.

Wildeforde shook her. Just hard enough that he had her focus. "Your father is a grown man that no doubt started this cursed mess. Go home on your own, or I'll toss you over my shoulder and take you there."

She was going to refuse. She was every bit as stubborn as Amelia—no doubt why the women were fast friends.

Benedict stepped between them, drawing Fiona away. "He's right," he said calmly. "Maybe not about the tossing you over his shoulder part, but this is not a safe place for you, and it won't be safe for us to go into this riot worried about whether or not some drunk bastard is putting you in danger."

She pursed her lips but didn't protest. Wildeforde led her back to her horse, talking intensely to her. He held both her hands to his lips and kissed them before helping her mount.

Bloody prick. Hadn't Wildeforde done enough bloody damage to her over the years?

Oliver approached. He stank of whiskey, but his stride was steady, his eyes were clear, his voice low and hushed.

"I've been chatting to some of the older men, convinced them to head home. Some of the boys too—the ones who are still shit-scared of their mothers anyhow."

That was good. Oliver could always be counted on.

"What are your thoughts?" Benedict asked, his eyes still on the jostling crowd.

"If we don't calm it down, they'll march on the house. We'd lose maybe thirty that come to their senses on the walk over there, but that would still leave a large enough mob to cause trouble."

Benedict cursed. "I've sent for the cavalry," he said as Wildeforde joined them. "But they won't be here for another couple of hours at least."

Oliver frowned, shaking his head. "I'm telling you, we don't have that kind of time."

Goddamn it. What a fucking disaster. Anxious energy coursed through him, heightening his awareness, making his skin prickle and his heart thump.

Wildeforde straightened and shook out his legs and arms, just like he did when the two of them used to spar in the boxing ring. "Then we're going to have to do it alone."

Together they strode toward the gathered men. There was no denying that they were an imposing sight. All three taller and broader than most men and used to wielding power. Perhaps their size would give them an advantage.

Plenty of men stopped their conversation to watch them approach, faces wary. A handful left as the potential consequences of the night became more apparent with each step the trio took toward the mob.

"Tucker!" Benedict bellowed. "What is the meaning of this?" He stopped just short of the platform, trying to keep the confrontation from easy view of the crowd.

Tucker turned and sneered, gesturing toward Benedict and Wildeforde as he addressed the crowds. "Listen as the oppressors come to try to strip you of your rights." His tone was oily and snide. He faced Benedict. "There is no law against the gathering of like-minded folks."

"No law against a gathering, if a gathering is all it is." Benedict crossed his arms in an effort not to tear the bastard limb from limb. How had it gotten to this point? Men he'd grown up with protesting against him?

He stretched his jaw. No good would come from thrashing Tucker in front of this crowd. He needed a calm approach. He took a centering breath. "Why don't you tell me what the problem is? Perhaps we can solve this here." Anything to keep this pack away from Amelia, away from Cassandra, away from their home.

Alastair McTavish joined Tucker on the stage. His voice carried clear over the crowd. "Maybe if ye'd been working and drinking with us instead of hobnobbing with them bloody toffs, you'd already ken."

Benedict swallowed and kept his tone cool. "I'm doing business, Alastair. That's all. Business this village needs, as you well know."

"Doing business...with the Karstarks? They put our families—your friends—homeless into the streets and you do business with them?"

"No," Benedict said roughly, with more heat than intended. "Not with them. Never with them."

"But they're at your house, are they not?" Tucker asked. "Eating your food, drinking your wine, waited on by your servants. If not business, why are they there?"

Benedict scrubbed his hand over his face. "It's complicated."

Tucker turned to the crowd. "It's complicated, he says. Too complicated for simple folks like us to understand."

The crowd muttered and threw dirty looks Benedict's way. It was evident why Tucker had been at the forefront of so many rebellious outbreaks. He had a gift for rhetoric. A gift for swaying an audience and whipping up the tempers of men.

"Look at him," the revolutionary said. "All dressed in his fancy clothes. Are his buttons made of moonstone? Or the hopes and dreams of the men he's supposed to be friends with? How can you trust a man so clearly not one of you?"

It was a solid punch to the gut. He'd grown up with these men. Worked with them. Drank with them. Celebrated. Commiserated. All with them.

He was as much a part of them as they were part of him.

But then he looked down at the costume Amelia had laid out for him. The costume he'd never have worn a bare month ago. A costume he'd put on without thought this evening.

Idiot.

Impatient, Wildeforde climbed onto the platform, holding out his hands as if he could physically quiet the men with his presence. At least he'd had the sense to divest himself of jacket and waistcoat. His cravat was undone and limp around his neck; the pristine white of his shirt was marred by dirt. The duke, striving to seem accessible.

The crowd wasn't believing it. A bottle thrown from some unseen hand nearly clipped him on the ear. It was quickly followed by another.

Wilde's shock was palpable. He'd grown up the heir and then the duke. Few people dared to disagree with him. No one threw garbage at him.

Bloody hell. The crowd looked ready to rip him apart. Benedict climbed onto the platform to stand shoulder to shoulder, knocking a bottle aside as it flew toward his head.

"Brandon Stewart, that was a full bottle. Don't waste good ale. Finish the bloody thing first." He'd hoped a little humor might bring them back together. A couple of men laughed, but not enough to sway the hostile atmosphere.

Benedict pointed to one of the farmers standing toward the edge of the crowd. He had a grim look on his face but was steady on his feet and less visibly sloshed than much of the crowd. "Clayton, talk to me. What's this about?"

The farmer shoved his hands in his pockets, pushing out his chest. "It's those that live in big houses with fancy food not giving a bloody fig for the people that farmed their land and made them money."

There was a murmuring of agreement from the crowd and a handful of applause.

The farmer continued. "It's about having no job, no home in three months' time, while the rich sit there on a pile of money, never having to worry about nothing."

The murmuring turned into shouting as Clayton's words spurred another wave of anger.

"You will have a home," Wildeforde called out, raising his voice to be heard over the crowd. "I've been in discussions with Karstark and he's agreed to hold off his...renovations...until we've built suitable alternatives in the village."

The local pig farmer called out. His eyes were glassed over, and he swayed as he spoke. "Give up our land for a poxy cottage on a tiny block? The hell we will."

The statement was met by the rhythmic pounding of feet on the ground and a clapping that shook the foundations of the rickety stage on which they stood.

As the mood worsened, Benedict's chest tightened, vise-like. The situation was quickly getting out of hand. He needed to calm them down before they put Cassandra and Amelia in further jeopardy.

"What do you plan to do about it?" Benedict yelled over the din. "Take the land by force? How long before the army shows up?"

Too long, he knew. They were hours away at best. And if they did arrive to such a hostile crowd, the end result would be bloody.

"Bollocks to the army," came the reply.

"We just need to stand our ground," came another.

"Stand your ground?" Wildeforde yelled. "You all heard what happened in Manchester. St Peter's Field ran red with blood not four months ago. Fifteen men dead, seven hundred injured, and for what? Standing their ground."

The Peterloo Massacre had made headlines for weeks but

done nothing to ease the tension between the workingman and the parliament. Women and children had been killed in the carnage, and all for nothing.

Abingdale would not be another Peterloo.

Tucker stepped in front of them. "We're talking about the liberation of the working class, throwing off the yoke of the oppressors. This isn't just about today, about the men on this field. This is about men across the country. Sometimes sacrifices need to be made to change the world. Who's with me?"

He raised his fist into the air, a gesture met by the raising of torches, a terrifying sea of fire in a perfect storm.

And Benedict could take no more.

He grabbed Tucker by the shirt front, lifting him until the Irishman's toes barely scraped the ground. "You talk about sacrifices, you worthless bastard. You talk about standing together. But where were you when the soldiers charged at Peterloo? Where were you at the Pentrich Rising, Spa Fields riots, or on the streets of Littlefield? You're a man of many fine words, but somehow when the cavalry charges and the arrests begin, you've disappeared."

He hated this man. Hated what he'd done to Benedict's community. Hated himself for being the fool that had brought him here in the first place.

Despite hanging in the air, Tucker smirked, as if holding a trump card that would win him the night.

By this point, the crowd had gone eerily silent, desperate to hear the exchange. The only sound was the crackling of the fire.

Tucker spat, saliva dripping down the side of Benedict's face. "Fine words from a man that turned his back on the cause, married himself a lady-wife, got himself a title, and betrayed those who stood by him."

The words were a knife to the chest, but it was the muttering of assent from the crowd—the people he'd grown up with—that twisted the blade.

"Bollocks. I've done only what was needed. I've betrayed no one," Benedict said, dropping the man to the ground. Tucker fell but stood quickly, brushing the dust from his knees.

"Then where have you been, *my lord*?" Jeremy had pushed his way to the front of the crowd and regarded him with a look so full of loathing that Benedict barely recognized the boy.

Devil help him, he had made a mistake.

The signs had been there for weeks. He simply hadn't acted on them, writing off Jeremy's behavior as youthful petulance—an annoyance that he'd not bothered to address. And now the kid had been twisted and turned into a blunt weapon for two older, malicious, and manipulative men to wield.

"Because it hasn't been at the firm," Jeremy continued. "Unless it's to swan around with some bloody toffs, showing us off as if we were pigs at a show."

Benedict's soul ached to see the damage his negligence had wrought. There had to be some part of the boy he knew left. Some part he could reason with. "Jeremy, I've been working to ensure the firm has work for everyone."

"But if a better deal comes along, you'll take it, right?" Jeremy sneered. "Because jobs for us don't matter as much as cash in the pocket, am I right?"

The roiling unease that was churning in his stomach started to rise. Started to make its way up his chest, his throat. "They're big accusations for a boy barely out of the schoolroom."

"It's true though, isn't it? You made the big deal. You got the money. But the jobs will go to some lucky bugger in America, not us."

There was a collective gasp from the mob. Oliver had been winding his way through the crowd—a word here, a slight push there—slowly winnowing out anyone who might be convinced to go home before it all went bad. He'd worked his way to the front of the crowd, and now put a big hand on Jeremy's shoulder. "That's not true, lad. You know it."

Benedict could try for a hundred years and still never deserve the unwavering faith of his foreman.

Tucker began to laugh. "If you're so sure of this, why does Asterly look as if he wants to vomit?"

Oliver looked to Benedict. "Just tell them it's not true."

He *did* want to vomit. He shifted from foot to foot, unable to look Oliver in the eye. "It's been a busy day." It was all he could offer his friend, and as the words came out of his mouth, he heard how thin and mealy they were.

Oliver's face slackened. The crowd shifted behind him as he stepped back in shock. "You...I can't..."

"I have a plan." But the plea didn't lessen the look of horror on Oliver's face. Or the clear betrayal.

This time it wasn't bottles the men threw, it was mud. A handful of it hit Benedict in the side of the head, splattering his face.

He stared out into the faces of men that he'd grown up with. Men that he'd tried so damned hard to protect. Men that he'd failed.

The crowd pressed forward, hungry for blood, and the makeshift stage swayed under the pressure.

"You've got to go." Wildeforde clapped him on the shoulders and pushed him toward the side of the stage. "You can't help matters now."

Benedict stumbled away, flinching as a boot hit square on his back.

Behind him, the war cries started.

Chapter 31 ─────────────────

Benedict raced up the drive, hoping to make it from the front door to his study without being seen by any of the thirty-odd guests that had taken over his home.

He needed to fortify the house in case Wildeforde and Oliver couldn't talk down the crowd.

He needed a drink. He needed to be alone. He definitely did not need to make nice to a room full of the toffs who had caused the damn problem in the first place.

And he did not need to see his wife.

Life had been running fine until she showed up. Now he barely recognized himself. How could he blame the men of the village for their anger when he himself found his actions reprehensible?

His foot had just touched the top step when Greenhill opened the door.

"Damn it, man. I can open my own bloody door."

Greenhill just bowed. "Of course, sir. Might I enquire as to the state of the village?" His words, though calmly said, had an urgency to them. Of course there bloody was. He had family in the village. Friends.

Benedict raked his fingers through his hair. "The women and children are indoors. The riot is contained to the village square. Wildeforde and Oliver are working to ensure it stays there."

The tension around Greenhill's jaw and eyes remained. It mirrored what Benedict assumed was his own.

He clapped a hopefully reassuring hand on the old man's arm. "I'm sure it will be fine. Let's just take some precautions. Send Daisy up to Cassandra's room. Don't tell Cass what's happening, just find some way to get her dressed. If we evacuate, she needs to be the first one out of here."

He didn't give a toss about their guests, but the thought of his sister in the house, while drunken men with torches surrounded it, was like glass shards spearing through his chest. She trusted him, and his choices had put her in danger. It was unforgivable.

"Will it get to that, sir? Evacuation?"

Benedict tried to give the old man an encouraging smile. "I hope not. Gather all the footmen, the men from the stables, any able body that isn't wearing a dress. Tell them to meet me in the servants' hall with whatever weapons we have."

"Does that include the guests? Should we warn them?"

Benedict paused. This damned party had been Amelia's dream for months. He hated that it was even a consideration, but it was. "No. There's no point causing a stir if it isn't needed." He'd let her have this last thing before he left for America and she returned home to London. Before he never saw her again. The thought flayed him, but he shoved it away.

"Shall I fetch Lady Asterly? She was very concerned when you left."

"No." The word came out desperate and barely human.

Greenhill frowned.

"Let's not worry her. The less she knows, the better."

A tight cough sounded from behind him. He didn't need to see Greenhill's face to tell him it was Amelia. Of course it was.

He faced her.

To an outsider, she might have seemed relaxed, her hand casually resting on the banister. But there was nothing gentle in her expression. Her lips were thinned, and her head cocked. "I can assure you that a state of not knowing does not make any woman feel 'better.' Particularly under these circumstances."

She looked him up and down. Her anger turned into fear, hurt, and empathy as she took in his appearance—the mud on his collar, the graze on his forehead, his wild hair.

"It's bad," she said. It wasn't a question but a flat statement.

He sighed. There was no point keeping it from her. She'd uncover the truth soon enough. "It's not good." His voice sounded bleak. Hopeless, even to him.

Her face softened, and she crossed the room, gathering him into her arms. He couldn't bring himself to return the embrace. He didn't want her comfort, and he sure as hell wasn't in a place to provide any. If she noticed, she didn't show it.

"I really thought they'd listen to you," she said into his chest, her words muffled by his coat. "You're their leader."

Benedict laughed darkly. If only she had seen the way they'd run him off that stage—and the disgust and loathing with which they did it. "I was never their leader, but I used to be one of them. Not anymore."

He pried her arms from around his waist and held her back. There was enough to do, right now in this minute, without having to console her. And he couldn't watch her cry.

He'd done this. All of this. She hadn't wanted to marry him, but he'd insisted. Because he wanted to be good, to be a gentleman. He could have stopped the spectacle that was their house party, but he hadn't. Because he'd prioritized her wants over the needs of those he should have looked out for.

He'd done this to all of them.

"Go back to your party, princess. You're just in the way."

Shock flitted across her face, disbelief. For a moment, she looked as if she was going to argue, her eyes bright and lips pursed. But then he drew back farther, released her arms, and severed all connection to her. He saw it, the moment she realized that he didn't want her. Her expression turned to stone, cool and emotionless. She inclined her head and retreated to the drawing room, perfectly poised as she moved.

He was a cad, and every fiber of his being wanted to go after her, but he forced himself to ignore that weakness and turn to Greenhill instead. "Ten minutes and I want everyone in the servants' hall. Be discreet."

Walking through to the library, he was sickened by the decadence of what was happening in his home—the giggling debutantes in their silks and pearls and the footmen with platters of hors d'oeuvres. Only miles away, men fearing their loss of livelihood, the ability to put clothes on their backs and food on the table, were driven to violence.

A voice in the corner of his brain—one that sounded suspiciously like his wife's—reminded him of the good that men in his position could do. Did do. That except for the odd bottle thrown, Wildeforde had not been a target at the rally. In fact, none of the men in attendance were Wildeforde's tenants.

He shoved the voice away along with any evidence that countered his current frame of mind. The aristocracy were the bad guys. Money and power corrupted men.

Even him.

The door to his study was already cracked open. He pushed it wide. The men inside did not hear his approach. They couldn't have, or they wouldn't have said what they did.

"A savage. But clearly not an idiot. He's got money enough for this brandy." It was the dry, raspy voice of Lord Karstark. That bastard.

"Rich as Croesus, but I wouldn't want his wealth if I had to work for it. Ugh." Benedict couldn't see the man the thin voice belonged to, but he could picture him. Slight, soft, delicate, without the tan that marked Benedict as a man who spent time outdoors, without the bulk from heavy lifting or the calluses from working with his hands.

"Bournesmouth, please," Karstark said. "You'd sell your grandmother for enough blunt to buy a new stallion."

"Correction. I'd have my man sell the old biddy. That sort of transaction is beneath me."

Karstark snickered. "This entire weekend is beneath us. Face it, gentlemen, we're here for the entertainment, watching that unfortunate woman dance in an effort to win her way back into our good graces. Little fool. I saw her bosoms, you know. All splayed out for the world to see. Her nipples were like delicious drops of jam. Reminded me of one of the housemaids I enjoyed."

Benedict's vision went red at the edges—a roaring sound screaming in his ears. He covered the room between the door and the armchairs in three long strides, grabbing Karstark by his bloody neck ruffles and dragging him over the back of the chair.

Two others jumped up, yelling in alarm. Benedict ignored

them and smashed his fist into Karstark's face, feeling immense satisfaction at the crunch of bone and cartilage. He hit the man again as the lord's pale and pathetic fingers pulled at the hand clenched around his neck.

Benedict was vaguely aware of the yelling of the other gentlemen. One of them clipped him across the back of the head with a book, but he just laughed.

A book? Seriously?

Releasing Karstark and letting him crumple to the floor, Benedict grabbed the book-wielding man by the waistcoat, lifting him and slamming him against the wall.

The man whimpered like a small boy. Benedict could smell the brandy, *his* brandy, on the man's breath. How dare these men come into his home, mistreat his household, humiliate his wife, and then laugh with the hubris of the all-powerful. He leaned forward until his face was close enough to see each bead of sweat on the man's brow. Their breaths mingled.

"Benedict!" Amelia's horrified voice broke through the red fog encasing him. He dropped the man, who collapsed at his feet.

She was in the doorway, her eyes wide in horror, her hand pressed to her chest. For a moment, he saw himself as she must: a brute, a monster, hands bloodied, body shaking with rage. No better than an animal. His cheeks blazed, nausea tightened into bilious knots, and he turned away, unable to look at her.

"Go back to your party," he said. He pushed past her into the foyer, where all their guests had congregated. Lord Karstark had crawled there, holding his nose, his shirt now red with blood.

He pointed to Benedict. "Not fit to be around people, attacking a man my age."

There was a mutter of agreement from those gathered. Looking at Karstark, wig missing, clothes torn, he looked frail and feeble—like a victim rather than the predator he was. But he had all of these people fooled. Even Lord Bradenstock was looking at Benedict with disdain.

He wanted to defend himself, to expose Karstark for the vile, womanizing, abusive bastard that he was, but he could read a room. He wasn't getting any sympathy for turning on one of their own.

"Probably time for you to go up, lad. It's over." The American drawl was ice down Benedict's spine. All his efforts—turning himself into another creature, filling his house with those he most despised—had failed. Grunt and Harcombe would not be signing that contract now. And all of those people who depended on him would see him for what he was: a failure.

Before he could think of some response, any response, Greenhill waved at him frantically from the door. The butler gave an exaggerated nod toward the outside.

Damn. Could he not just have one catastrophe at a time?

He pushed through the *tut-tut*ting guests until he was outside, drawing the cold air deep into his lungs, using it to brace himself. In the not-too-far distance, he could see torches—a line of them—coming toward the house.

"Get the guests into their rooms. I want two men at every window on this side of the building. Have Peter check to make sure every door and window is locked."

"Y-yes, sir." Greenhill waited for his master to precede him into the house, but Benedict could not go back in there. Not after what he'd just done. Not after he'd just shown himself for the animal he was. Not after he'd just destroyed everything Amelia had worked for. It was over between them now. How could it be otherwise? They were too different.

Their lives were too different. He'd been an idiot to think it could have worked.

"I'll remain out here. I'll try to talk them down. Tell the men to wait for my signal. These are our friends. We don't shoot unless we have to."

Amelia's face was bloodless as she stepped outside, but her voice was strong. "This is hardly the act of friends."

"I've hardly *been* a friend. I'd be a hypocrite to condemn them. Go back inside."

He moved her through the door and then shut it. He would deal with this alone. Taking a deep breath, he faced the approaching mob. They weren't close enough for him to pinpoint faces. They were at least ten minutes away. There was still time for disaster to be averted if he went out to meet them.

The explosion came without warning. First the ball of light, then the sound, and then the shockwave that knocked Benedict off his feet and rattled the door.

As he sat up, his ears ringing, he saw the red glow of a fire in the distance.

He stood, woozy on his feet. The line of torches had scattered, the little balls of light running in every direction— all away from the house.

The firm.

Chapter 32 ————————————

By the time Amelia arrived at the firm, after pushing past Greenhill and every footman who tried to hold her back, it was a mass of rubble and fire.

Ten-Tonne Tessie no longer existed. All that was left were twisted pieces of metal, many impaled into stone by the force of the blast. The main workshop had collapsed on one side, the roof falling in.

The stacks of coal and firewood that had been placed a far distance from the buildings were burning, sending vicious, choking plumes of smoke into the sky. It was the biggest bonfire she'd ever seen. Even fifty feet away, she was buffeted by the roaring heat. She threw an arm up to protect her face as she searched for Benedict.

Bright orange spots danced in her vision as she scanned her surroundings until she saw him, hunched over against the wall of the smaller workshop.

"Benedict!" She couldn't even hear her own voice over

the fire. She grabbed her skirts and ran to him, stumbling over fallen rock, cutting her hands on twisted metal, refusing to let the pain stop her from reaching him.

"Benedict!"

As she got nearer, she could see his shoulders heaving in heavy sobs. The palms of his hands were pressed into his eye sockets. He was shaking his head.

"No." There was more pain in that one word than she'd heard in a lifetime.

"Benedict." It was a whisper he couldn't possibly hear as she scrambled toward him, but he looked up nonetheless.

"He was so young."

Amelia recoiled. The mass of red at Benedict's feet was not a reflection of fire on scrap metal but a body. Her hand flew to her lips. The figure was unidentifiable, but there must have been something in what was left that told Benedict who he was because, as he cried, he kept repeating the name: Jeremy, Jeremy, Jeremy.

The sight of her husband in such sheer agony almost broke her. Her knees buckled and part of her wanted to collapse in a heap, wreckage on wreckage. But she couldn't. Because he needed her now.

"Oh, my love." She stepped around the body and knelt beside him, running her fingers through his hair. "My love." She went to press a kiss on the top of his head, but he moved out of reach. He scuffled away from her, refusing her touch.

"Benedict." Her throat tightened as she tried to hold back the tears. She bit the inside of her lip, looking to physical pain to keep the sharp stab of grief at bay. Gently, hesitantly, she reached for his hand.

He shook her off. "I did this," he said, his words choked. "I did this. I should have been around. I should have kept an eye on him. I knew that Tucker had his claws into him. And I did nothing."

"No. Sweetheart—"

"I should have spent my time with my workers, my friends, my people, instead of playing dress-up for your lords and ladies."

She shrank away from the viciousness of his voice. The cruelty of his words. This was not him. This was not the man she knew. "His death is not your fault." Despite desperately wanting to be calm and controlled, her voice wavered. That he would shoulder the blame was agony. But there was something else in his words that frightened her. He was pulling away from her. From them.

"Then whose fault is it?"

She paused, choosing her words carefully. "If he set the fire, then it's his fault." It was a stupid, stupid decision made by a reckless boy. And it could break all of them.

Benedict turned away from her, leaning into the wall, his arms caged around his head as if he could block her words out.

She approached him. Slowly. And sighed in relief when he allowed her to run a hand in circles across his back. It made no sense, but she was sure that the only way they'd get through this whole was if she didn't let him go. She needed to hold tight to him now, or it was over.

"Death is a high price to pay for stupidity," she said. "But it happens more than anyone cares to admit. You can't take this on. You're a good man, my love."

He snorted, turning his head so he could look at her. The bleakness of his expression made the blood drain from her face, her body sway off-kilter, and her feet turn to lead. He pulled away. There was no getting through this whole. The rift had already taken place.

His voice was strangled. "I used to think so. But then I let friends I'd grown up with wait on me. I pushed aside my distaste for people who willingly ruin the lives of others and invited them into my home. I accepted a business deal that made me a whole lot of money but took away the jobs I promised my people. I tell myself all of it will let me change lives in other ways, but I've just turned my back on who I am. And for what? You? A woman who's ashamed of who I am?"

Each word was a sharp, stinging cut.

"I'm not ashamed of you," she whispered.

"No?" His tone was cruel, mocking. His face was twisted in a hateful expression, and he didn't resemble the man she loved.

"You didn't pretend to your friends that you'd never done any work at the firm? Like work was a filthy secret?"

"I didn't want them to know *I'd* done that. But I love what you do. I love what you've achieved. I'm so proud of you." She gripped his shirt, desperate for him to hear the truth of what she was saying.

"You're proud of me? Yet you dress me up in silks and velvets because I wasn't good enough the way I was."

Guilt crashed into every corner of her. Because she *had* looked down on the clothes that he wore, the house that he lived in, the way that he'd spoken and acted. She had decided—twice—to turn him into a different gentleman.

"I thought it would be easier for you," she said. Whether he liked it or not, he was going to be an earl. He was going to have to move in those circles. She was trying to smooth out that course.

"Easier for me or easier for you?"

She couldn't answer because she didn't know what the truth was. It was all mixed up. So much had changed—her, him. Life had become a constant tumble, head over feet, over and over. She didn't even know what she wanted.

And her silence damned her.

He took another step backward, shaking his head as though that split second of non-answer confirmed something he hadn't fully believed. "Go back to London. You were planning to leave us soon anyway—just do it now."

"I wasn't planning anything of the sort." How could he possibly think that? That after all they'd achieved together, she would pack up and leave?

"You didn't ask Lord Roxburough if he'd be interested in selling his town house?"

"For the *Season*. Just for the Season. I assumed you'd come with me."

He stood, putting miles between them with every step he took away from her. "Well, I don't want to. You should go, though. I'm better off—we're all better off—without you around. You contribute nothing and just muddy everything up."

And there it was. The truth she'd fought against her entire life. She was no use to anyone. No use as a daughter, as a fiancée, as a wife, as a partner.

She'd tried. Lord knows she'd put every ounce of effort she had into proving her worth. She'd spent her days working tirelessly in the firm, helping build it into something bigger and better. She'd spent her evenings leading a household that she had become proud to belong to. She'd loved Cassandra like a sister, giving her all the support and guidance she could.

And she'd spent her nights and days simply loving him with everything she had.

And still it wasn't enough. He didn't want her around. He had plans to go to the Americas without her, and he hadn't even bothered to discuss it with her.

"Fine. If that's what you want, then fine. I'm leaving. And not because I don't like my life here. Not because I miss the balls and the theater and people. But because of you. I deserve better than your constant judgment, you damned hypocrite. I deserve someone who loves me without conditions. Who accepts me for who *I* am."

It felt good to get the words out. Her entire life had been about trying to live up to other people's expectations. Her father's. Her friends'. Now her husband's. Not any longer.

If the past months had taught her anything, it was that she wasn't perfect—far from it. But she was who she was, and she wasn't going to twist herself up into any more knots trying to be what someone else wanted her to be.

If she wasn't good enough for him, then she was done.

She waited a moment for him to respond. Instead he looked out over the rubble, as though she hadn't spoken a word.

She swallowed. "Good-bye, Ben." Her voice cracked but she squared her shoulders and turned back toward the house, picking her way through the debris and trying not to cry.

John was standing at the edge of the wreckage, horror-stricken. Tears ran down his face, creating rivers of soot. "Wh-where are you g-going?"

"Back to London. It has been a pleasure knowing you."

John grabbed her hand. "You can't leave him. He n-n-needs you."

She freed her hand gently. "He's made it clear that he doesn't. And I won't live like this."

Chapter 33 ————————————————

Benedict's muscles ached as he hauled rock from the ruins of the firm's primary building to the framework that had been built in the two months since the explosion.

It was dirty, sweaty work. His hands blistered, his arms ached, his back regularly seized up in protest. But he carried on because only exhaustion developed through tough physical labor granted him any sleep at night.

In those first few weeks after Amelia had left, he'd tried drowning his sorrow in brandy, whiskey, and ale. He hadn't been particular. But no matter how much he drank, he couldn't sleep without her next to him.

So he got back to work and worked until his body could no longer function.

Beside him, Oliver dropped his own stone into place, finishing off this line of wall. "Rain's coming," he said. "We'll need to get the tarpaulins out."

"Just ten more minutes."

"Ten more minutes and we'll be working in the rain.

Go home, Ben. Have a bath. Spend some time with your sister."

If Oliver had been angry about the contract with the Americans, it had only lasted until he'd arrived at the firm and seen Benedict cradling Jeremy's body. His foreman had been his rock since then.

It was Oliver who'd stood by him as he informed Jeremy's family of the boy's death. It was Oliver who had brought the workers back to the firm. It was Oliver who had dragged him home night after night from the pub when he was too sloshed to stand.

"I mean it, lad. Take yourself home. We'll start again in the morning if the weather clears up."

Benedict nodded to the men and boys that were stretching canvas sheets across the foundations. They gave him a wary nod in return. It would take time to win back their trust, but devil take him, he was going to do it.

He trudged home. The heavens did open. Rain beat down hard. He didn't turn up his collar or hasten his steps. He let the water trickle down the back of his neck. His boots became sodden, the hem of his coat heavy with mud.

He missed his wife. Every damn minute of every damn day. He'd been an ass. Worse than an ass, a downright bastard. Everything had gone wrong, and instead of accepting it and trying to move forward, he'd blamed the one person who'd supported him the most.

The truth was, he'd been afraid she'd leave. Afraid he couldn't be the man she wanted, so she'd hie off to London without a backward glance. And he couldn't be the one left behind again so he'd pushed her away.

But as much as he regretted losing her, he couldn't say it was a mistake. It was the best thing for her, to be in town with people who understood her unfathomable obsession with jewel-tone colors, who could dance without crowding the floor, who could talk with airs and graces.

Better to be with people who weren't clumsy behemoths who managed to get in more arguments than conversations with her ilk.

She was better off without him, even if he was miserable without her.

As usual, the door was open before he'd even made the top step. He took off his dripping coat and handed it to Greenhill. There was no point trying to go back to old ways with his butler. Amelia's influence showed no signs of abating.

"You've a visitor, sir. He's in the library."

Who the devil would be visiting him? A knot formed in the pit of his stomach. The letters from his grandfather, all sitting unopened in his bottom desk drawer, had been arriving with increasing frequency. Maybe the old bastard had grown tired of waiting.

"Who the devil is it?"

Greenhill scowled. If anything, he had become even more of a stick-in-the-mud since Amelia had left. Cursing was no longer acceptable regardless of your role in the household.

"The Duke of Wildeforde, sir."

An initial sense of relief turned quickly into unease. *Wildeforde. What the hell does he want?*

Wilde had left for London the day after the riot, without word to anyone. It wasn't surprising. A fistfight. A riot. An explosion. It was more fodder for gossip than the duke would tolerate. At least, that's what most people would assume. Only a handful of people had seen him with Fi that night. Only they would know he was running away.

"Why are you here?" Benedict asked from the doorway.

Wilde stood by the window, staring in the direction of

the firm. He looked over as Benedict entered and raised an eyebrow. "You're not doing much to counter your beastly reputation, are you? You look like garbage. When did you shave last?"

"Why are you here?"

Wildeforde sighed, crossed to the nearby armchair, and sank into it. "Very well, if we're not going to bother with conversation, I'm here on business. The Duke of Camden has requested an introduction. He has a proposition for you."

The Duke of Camden. Benedict had sworn never to work with an Englishman with a title. That had been the whole point of pitching to Grunt and Harcombe. But there was an entire village of people in need of work. While Fiona's latest project had potential, it wouldn't be ready for production for a year or more. And there was no money coming from the Americans.

"I thought your lot didn't do business," he said, refusing to move from the door. He would probably take this opportunity for the sake of his people, but he didn't need to welcome it.

"We don't do work, but we do money. Therefore, we do business. Camden has discovered a coal seam running through one of his more far-flung estates. He needs a way to transport it, and given his propensity to need the newest of everything, I suggested your *Tessie*. Although for the love of God can you give it a decent name?"

"He wants Tessie? Despite the fact that she's now five tonnes of twisted scrap metal?" His heart thudded at the memories of that night. The heat. The smoke. The slip of blood between his fingers. The heart-shattering agony as he watched Amelia leave. Benedict crossed to his desk and poured two glasses of brandy. He needed a drink to keep the visions away.

"I've told him the failure was not with the engine," Wildeforde said gently.

He knew then. The truth of that night. Of course he knew. Wilde made it his business to know what was happening in and around his estates, and Jeremy's death was no secret.

Benedict's grip on the decanter tightened until his knuckles whitened. "No." His voice was hoarse. "I was the failure."

They were hard words to admit, but Benedict didn't deserve the comfort of hiding his faults. It was his mistake, and he'd own it so the world could pass the judgment he deserved. His neglect had killed a boy and hurt those dearest to him.

The stark admission wasn't enough for Wilde. The duke waited for Benedict to elaborate.

"Jeremy sabotaged the engine. He was angry with me. I hadn't been around to notice."

It was why he was working such long hours at the firm now. Why he was drinking each night at the inn. He would never not be around for his people again.

"You know that it's not your fault, don't you?" Wildeforde asked. "Feeling responsible and actually *being* responsible are two different things."

"You sound like Amelia." He gave a glass to Wilde and sank into the vacant chair.

"She's an intelligent woman."

"Which is why she left."

Wildeforde didn't contradict him. He knew Amelia almost as well as Benedict did. He would have known from the start that Benedict didn't deserve her. That their union was destined to fail. The daughter of an earl and the son of a footman could never make it work. Not when they wanted such different things.

"So what are they saying about me in London?" he asked, swirling the brandy in his glass and watching it cling to the crystal.

"The usual rot. A violent brute that could crush a man's skull between his giant hands. Uncultured, volatile. Not exactly untrue, although I'm surprised you care." Wildeforde stretched out, kicking his heels up on the table between them, settling into the chair like it was old times. Like the past five years, the total fracturing of their friendship, hadn't occurred.

It was bittersweet. There was no overlooking the damage wrought in the past, but Wilde was here now. He'd always turned up when Benedict was hurting, without fail, and so he'd come.

"Amelia cares, so I care." And Benedict did. It would kill him to hear his temper had ruined her chances for happiness.

"If that's the case, if you really care, then why are you here and not in London?"

"Because as you said, I'm an uncultured, volatile brute. She's better off without me." Benedict drained his glass and took Wildeforde's when his friend offered it.

"She's not happy, you know. I mean, she's doing all the things the old Amelia would do—the parties, the dancing, the outrageous flirting…"

The crystal glass fractured beneath Benedict's fingers.

"But she's not happy."

She's not happy. Those words should be salt on an open wound. After all, didn't he want her to be content? To find joy in her life where he couldn't give it? Wasn't that why he'd pushed her away and put himself through this torture?

Instead the words planted a bright seed of hope. One that

needed stomping on. "I can't make her happy. I'm the son of a footman. I'm a working man."

"You're the grandson of a marquess. You're a future lord. You're richer than half the men of the *ton*, and you're a deuced fine man. A good friend and a good leader. But certainly, stay here ruining the crystal she purchased if you're happy to let her go."

Damn. He wasn't happy to let her go. It had been torture, every day, and Wilde was not helping his resolve. But it wasn't about him. "She loves your world. She loves the color and the music and the fabrics and even the people, though I can't for the life of me see why. She's better off there."

"Do you love her?"

"Of course I bloody love her. Frankly, I don't know how you were engaged to her for fifteen years *without* falling in love with her. She's intelligent and kind and completely aggravating. She's honest, brutally so at times, but it's always because she wants to make things better than they are. And I want her in my life forever."

I want her in my life forever. Saying the words out loud tattooed them onto his very soul. *I want her in my life forever.*

Wildeforde chuckled. "For a successful businessman and engineer, you can be completely cotton-headed, you know. If you want her, and you know that she wants to spend time in society, then your decision is made for you. It's not that complicated. Go to London. Put the effort in."

Go to London. His stomach tied itself up in knots at the thought. London would have been difficult enough before the blasted house party. To go there now, after everything he'd done, after all the damage and humiliation he'd caused. Could he do it? Could he face his wife again?

Could he live life *without* facing her again?

Benedict ran his fingers through his hair, gripping it tightly. "But how do I convince her that I mean it? I said some awful, awful things to her. I was the worst kind of cad. You have no idea."

"What's the biggest gesture you could make?"

Chapter 34 ————————————

Amelia's dance card was no longer the pleasure it had once been. Oh, it filled as quickly as it had before, and the same men still jockeyed for pride of place, but the dancing itself was no longer enjoyable.

She strained against Lord Lionell's inappropriate hold, trying to maintain the acceptable distance between them. But there was nothing she could do about the slow lowering of his hand below her waist.

"How is Lady Lionell? Is she still volunteering for the children's hospital?"

"Wouldn't have a clue," he responded. "She has her business. I have mine." His leer suggested that his *business* did not involve charitable work.

"She's so admirable, your *wife*. I must call on her now that I'm back in London."

He grinned. "Call on Thursday. She has some book group or needlework thing and will be out for hours."

Amelia shuddered. He was the third man to proposition her in as many hours. "Have you met my husband?"

"I don't think so." His voice was as dismissive as the slight shrug he gave.

"Oh, you'd remember if you had. He's six feet six inches with fists the size of Christmas hams. And you know those common-born types. Such hotheads. I once saw him destroy a door because it didn't open quickly enough. Split the thing in two. I'm forever having to replace furniture. I will pass on your regards."

The blood drained from Lord Lionell's face, and he released her as though she were burning a hole through his gloves. "There's no need...That is to say, I hope you didn't misinterpret...I..."

"Thank you for the dance." She swept into a deep curtsey to hide her smile. If she was to be subjected to constant solicitations, then she might as well enjoy making them panic.

Her friends were gathered halfway between the entrance and the refreshment table, framed by exotic plants and a chandelier—the perfect position to see everything and be seen by everyone. Men rotated in and out of orbit around them, hoping for a dance. A cluster of debutantes lingered a few feet farther out, desperate for some attention.

Amelia had a place there, right at the center. But she hung by the refreshment table, delaying her return. There was only so much petty gossip one could handle in an evening.

On the other side of the room—looking very comfortable on furniture by the wall with no flattering lighting—sat a group of women the old Amelia had dismissed out of hand. Women who had been too bookish, too unconventional, too frightfully uncaring of society's expectations.

I'd wager their conversation is interesting.

But the question remained, how could she approach these women who didn't give two figs for her?

Fiona would know. Fiona would just stroll on over and say something exceptionally interesting and thought-provoking, and these women would welcome her with eager arms.

What Amelia wouldn't give to have her friend with her now. What she wouldn't give to have anyone from home.

She and Cassandra had exchanged letters almost daily, but there had been nothing from Benedict. Not since she'd walked out.

Which was good. He was respecting her decision.

But also bad. Because she wasn't sure she'd made the right one. He hadn't been entirely wrong in his accusations.

She swallowed. A crowded ballroom was no place for emotion. She had hurt the one person who truly *saw* her, and losing him was something she was just going to have to live with—her penance for being too caught up in what other people thought.

One of the tepid swains who circled the room cleared his throat, trying to get access to the punch she was blocking. With a last look at the probably-interesting group of women, she made her way back to her "friends."

"Lord Lionell seemed to be enjoying the dance," Luella tittered as Amelia approached. "I've heard he's very generous to his mistresses."

Hmmm.

Benedict's temper had clearly rubbed off on her because she had to stop herself from slapping the girl. But she just smiled sweetly. "Manage to find a husband, Lulu, and an affair with Lord Lionell is yours for the taking."

Luella's eyes narrowed. "Not all of us will have husbands content to leave us so completely to our own devices. I'm quite jealous, Amelia, that your husband is so hands-off."

It was the perfect jab. A reminder of what she'd lost in a saccharine wrapping that didn't go unnoticed by those around her. Barely suppressed smiles had her shaking in anger and embarrassment. If she opened her mouth, it would be a firestorm of fury that poured out. So she kept her mouth shut and raised an eyebrow in the most condescending stare she could imagine.

The cluster of debutantes around them watched to see who would break first in this silent-staring struggle for dominance.

Luella was the first to capitulate, diverting her gaze, her ears flushing red. "There's Miss Penelope. I heard Madame Genevieve refused to dress her—thank goodness. There'd be no fabric left for the rest of us."

"What has she done, do you think?" one of the new crop of debutantes said. "Made a ballgown from the drapes?"

Amelia looked over at the girl hugging the wall. She was pretty enough, if a little fuller than the current prevailing taste. But hideously dressed. She sported too many freckles to be truly ladylike, and the half-smile she gave to anyone who walked past was too earnest to be fashionable.

Last Season, Amelia would have thought nothing of making some offhand derogatory comment. A flush of hot shame snaked up her neck. Last Season, she hadn't been a particularly kind person.

Was that why Benedict had pushed her away? Because he saw too much of that person still in her?

She would do better. For him, she would *be* better.

"Miss Penelope Ainslie, yes?" Amelia asked. "No mother, no sister, no aunts if I recall correctly."

"And no sense of style. Her first time in London, and she leaves the house in *that*."

No wonder the poor girl struggled in the sartorial stakes.

She'd been raised by men in the country. A lump formed in Amelia's throat. How incredibly lost Penelope must be feeling. It was a sentiment Amelia had never understood until her life had been upended by a broken carriage wheel. Ironically it was the same feeling that dogged her now, even though she was "home."

Lost and in the sights of a horrid young lady who needed to be taken down a peg or two. "I do believe your sense of style was somewhat lacking when you first debuted, Lulu. In fact, I seem to remember a highly amusing incident with an abundance of feathers."

Luella's cheeks flushed.

"Didn't it take two weeks of lessons and three trips to High Street before you stepped out in anything presentable? How grateful you must be that I rescued you from irrelevance."

There was a collective gasp from the girls around them, followed by utter silence as they waited for Luella's response.

But while she might have capitulated earlier, there was no surrender this time. "We may all have looked up to you once, Amelia. But that was before you debased yourself. There's another queen bee now."

Heads swiveled in Amelia's direction, eager for a response to the attempted social coup.

It was all rather sad, actually. None of these girls had any real sense of what really mattered in life. Benedict had shown her. He'd seen a kinder person in her and had taught her how to be that. He'd encouraged her to pursue work with the firm that had real meaning.

What other man would offer his wife a partnership in his business? Benedict's support had allowed her to make herself a better person.

What on earth am I doing back here?

Returning to London had been a mistake. Even if he wanted nóthing more to do with her, she could still have found a more productive, worthwhile life to live. She'd been naïve to think she could slip back into her old ways and be fulfilled.

Amelia took Luella's hand and squeezed it affectionately. They had, after all, been friends at one point. "You're welcome to the hive, Lulu. I hope it brings you joy."

Luella's eyes widened before narrowing suspiciously. "Just like that?"

She was tempted to try to explain it—the superficial nature of what they were focused on, how utterly irrelevant it was—but knew deep down that it took more than words to convince someone. So she smiled, a genuine smile for the first time that night. "I'm off to fly in a different field."

She curtseyed to the group—a thank-you for their respect back when that was what had mattered to her—and then walked away. The disappearing weight from her shoulders was utterly delightful.

It was time to leave London. Leave this.

She had enough funds to buy a small cottage, somewhere only a few hours' ride from Abingdale. Cassandra would be able to visit when she was older, and Fiona could come and stay when she needed time away.

Maybe, over time, Benedict would see that she was no longer the selfish, myopic girl he had married. Maybe, over time, they could repair the damage they'd done and start again.

The tenor of the room changed. A chorus of whispers drowned out the orchestra. People were staring at her. News of her showdown with Luella had travelled fast. Nevertheless, she held her head high. She didn't care. She was making the only decision that was right for her. The only choice that gave her some hope of a life with Benedict.

She turned toward the stairs and froze.

It was not her argument with Luella that made her the center of attention.

He had come.

Moreover, he had not come alone.

It was worse than Benedict had expected. All of London currently had its gaze pinned on him—the enormous violent brute dressed up like a bloody parrot. Standing there naked couldn't have attracted as much attention.

"The Most Honorable, the Marquess of Harrington and Mr. Benedict Asterly."

He swallowed and tried not to pull at the goldwork embroidery of his cravat as he waited for his grandfather to descend the short set of stairs into the ballroom. But the marquess was reveling in the attention and showed no sign of joining the crowd.

Face after face. The room was a kaleidoscope of irritation, amusement, and conjecture. The upper crust wondering what his appearance with the marquess meant. They'd mock him if they knew. It meant that he would do anything to be with his wife—even if that meant making peace with his grandfather.

Harrington put his hand on Benedict's back, an intimate gesture that doubled as a bold announcement. *Asterly is family.*

Was it a warning for Benedict to toe the line? Or was the marquess protecting him? Benedict didn't know. Their time spent together had been cold and stiff, full of broken conversation. Every word had been laden with decades of loathing and mistrust. Eventually, they'd reached an understanding—Benedict would listen to Harrington's advice in matters related to the running of an earldom—but beyond that the waters were murky, their relationship still undefined.

It wasn't easy to stand next to the man who'd destroyed his mother, but it had to be done. Partly because he had a responsibility to those he would one day serve but mostly because of Amelia. Because it would show her that he could listen, could change and that he valued her opinion. Amelia was why he'd finally opened those bloody letters in his desk drawer.

He scanned the room. When he finally saw her, he took the first full breath he'd managed in months. He drank in the sight of her, her head held high with her usual confidence, her grace and elegance that was at once gentle and steel-strong, her beauty derived less from her physical perfection and more from her intelligence and wit.

He took another full breath, the tension he'd been carrying dissipating into a calm serenity. He was whole. With her in the room, he was complete.

Amelia's hand pressed against her lips and her eyes shone. To hell with his grandfather and the peacocking. He couldn't wait another moment, another second, to have her in his arms. But as he stepped forward, she stepped backward.

Again, he moved toward her and she backed away. Her surprise quickly turned to an expression of horror. With an agonized look, she turned and fled through the crowd, pushing her way through the horde to the balcony doors, where she disappeared into the night.

"Amelia!" As he raced through the ballroom, the crowd parted before him, but by the time he reached the exit, he could see nothing but empty paths into the garden, strung with lanterns. There were two trails she could have taken, one that skirted the edge of the elaborately landscaped maze and another that plunged deep into the heart of it. He knew instinctively which she would have chosen.

"Amelia!" At every turn, he expected her to be just around the corner. At every turn the hollowness inside him spread. She had every right to be angry—he'd said cruel and hurtful things. But he had hoped that reconciling with his grandfather and stepping foot where he'd sworn he'd never tread would have earned him enough time to plead his case.

He ducked through an archway, moving toward a patch of light. Surely, she'd head for one of the lantern-lit groves. The bushes were tall enough that he couldn't see a clear way to her. He was blind and desperate. "Amelia, please," he called.

Finally, he rounded a corner, and she was there, sitting on a bench beneath a lamp, head in her hands. "Amelia."

She looked up. Tear tracks shone under the light, and his heart broke all over again. He'd made a mistake, coming here. He should have left her in peace rather than hurt her again. But the damage was done. All he could do now was ask for forgiveness.

He knelt before her, cupping her hands in his. "I'm sorry. I was a damned fool. Even worse than that, I was deliberately shortsighted. I didn't want to face my own failings or admit that I'd made mistakes, so I blamed you. It was spiteful and wrong and I'm so, so sorry. You were and always will be the best thing to ever happen to me."

She looked down at him, her eyes dropping to the carrot-colored cravat that had taken a full hour to knot properly, the contrasting blue and green quilted waistcoat and the bejeweled slippers on his feet. Horrendous, all of it, but he wasn't a man of words and so this was his love letter to her.

She shook her head, pulling her hands from his. "This is not what I want," she whispered.

No moment in his entire life had hurt like this one, not even the day his mother had left. A sharp ache formed in the back of his throat. He clenched his fists, digging his fingers into the barely healed blisters on his palms, channeling his grief into that pain.

But he wasn't going to stop trying to win her back. "I *need* you. We need you. I was wrong to say we didn't. Nothing works without you. Not the firm, not the house, not me. Every moment is just a fraction of what it would be if you were home. Whatever it takes, I'll do it. Whoever you need me to be, I'll be it."

His plea didn't have the effect he'd anticipated. She stood and walked to the other side of the small clearing, putting as much space between them as she could, hands wiping at her face as she did so.

He stood, straining against the need to go to her.

"I don't want you here, like this," she said, gesturing to his outfit. "I don't want you turning into something you're not just to make me happy. Can't you see how much damage I've already done?" She hugged her arms around her body as though she was trying to hold herself together.

The regret he'd felt over the past few weeks was tepid and shallow compared to what engulfed him as he realized she'd truly taken his hateful, shameful words to heart.

He covered the ground between them and gathered her into his arms, hoping that the feel of them holding each other once more brought the same sense of relief to her that it did to him. "No, sweetheart," he murmured. "None of it was your fault. None of it. It was a series of situations that did not go our way." His arms tightened around her and he kissed the top of her curls, breathing in the familiar scent of her.

"Everyone must hate me." Her words were muffled as she pressed herself into his chest and sobbed.

He hugged her close, trying to shore up all the pieces of her. "No one hates you," he whispered. "They all want you back. I *need* you back. Princess, come home."

She dragged in a few breaths, and her shaking slowed. She tipped her head back and looked up at him. Her eyes still brimmed with tears, but they held a flicker of hope. "Truly? You wouldn't prefer just to take your old life back? The one where you didn't have a wife upending everything?" Her breath hitched on the last note, a hiccup that snagged around his heart.

"Truly. My life needed upending. It was dull and lifeless and far too comfortable before you came along." He pulled a handkerchief from the inside pocket of his coat and wiped it across her cheek, the tears soaking it.

She swallowed hard and took it from him, blotting her tears and wiping her nose. "You need to promise that you'll throw this hideous outfit away."

Relief spread through him, a wash of light across the shadows. They were going to be all right. He stepped back, twirling with every bit of peacockness he could muster. "This? I thought you'd love it."

She smiled. That she was breathtaking was an understatement. She was the most beautiful thing he'd ever seen, even with her eyes watery and her hair all mussed. He didn't know what force had brought her into his life, but he was going to make damned sure he never risked losing her again.

She smoothed out the creases she had pressed into his

jacket, her hand pausing over the gold thread. "I love parts of it. In isolation. Perhaps with a diamond stick pin."

This was his Amelia. And God he was glad to have her back.

Despite the teasing, she was serious when she took his hand and pressed it against her heart. "I don't want you to dress differently; I know you hate color. And you don't need to make amends with the marquess. I can live without London."

He tipped her chin and placed a light kiss on her lips. "No, you can't. You love London. You love its energy. You love coming to horrendous parties like this. I don't want you to give that up."

"I haven't loved it lately. My friends are awful."

He chuckled. "In a city this large, I'm sure you can find some non-awful friends. And I'm sure I can find some men with whom I share some common ground."

She tightened her arms around him, sighing into his chest. "It's a deal."

The moment was wonderful but incomplete. He had come to London determined to bare his soul, and there was still one thing left to reveal. The words caught in his throat. Giving voice to what his heart felt could make the night perfect or turn it sour. Right now, as it stood, they were happy. He didn't want to jeopardize that. But he also needed her to know.

"I love you, princess." The words came out with more assurance than he felt. His heart quickened in the silence that followed.

The interminably long silence.

Maybe she hadn't heard him. Or maybe she had heard him and couldn't think of a response. Maybe he should say it again, louder. Or not and pretend the words had never been said. Blood rushed through him, creating a pounding in his head that matched any noise his steam engines could make.

Just as he was about to apologize, to take it all back and urge her to forget it all, she looked up at him, reached on her toes, and kissed him. "I love you too," she whispered. "Now take me home, please."

Epilogue ——————————————

Amelia hummed to herself as she watched the firm thrum and buzz below her. It had taken a year to get back to full production, but the work on the Duke of Camden's loco-motives was well underway.

She leaned back in the armchair Oliver had carried up to the mezzanine for her, gently stroking her belly.

"How did you even get up here?" Benedict asked as he climbed the stairs.

Amelia flushed. "Oliver might have helped." After she'd paused on the fourth step and come to a dead stop on the eighth, the foreman had sighed and lifted her like she didn't weigh the rough equivalent of a baby whale.

"There's a reason they call it confinement." Benedict dropped a quick kiss on her brow. "Are you feeling well? You should be in bed."

"I just wanted to see her fire up." They had invested every ounce of energy they had into forming new systems and procedures that would see Baby Tess delivered in sixty percent of the time it had taken to make the old Tessie, and nothing would keep her away from the first test run.

"Did John get off all right?" she asked. "He seemed awfully anxious before you two left—like he couldn't leave England fast enough. I worry about him in the Americas all by himself."

Benedict supported her under the arms as she shifted in the chair. "He's hardly all by himself. The factory is not far from Boston—not exactly the Wild West. And he'll have a team of people working for him."

"Still...I do wish we'd sent someone else to oversee the whole thing. There was no need for him to set sail for the other side of the world."

"Shhh, princess. You're going to miss it." He turned her head toward the new locomotive. The stoker shoveled coal into the firebox, and the engineer released the brakes. Slowly, Baby Tess began to move, the cast-iron wheels turning.

As she exited through the side door and onto the testing track, she picked up the pace. The crowd that had gathered, made up primarily of the men that worked for the firm but also their families, broke into applause.

They had done it. And this time Amelia had been there from the beginning.

"There," Benedict said. "You've seen it now. Can I please take you back to the house? You're giving me an apoplexy traveling around in your condition."

"Only if you promise to give me a foot rub."

He nuzzled into her neck, his breath sending shivers down her spine. "Oh, I promise I can do more than that. Let's get you into a hot bath."

Don't miss Wilde and Fiona's story,

How to Deceive a Duke

Coming Winter 2022

About the Author ———

Samara has been escaping into fictional worlds since she was a child. When she picked up her first historical romance book, she found a fantasy universe she never wanted to leave and the inspiration to write her own stories. She lives in Australia with her own hero and their many fur-babies in a house with an obscenely large garden, despite historically being unable to keep a cactus alive. *How to Survive a Scandal* is her debut novel.

You can follow her writing, gardening, and life adventures on social media or by signing up for her newsletter at SamaraParish.com/newsletter

SamaraParish.com
Facebook.com/SamaraParish
Instagram @SamaraParish
Twitter @SamaraParish
Pinterest @SamaraParish

Follow @ReadForeverPub on Twitter and join the conversation using #ReadForever

SOMEDAY MY DUKE WILL COME
by Christina Britton

Quincy Nesbitt reluctantly accepted the dukedom after his brother's death, but he'll be damned if he accepts his brother's fiancée as well. The only polite way to decline is to become engaged to someone else—quickly. Lady Clara has the right connections and happens to need him as much as he needs her. But he soon discovers she's also witty and selfless—and if he's not careful, he just might lose his heart.

A GOOD DUKE IS HARD TO FIND
by Christina Britton

Next in line for a dukedom he doesn't want to inherit, Peter Ashford is on the Isle of Synne only to exact revenge on the man responsible for his mother's death. But when he meets the beautiful and kind Miss Lenora Hartley, he can't help but be drawn to her. Can Peter put aside his plans for vengeance for the woman who has come to mean everything to him?

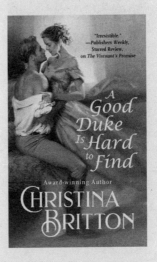

Discover bonus content and more on read-forever.com

Looking for more historical romances?
Get swept away by handsome rogues and clever
ladies from Forever!

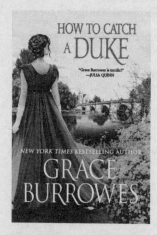

HOW TO CATCH A DUKE
by Grace Burrowes

Miss Abigail Abbott needs to disappear—permanently—and the only person she trusts to help is Lord Stephen Wentworth, heir to the Duke of Walden. Stephen is brilliant, charming, and absolutely ruthless. So ruthless that he proposes marriage to keep Abigail safe. But when she accepts his courtship of convenience, they discover intimate moments that they don't want to end. But can Stephen convince Abigail that their arrangement is more than a sham and that his love is real?

THE TRUTH ABOUT DUKES
by Grace Burrowes

Lady Constance Wentworth never has a daring thought (that she admits aloud) and never comes close to courting scandal...as far as anybody knows. Robert Rothmere is a scandal poised to explode. Unless he wants to end up locked away in a madhouse (again) by his enemies, he needs to marry a perfectly proper, deadly-dull duchess, immediately—but little does he know that the delightful lady he has in mind is hiding scandalous secrets of her own.

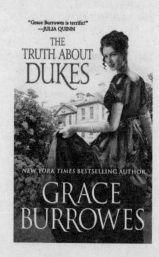

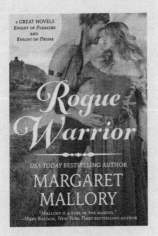

ROGUE WARRIOR
(2-IN-1-EDITION)
by Margaret Mallory

Enjoy the first two books in the steamy medieval romance series All the King's Men! In *Knight of Desire*, warrior William FitzAlan and Lady Catherine Rayburn must learn to trust each other to save their lives and the love growing between them. In *Knight of Pleasure*, the charming Sir Stephen Carleton captures the heart of expert swordswoman Lady Isobel Hume, but he must prove his love when a threat leads Isobel into mortal danger.

ANY ROGUE WILL DO
by Bethany Bennett

For exactly one Season, Lady Charlotte Wentworth played the biddable female the *ton* expected—and all it got her was Society's mockery and derision. Now she's determined to take charge of her own future. So when an unwanted suitor tries to manipulate her into an engagement, she has a plan. He can't claim to be her fiancé if she's engaged to someone else. Even if it means asking for help from the last man she would ever marry.

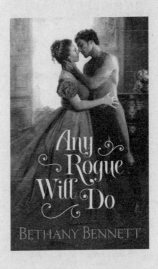

Connect with us at
Facebook.com/ReadForeverPub

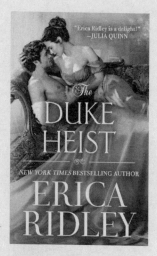

THE DUKE HEIST
by Erica Ridley

When the only father Chloe Wynchester's ever known makes a dying wish for his adopted family to recover a missing painting, she's the one her siblings turn to for stealing it back. No one expects that in doing so, she'll also abduct a handsome duke. Lawrence Gosling, the Duke of Faircliffe, is shocked to find himself in a runaway carriage driven by a beautiful woman. But if handing over the painting means sacrificing his family's legacy, will he follow his plan—or true love?

A ROGUE TO REMEMBER
by Emily Sullivan

After five Seasons of turning down every marriage proposal, Lottie Carlisle's uncle has declared she must choose a husband, or he'll find one for her. Only Lottie has her own agenda—namely ruining herself and then posing as a widow in the countryside. But when Alec Gresham, the seasoned spy who broke Lottie's heart, appears at her doorstep to escort her home, it seems her best-laid plans appear to have been for naught... And it soon becomes clear that the feelings between them are far from buried.

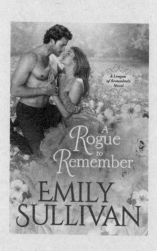